I spin away from him, tears threatening again. "You shouldn't say things like that," I mumble, rolling my pant legs back down.

"Yeah? Why not?" He sounds genuinely curious.

"You can't tell me you haven't noticed the way things are at school. I'm everyone's favorite loser. There isn't anyone more fun to pick on than me."

He's silent so long, I finally turn back toward him, and see anger on his face again, jaw clenching. I'm taken aback, worried that he's angry with me. I glance at the bank on the other side of the stream again, wondering if I can make a run for it with my knees so sore. I know I can, of course I can. I've had to run other times with worse pain than this.

"Yeah, I've noticed. It really ticks me off."

I choke out a strangled laugh at that. *He's* ticked about that? I shake my head.

"I want to be your friend," he says, and my stomach tightens.

"You can't be my friend. No one can be my friend. It's social suicide."

He reaches out and brushes his finger lightly over the bandage knotted on my hand, leaving an improbable trail of fire.

"I can honestly say that even if that is true, I don't care."

Books by Cindy C Bennett

Geek Girl

For my beautiful Lindsay, without whom this story never would have come to be.
I wished for you so hard, and have never been anything but grateful that I got even more than I wished for!

Acknowledgements

I would be remiss if I didn't give a couple of shout-outs here. To Jeffrey Moore and Camelia Skiba, authors extraordinaire, whose critiques and creative suggestions are *beyond* invaluable in making my stories so much better than they would have been otherwise. You, my friends, my comrades in arms, have my unflagging, eternal gratitude. And to Megan Rowley, who read the whole thing, as well, and helped me to see where I had drifted away from sense—or repeated myself. Megan (comma) you (comma) are (comma) the (comma) best (comma). To both my daughters, who have been my most vocal fans and biggest supporters, and to my sons who rarely read, but read what I write, anyway, and give me encouragement. To everyone who read *Geek Girl*, and gave me such positive reinforcement, and especially those of you who have repeatedly asked for more. And last, but not least, to my husband, who makes it possible for me to have the time I need to write.

Heart on a Chain

by Cindy C Bennett

Cover Design by Cindy C Bennett

ISBN-13: 9781456492410
ISBN-10: 1456492411

Prologue

Six Years Earlier

Henry watched Kate as she stuck her hand into the slotted opening on her sparsely populated Valentine's box, nerves thrumming—it was an unusual sensation for him, this insecurity.

He didn't take his life for *granted* exactly, but there wasn't a lot of conflict thrown his way, either, from his peers or from his family. He was too young to fully appreciate the blessing of having such a peaceful life, but old enough to understand that not everyone had it as good as he did.

He'd loved Kate for as long as he'd known her. She'd been his first friend on the first day of Kindergarten. He hadn't wanted his mom to leave him in the big, new, scary place full of strangers. Kate had come over as he fought the tears and placed her hand in his. With a smile, she'd led him to the coloring table and he'd been smitten from that day forward.

He'd never forgotten that; she'd been his comfort, his ray of sunshine in the dark storm of emotion.

Because of his sensitivity for her, he was one of the few who'd noticed the change in her over the past few years. She'd gone from a sweet, funny girl who always smiled, and could always make others laugh, to someone who was quiet and rarely smiled.

It made him sad, mainly because he didn't know why, and therefore couldn't fix it.

He never gave up. He thought if he just kept trying, he could find that girl again. Even more than that, though, he wanted her to know how he felt about her—how he *really* felt about her. He didn't think she could know how very much he wanted to be with her, how much he loved her. He hoped his special Valentine would make that clear.

Kate stuck her hand into her box, listlessly pulling out the small, store bought, generic cards that mostly sported cartoon characters on them along with some cheesy, false sentiment. She barely glanced at them as she set them to the side. He might have believed she was completely uncaring, removed from feeling anything about them, except for the tiny upturn at one corner of her mouth.

Finally she reached his. He could tell because the smile dropped from her face and her forehead creased in consternation as her hand was stopped in its retrieval progress. She tugged a little, then turned her hand at an angle to maneuver the large, folded piece of construction paper out of the opening.

Kate stared at the front. Henry suddenly felt embarrassed, unsure of his gift to her. Maybe it was stupid...it *was* stupid. It was idiotic and childish. Amateurish, the different colors of hearts layered one on top of the other on the red paper. He should have just bought one at the store—it would have been better. He balled his fists at his side as a flush stole up his cheeks.

Then she opened it, read the words he had written there, and his stomach clenched.

An amazing thing happened then. Like the sun rising on the horizon, her smile appeared, changing her countenance, lighting her face in a way he hadn't seen for too long. Her eyes came up to his, and in them he could see her answer.

She stood, and walked unsurely toward him, her smile wavering slightly. Then she turned into the coat closet, giving him a look that drew him toward her. He looked around to make sure no one was watching, waited a minute or so, then followed her in.

She stood in the back corner, waiting, worry puckering her brow, wringing her hands—until she saw Henry. Her face cleared and a small smile played across her lips.

Henry walked over to her, stopping directly in front of her. She glanced down, eyes slowly coming back to his as he leaned closer. She raised her mouth to his and kissed him. Surprise held him frozen for a long moment before he melted, innocently kissing her back.

She was his dream girl, and with her kiss she told him she was finally his.

Four months later Henry and his family moved away.

One

W*ham!*

The back-handed blow knocks me to the floor. I look up at her, determining in a nano-second whether I should stay down or get back up. I scramble to my feet, cringing slightly in anticipation of the next strike, guaranteed to come if I read her wrong.

I didn't. She turns away from me with familiar disgust.

"Clean up this mess you made, Kate," she grumbles, kicking at the plate filled with the remnants of her lunch that had been knocked to the floor from her side table as I fell.

"Okay, mom."

She turns back, threat in her pose.

"You sassing me?"

"No mom, I'm sorry." I hate the wheedling in my voice, but I am as helpless against that as I am in changing the tide of my life.

I scoop up the food scraps with my hands, piling them back on the plate and set it aside. I wipe a couple of the prescription bottles that had tumbled into the mess with the front of my shirt. I set the fallen bottles back on the table in their precise spot within the cluster of small brown bottles. She knows just what is in each one by their location.

Unbidden, the picture I have hidden under my mattress slides into my mind. In it, my mother stands in the backyard with me and my father, laughing and loving and looking young and beautiful—and very pregnant.

I was nine-years-old at the time, getting ready to start fourth grade, which was exciting because it meant that I was on the up-slide to being what I thought was the coolest of the cool—a *sixth* grader, oldest class in the school.

The day the photo was taken my father had brought home an early birthday surprise for me. My birthday isn't until February, but Dad couldn't wait. He wanted me to have it early so I could enjoy it before the snow fell.

As I carry my mother's dirty plate into the kitchen, I glance out the window at the long-ago birthday surprise. It's a swing-set, one of the sturdy, steel, A-frame kinds that you normally don't find in a backyard, but rather at a public playground. It was made to last for a very long time—even now it looks nearly the same; only the dulled shine gives away its age. Three swings hang from long thick chains. The burly men who delivered it made sure to cement the poles deep into the ground so that it wouldn't tip over. I was told I had to wait three days to swing on it to give the cement a chance to harden.

Three days is an eternity to a nine-year-old.

In three days, I learned, an eternity of changes can occur.

I quickly and as quietly as possible wash the plate—the dishwasher long ago quit working and the idea of paying a repairman or buying a new one is as foreign as a trip to the Taj Mahal. As soon as I'm finished I silently slip out the back door.

I'm well aware of how pathetic it is to have your only escape, your best friend, be an inanimate object—and a child's play toy at that—for someone who is seventeen years old and getting ready to begin her final year of high school. But it's all I have, so I hurry over, ignoring the light rain that begins to fall as I plant my feet into the well worn dirt, and shove off as hard as I can with a slight jump. The wind blows past me from both the speed as well as the storm kicking up. It cools the raw spot on my jaw that will leave me with a bruise to start the school year tomorrow.

Not that it matters. A pre-bruised punching bag doesn't make a difference to most of my tormentors.

As I sail higher, I feel the release of tension, the world fading away. I'm eased by the rush that comes as I push myself higher and higher. My mind empties as I give myself over to sensation. The only interruption comes when I hear my father stumble into the house—early tonight—and the yelling starts. Even that I can push away with little effort; I've had years of practice.

Luckily, there is no tell-tale sound of fist against skin when the yelling stops. My mind registers this in relief because it also means there's a good chance I won't have to be on the receiving end of her anger anymore tonight.

Sometime later, I become aware of lights being turned off in the house. It doesn't occur to either of them to wonder where I am, or to even check my room to see if I'm there. I don't have a problem with that—their lack of concern and attention long ago stopped being painful and became a positive thing if it means being invisible.

I continue to swing in the cool night air, hair damp now from the light rain. I wait for the peace to settle completely before letting the swing slow and then stop.

A deep breath, gathering courage, then I slip into the house as quietly as possible, not wanting to call attention to my existence.

I pull open my bedroom closet, and blow out an exasperated breath at the lack of options before me. Tomorrow I'm officially a senior; seems like that should qualify maybe just one new outfit, one thing that isn't a thrift store second that's worn out and ill fitting. I allow myself a two minute pity-party, then pull out the least worn items to put on in the morning.

Senior year.

Ugh.

I hate the first day of school.

Actually, I hate every day of school, but as this is the first day of my last year of high school, it somehow seems worse than all the others. There's a palpable excitement in the air from the other seniors, knowing that after this year they can start their real lives. I don't have a real life so this year is more frightening than all the rest—and that's saying a lot considering how every previous school year has been for me.

"Look out, freak."

I stumble but don't fall as I'm shoved to the side by one of the juniors. I see a couple of the sophomores look over in interest. Time will tell if these newbies will join in the game, or if they'll take pity and leave me alone.

I turn away from them and see Jessica Bolen coming down the hall, surrounded by her groupies. That's a really good reason for me to turn and head in the opposite direction. She hasn't noticed me yet, so I make a quick retreat down the nearby stairs, even though it means I'll have to hustle to make it to my first class. Tardies are something I avoid with a passion, not wanting more attention than is absolutely necessary.

Jessica is my main...nemesis, I guess, though there had been a time when we were friends. The summer before Middle School I had suddenly blossomed. My breasts began to emerge, I grew several inches, and suddenly nothing fit me. Shirts were too tight and pants too short. My mother couldn't be bothered by something as trivial as a growing daughter in her mad world, so I became a thief.

In the early morning hours before either of my parents had risen from their inebriated states I would sneak in and take a dollar or two from both my dad's wallet and my mom's purse whenever there was a dollar to be had. That was how I funded myself a "new" wardrobe; three shirts, two pants, one bra, three pairs of panties and one pair of battered shoes from the local thrift store. It cost twelve pilfered dollars and a great deal of guilt.

Though the clothes fit better than any other choice I had, they still marked me. Whereas in Elementary School I had been able to silently morph into a wallflower, unnoticed and largely left alone, Middle School saw me become a target.

It was Jessica Bolen who really started it, set the tone of what my life has since become—at least as far as school is concerned. For some reason she had begun to dislike me at the end of the previous school year. It had been close to the end of the year when she began saying derogatory things about me to my classmates, though there really wasn't enough time for the gossip to develop into more than a few lazily aimed barbs by her followers.

She had also blossomed over the summer and when school began she walked in as a confident, blonde beauty who had all of the guys noticing her—even the eighth graders and several of the freshmen. With her new confidence came a streak of cruelty and a perfect target for her to hone her skills on—me.

The first day of Middle School, I walked in wearing my second-rate clothes, and searched out the small group of friends I'd had in Elementary School, which included Jessica. As I approached, Jessica turned from where they stood in a circle, talking.

"What are you doing here? You don't belong with us," she sneered at me. I looked to the others, waiting for them to...what? Defend me? Instead, they all began laughing at my expense, and I turned away, humiliated.

Apparently she had overheard her parents talking about my family, and so the year began with her spreading rumors of my alcoholic father and drug addled mother. I couldn't even defend myself because no one knew as well as I did how true the rumors were. Of course, she didn't know the whole story and there was no way I was going to enlighten her and give her more ammunition. Not that she needed it since my clothes gave her that.

With her crushing any iota of self worth I might have pretended to have left I didn't fight back when she called me names, or knocked my books out of my arms, or tripped me when I carried a tray of food in the lunch room.

It was surprising how quickly the other students caught on to her games and joined in. Those who didn't join in soon avoided me like the pariah I was so that they didn't catch any of the bullets coming my way.

Every day since then has been a game of survival, like today, as I rush to get out of her path. I've learned to avoid areas where she or any of her friends might be, which is difficult since most everyone is her friend—or at least pretend to be.

I had hoped that High School might change the way things were for me in Middle School. I mean, the kids are older and more mature, right? While the teasing, shoving and name calling isn't as intense as my Middle School experience, it's still here, around every corner it seems.

My blonde hair has grown long over the years. I'm grateful for that because it makes a nice veil to hide behind. Unfortunately it also provides an easily grabbed handle for those wishing to pull it.

I guess I can always hope this year will be different.

It's while I'm hurrying to my second period class of the

day, walking with my head down but also observing those around me at the same time on alert for the warning signs of danger, that I see him.

Henry Jamison.

I stop cold where I am, getting bumped into from behind, but not shoved. I even hear a mumbled "Excuse me," though probably because they didn't realize who they'd bumped.

I'm frozen as I stare at him, mouth agape. The sight of him brings back a flood of memories that I had forgotten.

He had gone to my elementary school; I had known him from the first day of Kindergarten. I'd liked him in an innocent childlike way because he was never mean to anyone. He was the kind of kid that others flocked to naturally, popular without trying or even caring if he was. He made everyone feel as if they were his friend. I had admired that about him. Especially during those years when my life had gone dark and he had still treated me kindly.

He'd sat with me at lunch when I sat alone, which naturally brought others to my table as well. He'd always invited me to play kick ball when he saw me sitting alone, even though he knew I would decline. When I started to notice boys as something other than a complete annoyance I had thought he was the kind of boy I might really like—maybe even love—as more than just a friend.

The end of sixth grade made me think he might see me as something more as well when he gave me a special valentine—a card he had made and not just one of the cheap, small paper ones everyone else passed out.

The remembrance of that brings a remembrance of my

first kiss—my only kiss—in the coat closet. How bold I'd been. How nice his lips on mine had been. How much hope I had gleaned from such a simple thing.

My cheeks flush as I think of him holding my hand at recess, sometimes, after that kiss. We'd never kissed again, though I'd wanted to. I think we'd both been too shy and uncertain to make the first move.

He'd moved that summer. I didn't know, of course, until the next school year started.

Now here he is again.

He's grown, changed but there's no doubt it's him. He's tall, though he'd been close to my height when I'd last seen him. He stands taller than most of those around him and I'd guess him to be about six feet or so, maybe a little more. He has dark blonde hair, short on the sides and standing in odd spikes on top of his head, which I understand when he reaches up absently and runs his fingers through it. Rather than looking messy, though, it has a startling effect, looking as if he's spent hours getting it to look like that. His jaw is strong, square, masculine. The promise of the cute boy has become an amazingly gorgeous young man.

He laughs at something someone says and my stomach tightens in recognition. His smile is the same as I remember it, disarming and beautiful.

I stand here staring at him, forgetting to keep my usual watch for elbows or feet thrown my way, so when an elbow comes, I'm unprepared. It sends my books scattering across the floor—loudly—which catches his attention. His eyes meet mine and I see a flicker of recognition in their dark depths, a perplexed smile at the corners of his mouth. Horrified, I quickly scoop up my books and flee down the stairs, humiliated that he should have caught me staring, even worse having him see the new sport I've become.

Two

I spend the rest of the day hiding, even ducking my precious lunch, missing what is possibly the only meal I'll get today. Instead of looking for feet stuck out in front of me, I watch for him. As I settle into my last period of the day, photography, I breathe a sigh of relief that this horrible day is almost over. I sit alone at a table for two, confident that no one will sit next to me unless forced to. I sit with my head down, avoiding all eye contact with the precision I've developed over the years, which is how I see the large, white, athletic shoes stop by my desk.

A sick feeling forms in the pit of my stomach at the coming confrontation as it always does. But then—nothing happens. With a sinking feeling I realize my tormentor wants my whole attention, and won't leave until he gets it. I take a breath and lift my head—and feel my mouth drop at the sight of Henry standing there.

Dismay fills my chest.

Oh, no, please, not him too.

"Can I sit here?" he asks.

What? I cock my head a little, sure I haven't heard him correctly. I look around, seeing that there are a few other empty seats still available. I see a couple of the football players sitting toward the back, looking my way, snickering. I look back up at Henry and feel tears prick my eyes at the realization that it *is* him also—that he is somehow part of it, part of the torture, him sitting next to me is part of the game.

Before I can gather the courage to tell him no, he's placing his stack of books next to mine and sliding into the seat next to me. I immediately scoot away from him, hovering on the opposite side of my seat. He either doesn't notice or chooses not to comment on it.

"Hey, you're Kate aren't you? Kate Mosley? I don't know if you remember me; I'm Henry. Henry Jamison? We went to Elementary School together?" he ends on a question and I just stare at him like an imbecile—like my mother, when she's taken a few too many of her chill pills.

This is a new tactic, one I haven't dealt with before. I look around again, to see who else might be in on it, but just then the bell rings and the teacher rises from his desk, commanding our attention for the rest of the class—or trying to anyway. For my part, I can't concentrate at all on what he says; all of my attention is straining to the left.

I'm on guard even more than usual. My emotions are on edge, because though I don't know Henry now I had known him when he was younger. I had admired his kindness so much, even more so once any shred of kindness at home had disappeared—and had dimmed in my school mates. But apparently time has changed more than just his size and looks, it has changed his nature and he's quickly taken up the "torture Kate" game.

Each time he moves I jump involuntarily. I feel his eyes on me, but I refuse to be baited. I keep my eyes fixed resolutely on the open notebook in front of me, blank in spite of the teacher's lecture. He's telling us which supplies we will need for the class. I can't even concentrate enough to try to plan a way to get the impossible items. The only thing I look up for is to watch the clock. As soon as the bell rings, I'm ready.

I spring from my seat, scooping my books off the edge of the desk. By divine intervention, I don't drop them. I run from the room, not caring who I bump into on my way out, scrambling to keep my feet beneath me as I'm bumped and shoved.

I scramble past the area where the buses are parked, even though my house is five miles from school, which qualifies me for a ride on one. I quickly discovered the bus is just a persecution chamber with no hope of escape for those same five miles.

It's worth walking. Plus, there's the added benefit of walking taking more time, which keeps me from home a little longer. Today I walk quickly, at least until I'm past the boundaries of the school, beyond where most kids who have to walk have turned off. A few cars pass with windows rolled down, students hurling insults my way, but I ignore them.

I still can't believe he's part of it. I'm not sure why it should bother me so much. There are those who ignore me, of course. I would have preferred him to be one of those, though honestly I guess I'd hoped he might be the same as he had been all those years before.

I worry over this all the way to my house, the sight of which brings a tightening in my abdomen, as usual, and my attention is drawn from wondering about Henry Jamison to the reality of what lies ahead.

I wonder what mood *she'll* be in today. I actually prefer it when she's in a melancholy mood, even though it means a lot of crying. It's better than her violence, which I'm always on the receiving end of for something as simple as walking the wrong way or swallowing too loudly. I hurry inside, setting my books down, and removing my shoes to keep down the chance that she'll know I'm home.

I rush into the kitchen to start my chores, which means cleaning up the messes she made today. There are several plates and bowls piled in the sink, as well as the glasses from Dad's binge last night. I quickly wash, dry and put them away. I sweep the floor which is littered with food crumbs, and wipe the table. I throw away the empty liquor bottles, returning the others to the cabinet.

I hurry upstairs into the bathroom, gathering up the damp, smelly towels from there and from in front of my parents' bedroom door, and take them back down to the laundry room. I'm headed back to the bathroom to scrub the already-clean tub and toilet when I hear her.

"Kathryn!"

Stomach clenched, I walk into the living room where

she sits watching a small TV. It sits on a small, rickety table where there used to be a large screen that's been repossessed. I remember that day with crystal clarity because it was the first and only time I've been hit by my father; previously and since it has only been my mother who doles out punishment.

She sits on the couch in her usual, worn spot. She should be overweight, due to her diet of mainly junk food that she hoards jealously—and counts. If any are missing I catch hell—even if she *imagines* any missing. But the drugs keep her metabolism flying which keeps her thin. I think that I could probably outrun her if I wanted to, but she's done her work on my mind pretty thoroughly, starting when I was younger and more impressionable. Even knowing that it's all a mind game, I have no more courage to run from her than I do to stand up for myself at school.

"Where you been?" she demands, words slurred. "I have been calling you for hours!" Which could literally mean hours, or it could have been just a few minutes.

"I had school, remember? Today was the first day."

"Oh." That takes a little wind out of her sails, but she finds a new objective quickly enough. "Well, tomorrow before you leave you better make sure you get this house cleaned up. I can't live in this pig sty."

"Sure, mom," I reply, already cleaning up around her. Her clench-fisted swipe above my ear shouldn't surprise me, but I'm a bit off my game today. I stumble sideways onto my knees, hitting my head against the side table and nearly knocking the lamp off. I'm scrambling up and righting it before it can fall.

"You being a smart aleck?"

"No, mom, no. Sorry. Sorry." I breathe the word on each exhalation even as I feel the flush of humiliation at allowing her to treat me like this and then apologizing for it, but the routine hasn't changed much in the last eight years and habits are hard to break.

I hurry to the hall closet to grab the duster. I begin dusting around her items on the table, quickly but unobtrusively, knowing better than to upset her things.

"Oh. Leave off," she tells me, disgust in her slurred words. I stand back, waiting to see what else she has to say. "Quit staring, you give me the willies," she says. "Go to your room. I don't feel like seeing you today."

I merely nod and replace the duster on my way up the stairs. So it's the brush-off mood today—the best one of all. Staying in my room means no chance for dinner. It's a trade off, I suppose. Usually I'm commanded to make dinner, then not allowed to eat it. Sometimes I manage to sneak a little food if I cook. Being in my room means no possibility of that, but it also means I won't be hit.

So I'm relieved. I won't be able to sneak back down until they're asleep to retrieve my books that I've forgotten to grab on my way up. I always complete my homework, but sometimes throw it away instead of turning it in, in order to keep my grades average.

Unfortunately, that gives me a lot of time to think about Henry Jamison and wonder what he was up to today. Bitter disappointment in him returns and I sit by my window, gazing out at my swing-set where I wish I could be.

Three

"Hey, Kate."

I stumble and nearly fall at the words, bringing a round of derisive laughter from somewhere nearby. I glance back, and see Henry watching me. If I didn't know better I would swear he almost has a look of concern on his face.

I hurry away, clutching my books tighter. What did he mean by that, I wonder? His tone of voice sounded neutral, almost friendly. I truly thought there weren't any new games that could be thrown my way, that I had suffered every possibility of humiliation.

I was wrong.

I seriously consider ditching photography, but I don't dare. When I walk in, there he sits, already at our shared table. That's bad enough, but he's surrounded by two girls and another boy. I know the girls, popular cheerleaders, but ones who have left me alone. The boy is one of the kids who tormented me constantly throughout Middle School. He's now on the football team and hasn't bothered me much the past few years, but that doesn't exactly comfort me.

I debate sitting at another table, but a quick glance tells me there aren't any seats available that would be any better than next to him.

"Kate!" he calls as he waves at me. I stop, frozen in my tracks. The two cheerleaders stare at me, gape-mouthed, and the football player stares at Henry as if he's grown two heads.

"Okay, people, let's take our seats," Mr. Hurley, the teacher, commands. I'm forced to take my dreaded seat next to Henry, who smiles openly at me. I cringe and turn away.

"I have slips here for those of you who qualify for free or reduced lunches to exclude you from the class fees."

Oh no! My cheeks burn at what I know is coming. Sure enough, he walks over and lays one directly in front of me. Embarrassment floods my body at the humiliation of having Henry see this.

"Who else?" Mr. Hurley says, waving them in the air. "No one? Okay, then for the rest of you, I need a receipt showing you've paid your fees to the main office before mid-terms. Janna," a girl in the front row looks up at him. "Pass these out to everyone for me." He hands her a stack of slips.

Janna stands and begins handing out the slips as Mr. Hurley moves to the front of the room to begin lecturing. As she comes even with Henry, she hands him the slip with a smile, clearly indicating her interest in him.

"Hi, Henry. I'm Janna." There isn't any doubt by her tone that she's being more than just polite. He does an odd thing; he glances my way then quickly away. He smiles courteously at her, eyes averted.

Janna's smile hardens as she looks at me. Then it returns full force, mockery in every line.

"Here, freak," she oozes, handing a slip of paper my way, then jerking it back. "Oops, sorry, I forgot *you* don't need one of these."

She laughs cruelly, looking at Henry, expecting him to join in the joke. I can't see his face because he's turned slightly away from me toward her—that and the fact that I am now ducking my head, trying to hide my face but also trying to see his reaction. So I can't see what she sees, but whatever it is, it freezes her laughter. The smile drops from her face and she swallows loudly, cheeks flushed as she moves away.

Henry turns back toward me, but I quickly lean forward, pulling my hair down as a shield, mortified at the whole exchange.

I wonder how hard it will be to change my classes around.

School becomes even more of an exercise in torture—though I would not have guessed that was possible—because *he* has been added into the mix. Sitting next to Henry in photography is the worst, because he always sits and says hello as if we're friends. Most days he's surrounded by others, and either he's completely oblivious to their looks as he acknowledges me, or he just doesn't care.

I know what he's about because it's not exactly a new game. He's just better at it than those who've tried the same thing before. Get the freak to think you are her friend so that you can set her up for some major humiliation. I didn't learn the first time, and had been duped a second time, but I haven't fallen for it again; I won't this time either.

Always before, though, it hasn't seemed personal somehow. I know the others really don't think of me as a real person so while it hurts, it isn't the most devastating thing. This is worse because he'd been my friend once upon a time, and maybe even a little more. I have to admit, part of it is that I'd thought he was so much better the rest. It's a painful reality to see that he isn't.

In photography he sits, sometimes trying to start a conversation, but I keep my back turned and refuse to be drawn in, steadfastly ignoring him, keeping my hair between us.

Even knowing what he's up to, I can't help but be drawn to him in spite of myself. Because of our history, I suppose. So I watch him surreptitiously—just his hands, at first, as they drag a pen across the page while he takes meticulous notes. They're large, forming neat writing and not the messy scrawl most teenage boys create. Strong hands, long fingers, neatly trimmed clean nails, a thin scar across the back of his right hand. He's left-handed, but he doesn't write with his hand held at an awkward angle as I've seen other lefty's do. Rather, he holds his hand at the same angle as someone right handed, only in reverse, though he turns his page almost sideways to write.

Sometimes I even let my imagination wander and imagine his scarred right hand reaching over and enfolding my own. I wonder if it would be warm or cool, soft or rough with calluses. I can't recall how they felt all those years ago. I haven't been touched in a kind way by male hands for as long as I can remember—probably since he last held my hand—though I feel sure there was a time when my father touched me with love.

That's most disturbing of all, the fantasy of kindness from him.

Then I remember what Henry is about, that his kindness has died and that those hands will never touch me with anything other than for the purpose of humiliation, or worse, with revulsion. Each day after class I flee from the room, and from the building, waiting until I'm beyond school boundaries to slow down.

The first few weeks of school pass, and though Henry has quit trying to make conversation, he still says "hi" each day when he comes in. I never answer, but when he makes no further moves I at least begin to relax and not sit so far off the edge of my seat. He hasn't made any jokes at my expense in the hallways either, at least none I know about, and hasn't yet tried to humiliate me openly.

Oddly, it seems as if some of the other students who previously enjoyed tormenting me are losing interest in the game as well. Not all of them, of course, but some.

Then one day, as September gives way to October, the air beginning to cool, and leaves beginning to turn a brilliant yellow, something happens to change everything again.

I sit at lunch, in my usual spot on the floor in the corner, eating my free state-sponsored lunch, when Henry comes and sits at the table nearest me. I freeze in the act of lifting a bread stick to my mouth as he sits down at the table, which is usually reserved as a catch-all for the "losers" of the school (though obviously they're still not as big of losers as me, as they at least have a table).

He turns my way, looking directly at me. I stare into his dark eyes, the first time I've made eye contact with him since the first day of school. An electric charge runs through my body. Every nerve is standing on end, and a flush steals over my body, warmth flowing through my abdomen. I clearly recognize the fight or flight feeling.

He seems to be waiting for something, but I can't breathe, let alone think what he might want. He sets his tray down without breaking eye contact, then takes a step toward me.

That thaws me. Flight, it is.

I scramble to my feet, refusing to wait and see what he might do to me or my food. He calls my name, but I'm already hurrying toward the tray drop off area to dump my precious, uneaten lunch. I stumble in my hurry and nearly drop my tray, ignoring the mocking laughter near me along with calls of "idiot" and "freak." I don't even look to see who they come from. Those words no longer mean anything to me, but knowing that he's probably watching my clumsy retreat makes my cheeks burn brighter.

I ditch the rest of my classes. I've only ditched class once before in Middle School when the ridicule had reached extreme cruelty from a particularly tough girl and I was actually a little afraid for my life, so I'd left school early and went home. But when the school called home to inform my mother I had missed class, it had happened to be on one of her violent days. I'd had to return to school the next day with a black eye, swollen lip, sore ribs that felt possibly broken, and red finger marks on my neck where my airway had been cut off until just before losing consciousness.

When I came back, the tough girl had seen me, and some form of recognition and kinship had sparked in her eyes. After that she no longer gave me a hard time. In fact, I think there was a possibility that she had put out the word that I was to be left alone because no one gave me a hard time after that for quite some time. Then she had been arrested and taken to juvie—or so I heard—and within a short time she was forgotten. I was not and the persecution resumed.

On this day, I feel the risk to be worth it. I can't face him. And I feel at least a little safe since we no longer have a phone of any kind, so my truancy will require a note in the mail. I'm the one who has to bring the mail in so it won't be much to slip it out and drop it in the trash can outside before it can be seen. I wish I could go home and swing, but I can't risk being seen by my mother, so I hide out in a thick copse of trees that grow near my house until school is out and I am forced to go home.

However much I wish against it, though, another day comes and I have to get up and go to school. I had hoped that he would leave me alone, but at lunch I see him again coming toward my corner. Hunger wins out over my fear since I didn't get dinner again last night, and I curl protectively over my tray when I see him coming. Rather than looking directly at me or coming my way, he simply stops at the table and sits.

The few students who're gathered at the table look at him as if a viper has chosen to sit among them. I watch, my body still hunched protectively over my tray as he places his napkin on his lap, then makes sure to say hello to each person sitting there, introducing himself as if each one of them aren't exceedingly aware of just who he is.

You'd have to be blind or deaf to not know Henry Jamison. He has definitely not lost his ability to draw others to himself without even trying. Within days of his return to school he's become popular, sought after; by the boys to be a friend, and by all the silly, swooning girls to be much more.

After a few moments of silence, they resume their conversations, ignoring him mostly, but still glancing at him occasionally as if wondering why he's there.

A couple of Henrys friends saunter over, looking at those already seated, then eyeing Henry to gauge what their reactions should be. He introduces his friends to the "losers", amazingly remembering their names. His friends just nod, sitting and proceeding to ignore the others as if they aren't even there.

The others seem intimidated for a few minutes, shifting uncomfortably and wondering if they should move.

Finally, they decide to follow suit and ignore Henry and his friends.

I watch all of this with wonder and suspicion. What is he up to? When he does not as much as glance my way, I finally ease my hunched stance and begin to eat. I don't take my eyes off of him, though. I still wonder what he's up to, but I haven't eaten since my half-abandoned lunch the day before. I'm actually feeling somewhat faint from lack of food and that gives me the impetus I need to eat in spite of his proximity.

In photography I studiously ignore him, resuming my edge-of-seat position, refusing to even allow my eyes to wander to his hands. He had said "hi" when he sat, which is usual, but I feel tension emanating from him, which makes me nervous.

A new routine begins where he sits at that same lunch table each day, the table that's now filled half with the "losers", half with Henry's friends (both the original two from the first time and adding more it seems each day), each half ignoring the other but finding a strange sort of uneasy camaraderie. This new practice makes me stiff with anxiety. I consider changing where I sit, but have a feeling he'll follow me anyway. I just can't figure out *why*.

We pass another week without incident, my apprehension lessening a little, when an extraordinary thing happens. A boy who has been one of my worst tormentors both throughout Middle and High School comes into the lunch room. My stomach squeezes with fear.

Usually Frank and his buddies leave campus for lunch. When they stay there's a purpose, and that purpose is usually me. I cringed as I think of the times I've been forced to either dump my prized lunch because of something he spit or dropped into my food (once it was a small brown nugget of dog poop), or to try to eat around it. He takes great joy in my humiliation and I guess eventually he would start to miss my burning shame. Today is the first time this year he's missed it, apparently. I watch him immediately zone in on my sitting place, a grin splitting his face.

My eyes fly instantly to Henry, who's involved in listening to a story being told by one of his friends. *Oh please,* I beg silently, *please don't let him see this.* I'm not sure if I want him oblivious in order to keep him from getting a new idea for afflicting me, or whether I just don't want him to see my degradation.

I look back at my tormentor frantically, knowing from firsthand experience that trying to protect my food will only result in him pushing the tray against me, and then having to spend the day walking around vainly shamed that my front is smeared with the stains of my lunch.

I feel Henry's eyes on me and my gaze is drawn to his against my will. His brow is furrowed as if he's trying to figure something out. I can't keep my eyes in one place, though, gaze alternating between the two of them. He follows my flicking gaze to my tormentor, then back to me again. I watch as understanding dawns, but instead of the anticipation I expect to see when he figures it out, I see his face harden, anger darkening his eyes, jaw clenching.

Automatically assuming the anger is for me as I've been conditioned to for most of my life, I cower and keep my eyes on him, knowing he's the more immediate danger. He stands abruptly, causing every person at his table and even a few at nearby tables to stop conversation immediately and look his way. I cringe instinctively. Instead of coming my way, he turns toward Frank and steps in front of him, blocking his progress, back to me.

"Can I help you?" his words reverberate with fury. I hear it clearly from where I sit, but somehow it doesn't seem to register with Frank, who smiles cockily.

"No, man, I'm good."

He takes one more step, and suddenly Henry clamps a large hand down on his shoulder. Henry is at least six inches taller than Frank, and he doesn't lay it down softly, but rather drops it like a stone. Frank looks up at Henry and suddenly notices the clenched jaw. He hesitates for just a second, wariness creeping onto his face, to be replaced with an arrogant smirk as he realizes his friends are watching.

"Can I help *you*?" Frank asks sarcastically, which garners a snicker from his own friends.

"I don't think there's anything for you over here," Henry snarls at him, frightening me. Frank takes a slight step backward, glancing nervously over his shoulder, trying to retain his swagger. "I think you and your friends," Henry grits out, "should move on. I don't think this is the place for you to be—now, or anytime in the future for that matter."

Frank swallows nervously, holding up his hands in submission with a laugh meant to sound careless but which comes out sounding panicky. He throws a perplexed glance my way past Henry's impressively bulky arm.

"Alright, man, no harm no foul, right?"

Henry still has not removed his hand from Frank's shoulder and I watch as he squeezes, causing Frank to wince slightly.

"Not today, anyway," Henry growls ominously, glancing back at me, "but I'm guessing probably in the past." He leans in, putting his face closer to Frank's. "Not anymore, either. Capice?"

Frank gives a jagged laugh. "You're kidding, right, man? You're protecting *her?"* This is spit out as if I were less than a bug. I watch as his friends bristle behind him, affronted that they're being kept from their fun.

Then, amazingly enough, some of Henry's friends stand, all big football player types, clearly not understanding what's going on, but willing to back up Henry anyway. They don't move from where they stand next to the table, but Frank's friends immediately back down.

So does Frank, backing away from Henry's grip. His eyes dart my way and in that brief look I see something worse promised. Just as quickly he looks back at Henry, face carefully blank as he turns and walks away, trying to resume his careless swagger, but failing at least a little.

Henry's friends sit back down, muttering about punks, and the other kids at the table look somewhat awestruck at the scene that's just played out, that someone who is considered cooler than *them* has been taken down by these guys, while *they* are being allowed to share a lunch table. A couple of them shoot me confused glances, wondering what about *me* could have earned such defense.

I observe this from my peripheral vision, however, as I'm staring at Henry myself, awed. He's turned toward me now, and gazes back evenly, an expression in his eyes that I can't decipher. He doesn't seem to be angry with me, even though his breathing is still accelerated. As I watch, he takes a couple of deep breaths, mouth relaxing from anger to grim, clenched fists loosening. He nods tightly at me, resuming his place at the table.

I'm no longer hungry, but I don't move from my place, openly watching Henry. I can't help it. It almost seemed as if he...*protected*...me, as Frank had said. But...why would he do that? I'm confused, perplexed. A couple of times he glances covertly at me, but in those looks I can no more garner a reason than sprout wings and fly to the moon.

For the first time all year, I spend the afternoon looking forward to photography. I can't get the drama of lunch off my mind. No matter how I look at the situation, it still looks like he stood up for me.

Why?

When he comes into the classroom, I'm looking directly at him, trying to read his face. He stops next to the table when he sees my questioning look, looking at me with the same unreadable expression he had had earlier. A flush creeps up his cheeks, and he looks away, jaw clenching. He gives me another tight nod, for the first time not saying hello and I suddenly understand.

He's bothered and embarrassed that he *had* stood up for me, and in front of not only his friends but other students, among whom the story has spread like wildfire. I'd heard it being talked about when others didn't know I could hear, and people have been looking at me as if trying to figure something out. Now he's obviously sorry he had done it.

Tears prick the backs of my eyes as I turn my head back down toward the desk. For just a little while I had felt the elation of having a guardian angel, having someone who wouldn't let someone else be mean to me. Those couple of hours of feeling that safety only makes it more painful to have it taken away.

As soon as the bell rings, I quickly scoop up my books, ready to flee. I feel a hand clamp down on my arm. Heat floods from the point of contact as I still, staring at the hand that now holds my arm firmly. The same hand I've studied so much, with the light scar across the back. His grip is solid, and yet gentle enough that I know I could easily break contact.

"Kate," Henry says softly, and my heart lurches at the sound of my name coming from his mouth. "Please, I want to tell you—"

I don't wait to hear what he wants to say. I run, pushing past the other students in the doorway. A few people shove at me as I pass, but I manage to keep my footing.

Four

I run through the halls, pushing and shoving through the thick throng of teenagers until I reach the safety of the doorway. I leap down the steps, running toward my escape. I'm not sure if my feet tangle up as I reach the sidewalk or whether someone trips me, but suddenly I'm sprawled on the sidewalk, my books and papers scattering.

"Kate!"

I hear him call my name and look back to see him coming out of the door. I scramble up, leaving my books and papers where they lay. Taking the time to gather them will only give him the chance to catch up. I run faster without the hindrance of them anyway, ignoring the mocking laughter from behind, not knowing if part of that laughter is his.

I don't stop running until I'm halfway home, until my lungs are screaming and I have a stitch in my side, forcing me to stop. I lean over, hands on knees trying to catch my breath. It's only then I realize I'm crying. I stand up, putting my hands on my cheeks, feeling the wetness there. *Ow!*

I pull my stinging hands down, seeing that they're scraped and bleeding, peppered with small pieces of cement and rocks from when I had fallen. That stops my tears.

"*Idiot*!" I curse myself. Luckily, I'm near a small stream that runs along the side of the road. I take a step and nearly fall again, my throbbing knees buckling, adrenaline no longer carrying me. I look down and see that my left pant leg is shredded midway. "*Great!*" I mutter. I roll my right pant leg up above the knee. No scrape but a bright red mark that means a bruise tomorrow. I lift my left pant leg and see this knee is in much the same condition, only with an angry slice just below my kneecap which oozes a small amount of blood.

I limp along the road until I find part of the bank that looks safe enough to climb down to the water's edge. I half-slide sideways down the bank to the edge of the stream, knees screaming in protest. I sit on a flat rock and lean over to rinse my hands. I wash them as best I can, trying to dig the little rocks out, scrubbing the blood off. I splash water on my face, drowning the tears in the cool water.

A car drives by slowly above me, which wouldn't have caught more than my passing attention except that I hear the brakes, then the car backing up to stop directly above me. I look at the stream and the bank on the other side, gauging how hard it might be to make a run for it.

"There you are!" I freeze, stunned that *he* has found me here. "I have been looking for you *everywhere.*"

I force my legs into action, ignoring the pain from my knees as I stand. I crawl back up the bank toward the road, pretending it isn't hurting me at all. I have to use my hands to help me up the steep slope, grinding dirt back into my newly clean hands. As I come to the top he reaches for me, but I dart to the side, hurrying away, trying not to limp, failing miserably.

"Please, Kate, will you just stop for a minute? Wait—are you hurt?" he almost sounds genuine. I growl silently. "Kate, please, stop, I want to talk to you, to ask you—"

I round on him.

"What!" I demand angrily. "What do you want from me?" I limp-stride back over to where he stands, mouth agape at my outburst. "You've been gone for so many years...why now? Why can't you just leave me alone? Why do you have to be just like them, but worse because you were *better*!" I'm yelling now. I shove him on the solid wall of his chest with both palms, leaving muddy, bloody smears.

"Go away!" I command, as tears begin to fall.

He's staring at me, that odd expression in his eyes again. It makes me furious and with a yell I slam my hands flat against his chest again. He catches them and holds them there when I would have pulled back, and then suddenly his arms are around me, pulling me tight against him as I sob. Unthinkingly, I bunch his shirt front in my fists which are trapped between us as he holds me. His hands sooth down my back, chin resting lightly on the top of my head.

The feel of arms around me, in comfort rather than as restraint or in harmful intent, undoes me. I cry for all the years of mocking and teasing received at the hands of my peers, for having been born to hateful, careless parents. I cry for the fact that this one good, kind boy has joined the game. And *that* makes me think it's hopeless to find any good in anyone, which only makes me cry harder.

Gradually I become aware of where I am and whose chest I'm buried in. Mortification floods me. Still, I stay where I am for just one second longer, for one second reveling in the feeling of being held, touched with tenderness, even if it isn't real.

I push away, and he loosens his hold but keeps his hands on my shoulders. He ducks his head to look into my face and shame rises in my cheeks. I keep my eyes downcast, not wanting to see his expression which is likely disgust.

"Hold on a sec," Henry says, letting go of me, hurrying towards his car. I immediately miss the pressure and warmth of his hands, sure he's leaving now. Suddenly, he's thrusting a napkin at me. I take it cautiously, still unsure of his motives. I use it to wipe my face and nose with mumbled thanks.

I look, horrified, at the mess I've made of his shirt with my hands. I nod toward it. "Sorry about that," I concede, sure that this story will make the rounds tomorrow.

He smiles, and my heart skids to a halt before lurching into a staccato drumming. The smile actually looks genuine.

"It doesn't matter," he says, kindness in his voice, throwing me further off kilter. Then he looks down and sees the blood smears. He looks back at me, horrified. "You're hurt," he accuses.

I ball my hands into fists and shrug, taking a step backward in case he's angry now that he's seen his ruined shirt.

"I'm okay."

And I am, compared to some of the other injuries I've had in my lifetime. He steps forward, pulling my hands towards him, gently uncurling my fists, ignoring my flinch at his touch.

"Come on," he tells me, leading me gently back down the embankment. It's an easier descent with him steadying me, though definitely more terrifying. I still don't know what he wants from me.

He sits me back down on the rock I'd been sitting on before, then tears a strip of his shirt off. At my shocked gasp he grins and shrugs, causing my heart to speed up again. He dips the cloth strip into the water, and begins wiping my hands clean. Though he's surprisingly gentle, it stings and I suck my breath in through my teeth.

"Sorry," he says, leaning over to blow gently on my palms. It relieves the stinging there, but causes a burning to begin in the pit of my stomach—it's unlike anything I've experienced before. He continues the wiping and blowing with both my hands, until I feel like I'm on fire. I think I even groan because he suddenly looks up at me, eyes unreadable. I duck my head in shame. He then cleans my knee, which is still exposed by my rolled-up pants.

He tears two fresh strips from the back of his shirt, which is still clean, and uses those to bandage my hands, tying knots like a professional. When I raise my eyebrow at the knots, he grins again and says, "Eagle Scout. First Aid merit badge is required, you know."

I look at my hands, clean and bandaged, then back up at Henry.

"Why are you being nice to me?" I ask, bewildered by his attention.

His puzzlement matches my own as he says, "I don't really know."

My heart sinks at his answer. He must see that on my face, because he holds his hands up, palms facing me.

"That didn't sound right." He stands, pacing away, running his hand through his hair, causing his hair to spike up again. "When we were in Elementary, we were friends right?" He turns back, looking at me, but doesn't wait for an answer. "I can't really explain it, but I always felt, I don't know, *protective* of you."

He glances at me to see what I think of that. When I only sit, watching him warily, he continues, "When we moved, I missed you." This is said matter-of-factly, as if he's telling me the sky is blue, but his words rock me. Someone *missed* me? Not just anyone, but *him*? "I thought about you sometimes. Wondered what you were doing, if you were still here. Then I found out we were moving back. I was hoping you'd still be here, that I'd get to see you."

I couldn't be more stunned if he'd said he just swam across the ocean. The only thought anyone had ever given me had been when they saw me and thought of a way to hurt or humiliate me—peers and parents alike. To have someone think about me outside of that, to *miss* me, is beyond imaginable. I study him, trying to decide if he's just teasing me, setting me up for some elaborate prank, but honestly, he seems sincere.

"Then I saw you that first day and you ran away, and I've been trying to talk to you since. You don't seem very open to conversation," he says somewhat wryly. He looks at me, waiting for me to say something. I sigh.

"Things change," I say. He cocks his head, trying to understand what I mean. "Life here isn't the same. I'm not the same."

He nods, accepting this. He comes and squats in front of me.

"Yeah, you're a lot taller," he says gravely. I look up at him, and see his downturned mouth, then he glances up at me through his lashes and I see the gleam there. I can't help it—I laugh. This brings a smile to his face and I quickly cover my mouth to stop the sound. His smile falls, and he reaches up to pull my hand down.

"You shouldn't do that. I had forgotten what a great smile you have."

I spin away from him, tears threatening again. "You shouldn't say things like that," I mumble, rolling my pants back down—a gesture not without pain.

"Yeah? Why not?" He sounds genuinely curious.

"You can't tell me you haven't noticed the way things are at school. I'm everyone's favorite loser. There isn't anyone more fun to pick on than me."

He's silent so long, I finally turn back toward him, and see anger on his face again, jaw clenching. I'm taken aback, worried that he's angry with me. I glance at the bank on the other side of the stream again, wondering if I can make a run for it with my knees so sore. I know I can, of course I can. I've had to run other times with worse pain than this.

"Yeah, I've noticed. It really makes me mad."

I choke out a strangled laugh at that. *He's* mad about that? I shake my head.

"I want to be your friend," he says, and my stomach tightens.

"You can't be my friend. No one can be my friend. It's social suicide."

He reaches out and brushes his finger lightly over the bandage knotted on my hand, leaving an improbable trail of fire.

"I can honestly say that even if that is true, I don't care."

I let out a frustrated groan. "Of course you care. Everyone cares. Do you want to be treated like me? Trust me when I tell you that you don't."

"Trust *me* when I tell you I don't care. I think you give both yourself and some of these people too little credit. Besides, if they're that immature, who cares?"

"Spoken like someone who's never lived in my shoes." I look off to the east, staring at the rugged mountains.

He's silent for a minute, head down. "You're right. I haven't been there. I'm not asking for a sacrifice by either one of us. I'm just asking for a chance to be your friend." He gazes back at me, compelling me to meet his eyes.

"Why?" I ask, barely above a whisper. "You don't even know me anymore."

He smiles, and I feel my resolve weaken. "Yeah, but I'd like to."

I shake my head and grimace. "You don't know what you're asking."

"I'm not asking for anything. I won't expect any more than you want to give. Mostly just for you to not ignore me during photography."

The corners of my mouth lift a little at that. "I was kind of wondering how I was going to do that when we had to partner for labs."

He grins.

I look at him dubiously. "I don't know about the friend thing, though..."

"Yeah, you might be right. You might not like me too much when you get to know me," he teases.

Fat chance.

"Or you me," I return, dead serious.

"I doubt that," he's smiling, but his voice is solemn. "But we won't know if we don't give it a chance, right?"

A thousand reasons why we shouldn't bubble up, but he squeezes my upper arm in supplication, much as you might with someone who really is a friend. The arguments die on my lips.

"It's your funeral," I mutter insolently.

He laughs, and then holds out his hand to me. "Friends?"

I stare at his offered hand, before finally placing my hand in his. He gently squeezes, careful of the injury, then stands, drawing me up with him.

"Come on, friend, I'll give you a ride home."

"No!" he looks at me, surprised at my vehement refusal, but I can't let him drive me to my house. "I mean, that's okay, I like to walk. I walk home every day."

"Okay," he accepts this without argument. When I begin to climb the hill, my bruised knees that have been sitting in one position long enough to stiffen betray me and I groan involuntarily.

"What?" his concern is immediate, as he looks me over.

"Nothing, it's fine. I think I hurt my knee a little."

I try to play it off, intending to grit down on the pain and walk as if nothing's wrong. My body, never my ally, has other ideas and two limping steps give me away.

"Alright, enough of the martyrdom," he says, sweeping me up into his arms as if I were a small child. Surprised, my arms wrap around his neck to hold on, embarrassment causes me to duck my head. He strides easily up the hill, not putting me down until we reach his car. He sets me down, opens the door, moving a pile of books for me to climb in.

"These are yours," he says, handing me the pile. "You dropped them outside the school today." No reference to the fact that the reason I had dropped them—and skinned my hands and knees—was that I had been running from him.

"Thanks," I mumble.

He closes the door, walking around to climb in the driver's side. It feels surreal, riding in a car beside a boy, almost as if I'm normal. I direct him to within about a block of my house.

"Stop here, I'll walk now."

He turns to look at me, an argument ready, but something he sees in my face stops him. He nods, and pulls over.

"You sure you'll be okay?" he asks.

"Yeah, I'll be fine."

"Okay. Hold on," he says when I reach for the door handle. He jumps out, running around the car to open my door. I pretend that my knees aren't blaring at me, and he pretends not to notice as I clamber out.

"You know, you're a little taller, too," I tell him, amazed at my boldness.

He laughs as he gets back in, gives me a wave, turns his car around and drives off. I watch him go, wonder thrumming through me—right alongside the suspicion.

When I limp in the front door, I see immediately that my mother is asleep, snoring in a drug-induced slumber. Another first as I sneak quietly past her—not that she's sleeping but that I ignore my chores for the moment, going up the stairs. I walk into the bathroom, locking the door behind me. With some trepidation, I approach the mirror.

The mirror has become my enemy over the years, only required when I need to try to cover a bruise or black eye. Now I look in, pull my long, light blond hair back from my face, and try to see what Henry might see when he looks at me.

Rather unremarkable, I think. With a finger, I trace smooth skin (blessed with acne free, blemish free complexion), straight nose, eyebrows neither too bushy nor thin, an ordinary mouth, indented chin. I suppose my eyes are my best feature, wide and fringed with dark lashes. They're light blue, ringed with gold.

I shake my head and let my hair fall back into place. Nothing attractive, extraordinarily plain, but he still wants to be my friend. Okay, then.

For the first time in my life, school tomorrow is something to look forward to. As a matter of fact, I think I might not be able to wait for it to come.

Five

However, as morning dawns, I find myself tied up in knots. Had the previous afternoon really happened, or had I only dreamed it? Because I can't imagine that anyone would go out of their way to be my friend, let alone Henry. I wake early with excitement, but gradually my self-doubt chips away at it until I find myself dragging my feet, not leaving until the last possible minute.

Once at school I fall back into my old pattern of avoiding places where he might be. I'm not sure what I'll do if I see him and he ignores or, even worse, laughs at me.

By the time lunch comes, I'm taut with tension. I walk into the lunchroom, head down, stand in line to get my lunch, and then head for my usual corner.

And stop dead in my tracks when I see him sitting at the same table, looking right at me, smiling. At least, I guess he is smiling at me because a glance behind me doesn't reveal anyone there looking in his direction.

As I come closer, still hesitant, he steps out from his chair. I stop again, frozen, tense, waiting for… what? For him to flip my tray out of my hand? For the joke to come at my expense? For his mocking laughter?

He walks toward me, a questioning look in his eyes, the smile on his lips faltering somewhat. He runs his fingers through his hair, stopping when he's standing in front of me.

"Hi," he says.

The sound causes me to twitch nervously, and I quickly glance around to see if anyone has heard. He still has a chance to back away. He takes another step and raises his hand toward me. I step backwards, ready to duck if he pushes my tray upwards. He halts the motion, color draining from his face. He stares at me, and I feel my cheeks flush with chagrin.

"Let me carry that for you," he says, quietly, taking my tray. I'm reluctant to release my grip, having lost more than one meal in the past from this very tactic. Not wanting to get into a tug-of-war with *him,* I let go. To my surprise, he simply turns around and places it on the table next to his own—then pulls the chair out. I look at the chair, then back at him. Another tactic I've fallen prey to before, the chair being pulled out from under me as I go to sit.

Henry simply waits.

With some reservation, I start forward, gripping the edge of the chair as I sit to keep it from being pulled out, but I don't feel a backward tug on it. It's a little uncomfortable to be sitting at the table, and I look longingly at my usual spot on the floor. I feel very exposed. Henry sits next to me; his size and presence shelter me, offering some sense of security—false or not, I find it comforting.

"How are you doing today?" The question is unexpected, and I put down the slice of pizza I'd been about to bit into.

I shrug, "Fine, I guess."

He grins, "I meant your hands and knees."

"Oh." I glance down at my palms, and suddenly his large hands are there, pulling my hands toward him. His touch burns through me from the point of contact, all the way to my stomach. I've had more human contact in the last twenty-four hours than I've had for as long as I can remember—excluding the violent kind, of course—and it has all been from him.

He examines my hands carefully, as if he were about to make a diagnosis. He rubs the pad of his thumbs softly over the scabbing scratches, and I shiver involuntarily.

"They look better. Clean, not infected." He glances up at me, and grins again. My heart thuds and I pull my hands back. He doesn't seem offended, the smile never wavering. "You aren't limping so badly, either." This surprises me; I thought I wasn't limping at all. "Did you walk to school today?"

I nod, still tongue tied.

He shakes his head. "You miss the bus?"

"No, I never ride the bus. I always walk."

"Healthier, huh?"

I almost laugh at his words.

"Yeah." *Healthier with the decreased chance of being beat up!*

"Then you blow it all by eating that greasy crap," he teases, indicating my pizza. To him, greasy crap; to me, likely the only meal I'll get today and therefore beyond delicious. I can't say that, of course, so I shrug and pick it up again, taking a big bite.

Then I notice the others at the table. They're the "losers" and they're looking at me, mouths hanging open, shocked more than they would have been if Henry had sprouted a second head and started talking in tongues. I quickly look down, trying to ignore them as I eat, but hyper aware of their stares anyway.

As if that isn't bad enough, soon two of Henry's friends come over, dropping their trays loudly and high-fiving Henry. They glance aside at me, but I think that maybe they seem less surprised to see me here than the losers are.

"You know Ian and Kaden?" he asks me, and I only stare as they both jerk their chins toward me in greeting. Soon three other boys come and sit, Henry again making introductions, as if I haven't been attending school with these guys for several years.

With them come a lot of noise and talking, and I'm glad to sink into obscurity, eating quickly. Henry keeps glancing my way, as if to make sure I know I'm included in the conversation, but not trying to draw me in, for which I'm grateful.

Lunchtime passes both too slowly, and much too quickly.

After lunch, I have two classes before photography. I

go through the motions in those classes, but I'm counting down the minutes until photography. I'm earlier than usual, then try not to keep watching the door, looking for the familiar, dark blonde, spiky hair to come in. When I see his frame filling the door, my pulse quickens. As he sits next to me with his usual greeting, I can tell I surprise him when I look at him with a shy smile and say "hi" back.

Class starts and there's no chance for conversation, but I feel a kind of comforting satisfaction sitting here next to him. Today is the last day of note taking, and on Monday we begin labs. I'm looking forward to that so that I'll have an excuse to interact with him—and dreading it at the same time.

As soon as the bell rings, I start stacking my books, not in as big a hurry as I've been before, but still needing to get off campus before the bulk of the students do to increase my chance of being left alone.

"Need a ride home?" his words stop my movements. I think about how it had felt, sitting next to him in his car. Then I think about the looks and talk it will cause, not to mention how much sooner I'll arrive home.

"No, thanks, I'm going to walk."

"With your knees?" he's skeptical. "Come on, it's on my way." I still hesitate, anxious about the thought of walking down the hallway next to Henry, with everyone watching, wondering if I should suggest meeting him at his car—knowing I'd never actually show up.

He takes my hesitation as capitulation, and grabs my books, piling them on his own as he stands.

"I promise not to bite," he teases with that disarming

grin. Without that, I might have said no, but I'm sadly powerless against what it does to my heart. Head down, I walk out of the room beside him.

Once we're in the hall, I slow my steps a bit, walking just slightly behind him. It seems too brazen to walk right next to him. He slows his steps to match mine, keeping me next to him. I try to slow more, but he also slows. Finally, when we're barely moving, I realize the ridiculousness of it, and begin walking at a normal pace. I try, unsuccessfully, to ignore the looks and whispers that come our way as it's obvious we're walking together since Henry occasionally grabs my elbow to steer me through the crowds.

I'm grateful when we reach the car. He opens my door for me, handing me my books before shutting the door. As we pull out of the parking lot, I'm again aware of disbelieving stares and students pointing at us. Henry's oblivious.

"So, you have any big plans for the weekend?" he asks, attention on the road as he navigates the maze of teen drivers still pulling out of other lots and merging into traffic.

Let's see; housecleaning, laundry, cooking food I won't be allowed to eat, and maybe a beating or two. And, oh, yeah, swinging on my children's swing-set as a means of escape.

"No, not really. You?"

"Nothing to write home about. I'm sure my mom has a list of chores for me," this said with a lighthearted grudge in his voice and a smile on his lips. I wonder at those chores, certain they're nothing compared to my own. "I thought I might go to the football game tonight. You going?"

The football game? I have to think for a minute. Ah, yes, he must mean the high school's football game. I'm barely aware of the schools extracurricular activities as they aren't for me. No matter what game he's referring to, I won't be attending.

"No."

"Do you want to go...with me, I mean?"

I look at him, stunned. Is he asking me on a date? *No*, I laugh silently at myself, of course not. He's just trying to be nice, to be my friend. My silence spurs him to speak again.

"I could come pick you up. You know we don't want you walking on those sore knees for a few days," he teases, smiling at me.

"No, I can't." There's no answering smile on my face, and even I hear the quiet desperation in my voice.

"Oh, come on, it might be fun and—"

"No! I said no. I just...I just can't, okay?" He's silent following my outburst.

"Is everything okay?" His voice is full of concern.

I keep my head turned away, not answering, not trusting my voice because I can imagine it, imagine sitting next to him on the bleachers, drinking a soda, almost being a *normal* teenager. I feel his gaze on me, though he doesn't press me.

He stops at the place I'd had him let me off the previous day and I nearly leap from the car, not waiting for him to open it for me, slamming the door behind me, running toward home, ignoring my screaming knees.

Six

It's the most depressing weekend I've had—and I've had plenty of depressing ones to measure against it. Before it's all been about what was at home for me, where this one is about what could have been *away* from home for me.

A week ago, I wouldn't have even thought of it, but now I do. I can imagine it and it's Henrys fault; he treated me like I was the same as all the other girls when he asked. I don't know anything at all about football, don't know if it's something I would like or hate, so that isn't the thing that has captured my imagination. It's just the being there, among my peers, sitting next to Henry.

It doesn't even occur to me to worry about the teasing or humiliation I might suffer by showing up in a social place where there's less supervision than even at school, because somehow I know that if I'm with him, no one would bother me.

Mom's particularly ferocious this weekend as well, probably because Friday had been Dad's payday. He still hasn't come home from work by Saturday night which means there won't be much money left when he does get home—if any—because he will have drank most of it away. This means that on top of my misery at missing out on being with Henry at the game, I also have the added fun of being her target.

Dishes not being washed and put away quietly enough result in fingerprint bruises on my upper arm; causing dust motes to fly in the air earn me a punch in the chest that leaves me gasping for breath. Finally, on Sunday as she stands screaming in my face because I had eaten one of her candy bars—which actually is true for once, though in my defense I hadn't eaten anything else all weekend and felt faint from being forced to stand in the corner for three hours straight—she reaches out and belts me below my eye, knocking me to the floor. Before she can harm me any further, we hear my father's car turn into the driveway.

"Go get cleaned up. You look a mess," she tells me quickly. I'm well versed in the hide-the-abuse-from-dad game. Not because he cares about me, but because it just gives him more excuse for beating on her. I'm not going to look this particular gift horse in the mouth. I hurry up the stairs, washing my face, seeing the already purpling bruise around my eye. I hear him come in, her accusations and then the yelling starts. I slip into my room, opening the window and crawling out to find refuge on my swing.

* * *

Monday morning I arise early and quickly shower and dress. I set a personal best record for being ready to leave, hurrying down my street and around the corner, where my feet skid to a stop.

In the drop off spot, Henry stands, leaning against the hood of his car, legs crossed at the ankles, arms folded and head down, looking for all the world as if he's in for a long wait. As if sensing me watching him, though, he suddenly glances up. When he sees me, a slow smile splits his face; he slowly unfolds and walks toward me.

"Hey," he calls, naturally, as if this is a normal occurrence for him to be sitting here.

"What are you doing here?" I ask suspiciously.

He laughs.

"Good morning to you too."

I smile and shrug, embarrassed at being rude. "Good morning." I look at him for a moment, and then ask again, "What are you doing here?"

He sweeps his hand to indicate the car. "Thought you might like a ride."

I shift uneasily.

"Did you think maybe I walk because I *like* to?" I ask, somewhat defensively.

He's taken aback by that.

"Really?" he's baffled. "You like walking that far to school twice a day, every day?"

I look away, and then give a half-truth.

"Yeah." I do like walking *most* of the time, but only because the alternative is so unappealing. Some days it's tedious, and sometimes my battered body makes it difficult, but it also gives me *me* time; time to think, to see, to feel and smell the world without anyone bothering me.

"Huh," he huffs, surprised and a little deflated. "Well, I thought maybe your knees..."

"They feel better now."

"Oh," he seems at a loss. The corners of my mouth lift slightly at his little boy look and I take mercy on him.

"It was a really nice offer, though. I appreciate it."

He still looks a bit pouty, and I can remember the boy he had been in our earlier years in grade school.

Suddenly he brightens and looks at me.

"Maybe I could walk with you today. I'll just leave my car here, and pick it up after school."

My brows furrow.

"But how will you get back here to get it?"

"I could walk back...with you...you know, if that's okay...." He trails off and with shock I realize he's feeling *unsure* of himself.

"Okay." My quiet answer surprises him—me, too, if I'm being honest. He gazes at me for a minute, gauging to see if I'm accepting because I want him along or if I just feel pressured. Whatever he sees in my face satisfies him, and he nods.

"Alright. Let me grab my books and lock up." He does that, hurrying back to my side. "Do you have a special route you take?"

I nod, serious. "Yes, I like to take the one that gets me there."

He looks at me for a minute. I can't keep the grin back. He bursts out laughing.

"Yeah, I guess that would be a good one."

He grabs my books from my arms, lifting his shoulders. "My mom would kill me if she thought I wasn't being an absolute gentleman for even one second." Well, that would explain his opening the car door for me.

He matches his longer stride to mine as we walk. He glances aside at me, opening his mouth to say something. The words never come. He stops abruptly and I stop with him at the alarmed look on his face, glancing behind me to see what has him worried. Has someone seen him walking with me? Looking back at him, I see it's me he's staring at.

"What?" I ask.

He reaches out, laying his hand lightly on my cheek, thumb lightly skimming just above my cheekbone.

"You have a black eye."

I jerk away from his touch, bringing my own hand up to replace his, covering the side of my face, making my hair a veil between us as I drop my head. I'd mostly forgotten about it. I had covered it with some concealer earlier, though apparently I hadn't done a very good job.

"What happened?" I hear the anxiety in his voice.

"Just being my usual clumsy self," I lie. "I fell against the doorframe." The lie rolls easily off my tongue, having told it many times before.

He reaches out and pulls my hand away, turning my face toward his, examining it with the same care and concentration he used before when he had examined my scraped hands. He looks skeptical about my story, but doesn't question me further.

"You need to be more careful," he chides gently. "Does it hurt?"

His unfamiliar touch is doing funny things to my head, making it hard to think, so I pull away again and continue walking.

"No. I had forgotten about it until you mentioned it." He steps quickly to catch up to me. I can feel his gaze on my face, my cheeks heating up. He's silent.

"Does it look that bad?" I ask when the silence lengthens.

He doesn't say anything for so long I finally risk a peek at him. He's looking at me with an intense watchfulness. He sighs.

"No, it's really not that easy to see."

"You saw it," I accuse.

"I'm pretty observant, probably more than what's normal."

We walk in silence for a few minutes.

"Have you ever thought of becoming a doctor?" I ask.

He jerks in surprise.

"What makes you ask that?"

"I don't know, you just seem sort of doctor-ish, you know, like today with my eye and last week when you were cleaning my hands. You just seem really concerned about injuries."

He smiles. "Actually, I have thought about that. I've thought about it a lot. Enough that I have my schooling planned to send me in that direction. My dad's a veterinarian, so I've spent most of my childhood watching him heal—animals, anyways. I always wanted to be like him, be a vet, you know? But even though I really like most animals, I'm not passionate about them like him, so I thought maybe I'd be better with people."

I try to imagine what it would be like to have a dad you admire so much that you want to follow in his footsteps.

"I remember your mom a little bit," I tell him. "She always came on field trips, and I remember her being in the classroom for parties and things."

"Yeah, she's a good mom. It's a good thing I have younger sisters, because she would miss having little kids to spend all her time on."

Tightness grips my throat. I vaguely remember my own mom once being like that. What a horrible child I must have been to have killed that kind of caring. I clear my throat, pushing those thoughts away.

"I remember one sister; your mom always brought her in a stroller. You have more now?"

"That was my little sister. She's ten now. I have another sister who's thirteen. Maybe you don't remember her because she was in school herself. And I have a little sister who's three; she was sort of an oops. Pretty embarrassing for a fifteen year-old boy to have a pregnant mom. But, what can you do? Besides, she's a really cute kid."

"No brothers?"

"No." He laughs. "My dad says he and I live in an estrogen ocean, which isn't too bad right now, but just wait until they've *all* hit puberty."

I laugh. He looks at me, embarrassed that he said that, then looks away.

"What about you?" he asks. "Any brothers or sisters?"

"No," I say, thinking as always of the little brother I should have had, the little brother who's death had destroyed my mother.

I still have memories of life when it was good. That's both a blessing and a curse, as the saying goes. A blessing because in the darkest of times those are what I cling to, what I dream about and re-imagine my life to be. Sometimes that's all that keeps me hanging on.

The curse is that those remembrances also make my life now seem that much bleaker because there was a time when life was light. The darkness began the day my dad lost his job—but really; people lose their jobs every day. Why had it been so traumatic for my father? That's a question I've never had answered.

In the beginning, my pregnant mother protected me from the worst of my father's fury. She was the calm in the storm. When we could hear his car coming down the road, she would shuffle me outside to play on my new swing.

It was there that I found my escape. With the wind blowing through my hair, blue sky above and green grass below, I found flight. I would imagine I was a bird, and that if I could just go high enough, I could let go of the chains and fly far away from the yelling, from the sounds that I refused to let my brain process, but that always resulted in a black eye or cut lip on my mother.

When she went into premature labor after a particularly violent fight just a few days before Halloween, I was outside trying to reach that magical flight. I had heard my father slam out the front door and drive away when I heard her painfully distressed call for help.

I ran inside and saw the pool of blood underneath her where she lay on the floor, holding her rounded belly and gasping in pain. About a month earlier some scary looking men had come during the day and taken her car. I couldn't have driven her anyway, being only nine and small for my age. Having no phone also diminished the options. It was expressly forbidden to go to the neighbors at all. When she slumped to the floor and I couldn't wake her up, I was desperate. I broke the rule and ran to the house next door.

The neighbor called 911, but apparently, that was where her help ended. She didn't even come to the house to see if she could help my mother, and even at that young age I could understand her reluctance to become involved. I would have happily uninvolved myself with my family if I could have.

Soon there was an ambulance taking her away. No one seemed too concerned that they were leaving a nine-year-old home alone with a large puddle of blood marring the kitchen's tile floor. I was afraid of my father coming home and seeing the mess, so I found some towels and wiped it up as best as I could. I had never actually used the washing machine myself, but I had seen my mother do it, so I tried to mimic what I remembered and placed the red soaked towels inside, dumping in what seemed like the right amount of soap, and twisting the dial until the water flow began.

I then pulled the mop and bucket out of the closet and finished cleaning up, scrubbing around the edges of the puddle where the blood had begun to dry in a hard line, until I couldn't see any remnants of the blood left. My father never did come home that night. He'd received the news somehow and had gone to the hospital. I stayed home alone.

I'd been out back swinging for quite some time before realizing he wasn't coming, and neither was she. So I went in, locked the doors and went to bed as if nothing had changed. Noises in the night when you are alone are much more sinister than when you have someone there with you.

She didn't come home the next day either, though my father came home briefly to tell me that she would be home the next day. I was surprised that he actually looked somewhat sad and something else—guilty?—when he stopped in. He brought a bag with a hamburger, some greasy fries, and a soda for me; a rare treat that I hadn't had since before the day he had lost his job. He left and I assumed I would be spending the night alone again.

However, I was awakened in the dark of the night when he stumbled in. I cowered down under my covers, afraid without the protection of my mother. His footsteps stopped outside my door, and ice crawled over my skin, freezing my body motionless, even my breath. Finally, he stumbled on, and I breathed a sigh of relief. I shook like a fall tree in the wind, unable to control the residual fear, tears running silently down my cheeks. Sleep was a long time coming.

He did go to the hospital the next day to bring my mother home. When she arrived her stomach was strangely flat, and she did not bring a baby. I was so happy she was home I threw myself against her, wrapping my arms around her waist. But she didn't hug me back, or even seem to notice I was there.

"Leave off," my father commanded roughly, a phrase both of my parents began to use with me quite often. I dropped my arms, looking up with a question. She didn't even look at me, and I noticed how sad she looked, the corners of her mouth turned down deeply, eyes red and swollen. She walked into the house and lay down on the couch, turning her back toward us, pulling the blanket which hung on the back of the couch over herself, covering her head.

"Mommy?" I questioned, calling her by the name I hadn't used in a long time. She ignored me and then I heard her soft cries coming from under the blanket. I looked at my dad, accusingly, which seemed fair since he had been the cause of all her other tears for the last few months.

He looked at me and I saw guilt flit quickly across his face again, then he looked away and replaced it with his usual scowl.

"Your mom lost the baby," he told me.

Lost it? Shouldn't we be out looking for it? He must have seen the confusion on my face because he clarified.

"The baby died. Your mom will be sad for a while so go outside and leave her alone."

I was stunned. The baby had died? How did that happen? He glanced at me briefly again, saw the questions on my face and turned away.

"I'm going out," he called over his shoulder as he pushed out the front door. I stared after him, tears pricking my eyes. I looked back at the huddled lump on the couch that was silently shaking and did as I had been told; I went outside where my trusty friend the swing waited to take me away.

* * *

"An only child, huh? Bet you're spoiled." Henry's comment jars me back from my bitter memories as we walk. A cynical laugh escapes me at his comment. I'm the furthest thing from spoiled there could be. He looks sharply at me.

"How was the game?" I blurt out, the first thing I can think of to change the subject. He watches me for a few moments longer, though I'm looking at the sidewalk, as if he might read my mind and see the truth.

"It was okay, I guess. Typical, lots of screaming kids not watching the game at all. It's more social than anything. I doubt more than a few of the people there could tell you the difference between a touchdown and a field goal."

I feel mortification color my cheeks, wondering if he knows that I don't know myself.

"I think most of the guys go to watch the cheerleaders, and most of the girls go to watch the football players."

He has no idea how great the whole thing sounds to me.

"And we lost anyway. Next week should be better, though. We play Jefferson." Jefferson High School is our schools biggest rival, though I never could figure out why they should be a rival more than any other school. "You should come."

Sensing the refusal I'm about to issue, he hurriedly jumps in. "Before you say no, just promise to think about it. If it's an issue with your parents not wanting you to go with a boy, you could just meet me there. I'll make sure there are girls with us so that you won't have to lie. I can even get someone to come pick you up—a girl I mean. It doesn't have to be like a date or anything, if that's a problem. Just friends, just for fun," he holds up a hand in supplication. "Just think about it? Please?"

I don't want to argue, or have to try to make up an excuse, so I just nod, knowing I'll have to say no on Friday afternoon. He smiles triumphantly, and I feel bad thinking about having to take away his perceived victory.

I have to admit, for the rest of the week, I fantasize about it. I imagine telling him yes, see again how it would be, sitting there like everyone else, as they all take for granted, being *normal.*

Seven

He doesn't mention the football game again the rest of the week. Part of me hopes he's forgotten about it and won't ask me again, forcing me to tell him no if he does.

A bigger part of me is dismayed at the thought that he's forgotten, or regrets asking me, and that he won't ask again.

He drives me home on Friday. Every day he has shown up in the morning. Sometimes we ride in his car, other times we walk. I like the walking better because it takes longer to get to school. Alone with him I can be myself and talk freely—or as freely as I can for someone full of secrets.

I'm tense on Friday, filled with dread over whether he'll ask again or not. He doesn't say anything about it on the whole ride home, granted the drive doesn't take all that long. So it's with both relief and disappointment that I say goodbye as soon as he opens my door and I climb out of the car.

"Wait," he says, grabbing my forearm lightly. "Did you think about the game? Will you come?"

I can't. Those are the words in my head, the ones I intend to say. Instead I hear myself say, "Okay."

What?

His face echoes the stun in my head, but he recovers quickly.

"Cool. Should I pick you up at your house or..."

"I'll meet you here." Not sure how I'm going to accomplish *that.* My throat closes with fear.

"Okay. How about six-thirty?"

I nod, not trusting myself to speak, walking quickly away instead of waiting for him to drive off like I usually do. I hurry home, wanting to finish my chores as quickly and efficiently as possible to hopefully avoid Mom's wrath. I feel like I might throw up from the tightness that seizes me from the top of my head to the tips of my toes. I'm praying for something like a miracle to pull this off.

When I get home, it's to find Mom showering. This throws me since she never showers in the afternoon. It's rare she showers in the morning but it's never occurred in the afternoon.

I stand in the kitchen, unsure of what to make of this.

"Kate?" she calls a few minutes later from her bedroom. At least she's calling me "Kate" instead of "Kathryn." When she calls me by my full name, it never ends well.

With trepidation, I approach her bedroom door. I knock softly, and she calls for me to come in. I stare at the door with terror. I'm never allowed even near her bedroom, let alone within. My hand is on the doorknob, afraid to turn it, afraid not to.

"Kathryn, get in here," she demands.

I open the door, but stay on the threshold.

"There you are." She stands in front of her closet, dressed only in underwear and a bra. I look around, wondering if I've stepped into some twisted version of the real world.

"I need your help. I've gotta get ready for dinner." Like this is a usual request.

"Dinner?" my voice is a strangled whisper.

"Yes, dinner." *You idiot,* is the clearly unspoken rest of that sentence. "You know what that is, right? Food you eat in the evening, after lunch, before bedtime." Her voice is derisive.

I've heard of that, yes, I just usually don't get to have that myself. I imagine the consequences of speaking that sentence aloud. Instead, I say, "What can I do to help?"

"Your dad's boss is having some fancy shindig that the wives are required to show up for. You need to help me get dressed and fix my hair."

I wonder if she's suddenly speaking a foreign language, because her words make no sense to me. When I just stand there, she throws me a dirty look.

"Don't just stand there like an imbecile. Get in here."

I step hesitantly into the forbidden realm, trying not to look around, though I can't help it somewhat. Dirty laundry and paper clutter the room. *Well,* I think, *if you don't let Cinderella into the castle, she can't clean it up for you.*

She puts on a button-up blouse with a wrap around skirt, which I help her tie. She sits while I use the blow dryer to dry her hair. She wants me to put hot rollers in for her, but the close contact with her makes me a nervous wreck, and I keep dropping them. Finally she swats my hands away.

"You're useless," she tells me. "Go...clean the kitchen or something. Try to make yourself useful."

I don't wait to see if she's going to change her mind, having been handed this reprieve. I go to do what she commands, cleaning quickly but thoroughly so that she won't be able to find immediate fault.

When my dad pulls into the driveway, my stomach begins convulsing again. He hasn't been home this early for as long as I can remember. For the most part, it feels as if no one lives here but my mother and me.

He comes in, glancing at me but ignoring me as completely as if I were invisible. I hear the shower come on again and a few minutes later they both emerge from their room, looking for all the world like any other married couple going out to dinner. I'm sure my mouth is hanging open.

"Finish up your chores, then go to bed," is all the instruction or information I get as they walk out the front door. I walk into the living room, watching them through the window as they climb into dad's beat up old car and pull out of the driveway. It's not until they pull away that I realize what this means for me.

I'm going to a football game.

* * *

I finish my chores in record time. There isn't much I can do about myself besides run a brush through my hair, and pull the least trashed shirt that I have out of the five that I *do* own. Afraid they'll come back early and stop me, I run down the street and around the corner—and nearly barrel Henry over.

He catches me by the arms, taking the weight of us both against a telephone pole, managing to keep us from sprawling on the sidewalk. Embarrassment floods me as he sets me back from him.

"In a hurry?" he asks with a grin.

"Sorry, I didn't think you'd be here yet."

Confusion flits across his features.

"Then why the hurry? Were you trying to come and go before I arrived?"

Surprised at the way his mind works, that he would think *I* would be trying to avoid *him*, I shake my head.

"Of course not. It would have been nice to be the first one here, though. No matter how early I leave my house, you always beat me here." Not a lie, just a different truth.

He laughs. "Sorry. It must seem like I'm some weird stalker or something, just sitting here waiting for you to happen by."

I shrug. "I don't mind. It's kind of nice to have someone waiting for *me.*"

He cocks his head, dark eyes intense.

"Well, those who aren't waiting for you don't know what they're missing."

My breath catches in my throat. It almost sounds like he's flirting. I shake my head and give a (nearly) silent guffaw; that's foolish. He's just being his usual gentlemanly self as his mother taught him, the same as when he carries my books or tray, pulls out my chair at lunch, opens my car door. His steady gaze hasn't softened, watching me as if expecting something, a response or reaction. I have none because I don't know how to respond to this kind of teasing.

"So," I say, sweeping my hand toward the car, averting my eyes from his, "are you going to open my door or do I have to do it myself and tell your mom on you?"

He chuckles, the spell broken, striding over to the car. He opens the door, bows with a flourish and sweeps his hand toward the car. I smile shyly as I pass him.

We arrive at the high school well before the game starts, but the parking lot is already crawling with students. There are students here not only from our school but also from Jefferson. There's a lot of good natured taunting going on, but the police officers walking around give the impression that it could turn into more. Henry comes around and opens my door, of course, calling greetings to some of his friends. I recognize a few who sit with us at lunch, and I wave back, surprised, when they call out a hello to me.

We head toward the entrance to the field. I see a couple of the girls who are on the Spirit Squad sitting at a table, checking student ID's or taking money for tickets. They both gape when they see me walking up to the table. Their eyes nearly bug out of their heads when Henry grabs my hand, twining his fingers with mine and pulling me to him, making it obvious that I'm with him.

"Hey Celia, Amber. How you guys doing?" Henry says. I might have smiled as I watch Celia pull off two tickets and hand them to Henry without asking for his student ID, her eyes darting back and forth between us, except that I'm beginning to feel like this is a mistake; I should have stayed away as I always have. A cold pit forms in my stomach.

Henry doesn't let go of my hand, keeping me firmly by his side as we enter the gate, giving his tickets to yet another Spirit Squad girl who gapes as openly as the first two. He just keeps on smiling, greeting everyone, acting as if there isn't anything unusual about being there with the schools biggest loser.

There's a feeling of heightened excitement inside the stadium, students milling about everywhere. Students, parents and school faculty are all dressed in their own school colors depending on which team they're here to support. Even Henry is wearing our school colors. I look down at my yellow shirt which represents neither. Appropriate somehow; an island unto myself.

I'm very conscious of the feel of his hand pressed against mine. I know this isn't a date, just friends hanging out. Knowing that doesn't change the speeding of my heart—I haven't had my hand held since...well, since I held hands with Henry in sixth grade. We walk over to the stands, teeming with a writhing mass of over-excited humanity and I'm doubly glad he's holding onto me, because it would be a simple thing to get lost in all these people.

He pulls me behind him up the bleachers in a place where there doesn't seem to be a path, and finds us seats among a group of kids who I know by name, several of whom have been my tormentors at one time or another in the past. He high-fives the guys, says hi to the girls and I stand behind him, wishing that a big hole will open beneath and swallow me up. I keep my head down, even as Henry brings me in front of him, letting go of my hand and placing both hands on my shoulders.

"You guys all know Kate, right?" he asks with a cheerful, positive tone, shaming them into acknowledging me and saying hello. I peek up at each face, nodding slightly in reply, seeing they're clearly as uncomfortable as me, the knowledge of our histories between us, only Henry unaware.

Though it doesn't seem as if there's room for one more person where we stand, Ian and Kaden, our lunch companions, push their way in and start a loud, laughing banter with Henry and the others standing here. I'm thankful for their exuberance since it takes the edgy focus off of me.

The football teams make their way onto the field and the crowd grows frenzied. In spite of my anxiety, I feel myself caught up in the excitement. I don't go so far as to scream and yell like the others, but I find myself grinning. Henry's whistling loudly next to me, and he shoots me an impish smirk that causes me to laugh aloud. Even those surrounding us seem to have come to terms with my presence and are no longer shooting me sidelong looks, ignoring me now to join in the cheering.

There's a coin toss, though I could only tell that it was in our favor by the cheering that erupted all around me. After that, the teams line up at opposite ends of the field and someone from the other team kicks the ball towards our team. To my surprise, everyone running toward him suddenly stop when he kneels down. I'm confused; my limited knowledge at least knows there's supposed to be tackling involved.

Henry chooses that moment to look over at me, and seeing the confounded look on my face, leans toward me. Yelling to be heard over the crowd, he asks "Have you ever been to a football game before?"

I shake my head.

"Watched one on TV?"

I shake my head again.

"Do you know anything about it?"

"I thought I did. I thought they were supposed to tackle each other."

"Mostly that's true."

"So why did they all stop?"

So he explains it to me—and explains each play after that. I listen intently, determined to learn. It's difficult to concentrate because the noise around us makes it hard to hear, so he wraps his arm around my shoulder with each explanation, pulling me close so I can hear better. It creates a private little cocoon, and I can look up at him, eyes locked on his without it meaning anything more than that I'm listening.

Not more to him, anyway; but so much more to me. After a while, he quits taking his arm down between explanations, leaving it resting on my shoulder.

When quite a bit of time has passed, he says, "Come on," grabbing my hand and pulling me up the stairs, this time to walk along the sidewalk at the top of the bleachers.

"Is the game over already?"

"No, it's almost halftime. But if we don't get to the snack stand now, we'll have to stand in a long line."

When we get to the snack stand, the line is a dozen people deep, and I wonder what he considers a long line. I hear the whistle blow, then both teams jog off the field and I assume that means half time has arrived. The line behind us grows, snaking out until I can see what he meant.

Just before we arrive at the front of the line Henry turns to me and asks me what I would like. Panic freezes me for a moment. I didn't bring any money. I don't have any to bring even if I'd wanted to. I simply shake my head.

"You don't want anything?" he's genuinely baffled.

"No, I'm okay. I...I ate earlier." Again, not exactly a lie since I *had* eaten—lunch, at school.

"Come on, you can't be at the game without a hot dog. It's *tradition*."

"No, really, I'm fine."

It's our turn so he steps forward and orders while I look around, pretending my empty stomach isn't grumbling at the smells. I can't help but notice the looks I'm getting from those standing in line who attend our school. The same looks I've seen on other faces all night. I ignore them, not wanting my night ruined.

Henry turns and hands me a soda and a hot dog, shoving them into my hands before I can refuse them, turning back to the girl at the stand to grab a matching pair for himself.

"No, I said I was—"

"I know, but since this is your first game, I don't want

to be accused of not giving you the full experience." His smile disarms me.

"Okay. Thanks."

He leans his head down toward me, eyes black in the night, and my breath stops. "You're welcome," he says, a smile in his voice.

We walk over to a table laden with condiments, most of which have been spilled across the table. We load our hot dogs with ketchup, mustard and relish and eat them, dripping condiments on the already splattered ground. It's the best food I've ever eaten.

We make our way back to the stands just as the teams came back out onto the field. There's more cheering, though not as enthusiastic as when the game first started. Henry stands next to me, only occasionally having to explain plays or rules now. Because he isn't standing with his arm around me—to my disappointment—I'm thinking more clearly and notice things I hadn't before.

There aren't very many people actually paying attention to the game. Most of them that are watching are the parents. Everyone else is milling about, talking and laughing, only turning to the game when a good tackle is made, or when points are scored.

It's as I'm looking around that I see her. Jessica stands a few rows above me and one section over. She's *glaring* at me. The ferocity of her look stuns me. Her gaze never wavers, even though her friends are talking animatedly to her. She must have been watching me for some time because none of them even seem to notice her concentration, or look to see what she's looking at.

I quickly turn forward, eyes on the game, but my mind on her. I'm not sure why she hates me so much. I have tried very hard to stay out of her way and to not aggravate her any more than necessary. Apparently, my showing up to a football game is enough to rekindle her hatred in full.

I try to follow the game, but now it's as if I can feel her eyes on me. Quick looks back confirm that she's still watching. After a few peeks, Henry glances down at me, then behind me to see what I'm looking at, then back at me.

"Everything okay?" he asks.

I look back and see that she's suddenly, intently interested in the conversation around her. My eyes narrow in suspicion.

I smile up at Henry. "Yeah, everything's great."

He smiles back at me. Our team scores a touchdown and his attention is drawn back to the field, whistling and cheering. I take a quick peek back and see that she's once again glaring daggers at me. I sigh. It would be nice to have just one easy day in my life.

Our team ends up winning in a very exciting tie-breaking field goal. The kicker is hoisted up onto his teammate's shoulders and carried off the field like that, the cheerleaders are jumping up and down, people are high-fiving and yelling—and all of that goes away when Henry pulls me into an impromptu celebratory hug, pulling my feet up off the ground as he holds me. I wrap my arms around his neck for security at the suddenly weightless sensation.

The feel of his warm solid body pressed tightly against mine is unlike anything I've experienced before. It's simply a bear hug to him, but in that moment I know that whatever consequences I'll face if my absence is found out will be well worth this moment.

It takes some time to make our way down from the stands with all of the celebrating going on. At one point Henry's hand is ripped from mine by the flowing tide so he tucks me under his arm, holding me tightly against his side. After a minute or two of trying to figure out what to do with my hand that's awkwardly trapped between us, I wrap it lightly around his waist.

Once we move out of the crowd, he might have released me, but instead he retains his hold. We reach his car and he relinquishes his hold to dig his keys out of his pocket. The loss of his heat and the cool fall night air cause me to shiver.

"You cold?" he asks.

I wrap my arms around me.

"A little, but I'll survive."

"Here, I have a jacket..." He opens his trunk, pulling out a zip-front hoodie. I push my arms into the way-too-large jacket. He reaches forward and zips it up, then rubs his hands up and down my arms.

"Better?"

"Yes, thanks. What about you, though?"

"I hardly ever get cold. My mom says my dad and I have built in furnaces."

He opens the car door, shuts it behind me, and jogs

around to his side. He starts the car, taking some time to turn the heat on.

"Did you like the game?" he asks as we work our way out of the parking lot, which is still jam packed with kids just sitting in their cars, flashing their lights and honking their horns.

"Yeah, I really did."

"You figured it out pretty quickly. My dad watches football on TV all the time, but after all these years Mom *still* has no idea how it works." This complaint is given with that same amused frustration I've heard before when he talks about her. I wonder how it would be to have a mom worthy of such love.

Even more, I wonder how it would be to be the recipient of such an emotion from Henry.

"It was a lot of fun. I'm really glad I came. Thank you for asking me."

He reaches across the seat and squeezes my hand which lies in my lap, and continues to hold my hand for the rest of the ride home. He stops at the usual spot, which starts the butterflies in my stomach at what I'm going to find at home. If my luck has held, they won't be home yet. *Yeah, right, since when do you have that kind of luck?*

Since he *came into your life*, another voice answers, surprising me with its truthfulness.

"This is your bus stop," he says as he opens my door. I climb out, starting to unzip the jacket to return it to him. His hand on mine stills the action.

"Keep it. I can get it from you later."

"Won't you get cold?" I ask.

"Internal furnace, remember?"

"Okay, well, I'll bring it Monday."

"Listen, I was wondering if you might want to go do something tomorrow."

Of course I want to, more than I've ever wanted anything in my life. That isn't my reality, though, having what I want.

"Sorry, I wish I could, but I can't."

Disappointment flashes in his eyes. He nods.

"You sure I can't drive you home? It's dark out here."

If he only knew the danger isn't here in the dark, but in the "safety" of my home.

"No, I'll be fine. Thanks again. I haven't had this much fun in as long as I can remember."

He smiles, pulls me in for a quick hug which testifies of his internal furnace, releasing me before I can even react enough to bring my arms up to return the gesture.

"See you Monday morning then."

"Okay. See you then."

I watch him drive off, then walk toward my darkened house. The car is in the driveway, but all of the lights being off are a good sign. I sneak around to the back and climb up to my window, which I had unlocked before I left. I quietly climb in, reluctantly pulling his jacket off to get ready for bed.

I pull back the covers, moving the pillows I had placed on my bed to make it look like I was in bed already. The chances of one of them actually coming to check on me were slim, but it's best to be prepared for anything, I've learned. Just before sliding into bed I pull his jacket off of the chair back and put it back on, zipping it up tightly.

I climb into bed, snuggling the jacket close to me. It smells like him, I think, as I take a deep breath in the folds of the material. I relive the night, pushing out of my head the bad parts, especially Jessica, slowly reliving each moment that found my hand in his, or me in his arms. With a contented, happy sigh, I slip into sleep.

Eight

If there can be such a thing as a peaceful weekend in my house, this is it. Whatever Friday night had been for my parents, it has somehow provided a small measure of happiness for my mom. Not that she's been immediately transformed into a kind, loving mother, but the put downs are few, the complaints about my work almost non-existent, and I haven't received so much as one pinch or slap.

I can't stop thinking about Henry. Monday morning can't come soon enough, no matter how unusually calm a weekend I'm having. I wonder where he is, what he's doing. I wonder who he's with, and I'm jealous of anyone being with him, no matter who it is.

I have never imagined school being something to anticipate, but here I am again, rushing to get ready and get out the door. I only wish I had something to wear that didn't look like the obvious secondhand item it is.

Mostly I own t-shirts and sweatshirts—shapeless, anonymous clothing. For the first time ever, I wish for something more feminine.

I run to the corner, then slow to a walk in case Henry is already there. He is. I smile, wondering just how early I'd have to show up to beat him here. I'm wearing his jacket in the cool morning air, having first hidden it under my books as I left the house. I could have just carried it, but I wanted the feel of it on me one more time.

"Hey," he calls.

"Hey," I say back, shyly, embarrassed, now, that I'm wearing the jacket.

I shift my books and begin unzipping it.

"Thanks for letting me borrow this," I begin.

He wraps his hand around mine, halting my unzipping.

"Keep it." My chilled hand is warmed by his.

"I can't—"

"It's cold out here." He squeezes my hands, "I can tell you're cold. Besides, I've got plenty of others."

"Okay, I'll give it back after school. I'm sure it will be warmer then."

As we ride in the warm comfort of his car, he holds his hand out.

"Here, give me your hand and I'll warm it up."

I warily place my hand in his, thinking this feels a little too much like simply holding hands, something I've never done with anyone else. Then I decide I'm overanalyzing the whole thing. Clearly, he's just trying to help, and I'm grateful for the sake of my cold hand, anyway.

"I wanted to tell you...I mean, what I wanted to say was..." his voice is oddly unsure, vulnerable. He clears his throat, then starts that thoroughly distracting thing of rubbing his thumb across my palm.

"I had a lot of fun with you Friday night."

"Me, too."

He opens his mouth, closes it again, jaw clenching once before finally saying, "I was wondering if you'd be willing to give me your phone number so I can, you know, call you sometime." I wonder if it's normal for it to be such a big deal to have someone's phone number. Having never had a phone—or a friend—I have no idea.

"I'd be glad to give it to you if I could."

He glances at me, brows furrowed with that charmingly puzzled look he sometimes has.

"You aren't allowed to give out your number?"

I duck my head, ashamed now. "We don't have a phone."

"Oh." That stymies him. He's silent for a minute. "Well, that sucks."

I can't help it. I burst out laughing. It sucks for him? How does he think it is for me? Although, admittedly, it wouldn't do me much good since there isn't anyone I'd want to call, let alone anyone who would want to call me.

He smiles at my laughter. "Saturday and Sunday were long days. I really wanted to talk to you."

I'm surprised at how his thoughts echo my own, but even more surprised that he even thought of me at all after the game. Surprised that it warms me so much to hear him say it.

"For me too," I tell him.

"You think you might be able to get out again this weekend?"

"When?" I hear myself asking, knowing it's completely impossible.

"Well, Saturday would be nice if you could. My mom is big on...well, pretty much every holiday. But since Halloween is almost here, she has her big annual Halloween dinner planned for this Saturday."

"You want me to come to your mom's dinner?" I'm taken aback.

"It's not a big deal, or anything," he rushes to tell me. "She has this big holiday themed dinner for most of the holidays before the actual holiday. Kind of a tradition, but kind of fun too, I guess. I just thought you might like it."

"Who would be there?" I ask.

"Just my family."

I feel a little queasy at the thought of being there for a family function—or anywhere for that matter. I haven't had a lot of experience in anything that has to do with normal families.

"But won't your mom be mad if you bring me to your *family* dinner?"

"Actually, she invited you."

"But... she doesn't even know me."

"I've told her about you and she'd like to get to know you." Panic floods me. Why would she want to know *me*?

Reading my mind he says, "She likes to know all of my friends."

"Oh." The dread eases a little. That makes sense, I guess. That's probably how most normal moms operate.

"I thought I'd tell you now so you can have the week to think about it again. I seem to have better luck getting you to come that way."

I laugh.

"Okay, I'll think about it," I promise, already disappointed that there's no way my luck will hold for another weekend, allowing me to say yes.

I probably would have told him no, except for an incident that happens on Friday.

After lunch I'm walking to my math class, not paying attention to my surroundings. Since Henry and I have become sort-of friends, the other students seem to have lost most of their passion for bullying me. I'm not sure of the reason for it, but I'm not going to call attention to it either by questioning it. I'm by no means full of confidence as I walk down the hallways, still keeping my eyes on the floor, but maybe not as watchful as before.

That's why I don't see Jessica. As I pass the girls bathroom, I'm suddenly shoved inside, falling as my books go skidding across the floor. I look up to see what happened and see Jessica with two of her cohorts standing, blocking the exit. One of them faces toward the hallway, keeping anyone out who might try to come in.

It's been so long since anyone has done anything to me, that instead of cowering as I usually do, I scramble to my feet, intending to confront her. Something in her face stops me.

Her eyes are narrowed, mouth pinched. She looks more than angry. She looks like my mom looks just before she inflicts some kind of violence on me. She sees my hesitation and begins moving toward me slowly, like a predator cornering its prey.

I take an involuntary step backwards, see her eyes widen with pleasure at that.

"I have a question for you," she says casually, but I can hear the menace in her voice.

I swallow over the lump in my throat, all of those feelings of fear and humiliation that I had almost forgotten about recently coming back full force.

She's still slowly walking, examining her nails. "I was just wondering..." her eyes shoot to mine, and I'm stunned by the power of the hatred I read there. "Just who do you think you are?"

I'm not expecting that. My face must reflect my confusion because she suddenly strides up to me, her face right up in mine.

"Do you think you're so great that you deserve someone like Henry Jamison?" When I don't answer her, her anger flares. With a half-scream, half-growl she punches me across the face, knocking me back to the floor.

"You are a loser!" she screams at me. "He is too good for you. Leave him alone!" She turns away, supposing that I'll obey her. I know better, know to leave well enough alone.

But something has shifted in me, ever so slightly, and before I can stop to consider the consequences, I open my mouth. "He's my friend," my voice is soft, but she hears it clearly.

She swings back toward me.

"*What?*" she screeches.

I sit up, wiping the blood that seeps from my cut lip with my thumb.

"I said he's my friend," my voice is surer now.

With another frustrated scream she jumps on me, straddling me, slamming my head against the cold tiles. Then she slams it twice more for good measure before I can recover enough to try and stop her.

She leans over me and speaks with gritted teeth, spittle showering my face.

"In what world do you begin to think he could be your friend, let alone love you? I've seen the way you look at each other. It's disgusting. I'm telling you right now that I won't let it be. *I* am the only one good enough for him, and I *will* have him when you quit…*tricking* him, or whatever it is you do to make him want you. If I have to tell you again, you'll be sorry!"

She slams my head again, then rises off of me. After a kick in my stomach, to make sure the message is clear, she strides out of the bathroom. I lift my head to watch her go. Both the other girls who are with her look back at me, and I swear they look almost apologetic.

I groan and lay my head back down for a minute. I hear the bell ring and groan again. Slowly, I roll onto my side and push myself into a sitting position. The room sways and I close my eyes against the sensation. When it stops, I grab the edge of the sink and pull myself up.

I look in the mirror, see the drying blood on my face at the corner of my mouth, which is already swelling. I turn on the water and carefully clean the blood off, rinsing my mouth out with a handful of water. I touch the back of my head, which is throbbing, wincing when my fingers brush the knot that's already forming there.

I might have cried then, that my tenuous sense of

security has been shattered, except for something she said to me. Something that sings through my blood and causes my nerve endings to tingle.

I've seen the way you look at each other, she said, and the possibilities that accompany those words bring a smile to my face.

By the time photography rolls around, my lip is swollen, but it can't keep the wide smile from my face. Henry looks at me in alarm.

"What happened?" he demands angrily. I'm beginning to understand that his anger isn't directed toward me, but rather toward whoever hurt me, so I'm not quite as alarmed by it.

"Doesn't matter," I say happily.

I can see the anger faltering, warring with something else.

"Are you *happy* that someone hurt you?" he is incredulous.

I shake my head.

"Then what's with the big smile?"

"I'm *happy* because I get to say yes."

"Yes?" he looks lost.

"Yes, I get to say yes—to you. For Saturday. If you still want me to come."

A grin fights to wipe the frown from his face, his eyes showing his confusion.

"You had to get beat up to say yes?"

I shrug, my smile never wavering.

"That's messed up," he mutters.

Mr. Hurley stands to begin class, as Henry leans over to me.

"So, what does the other guy look like?" he teases, and I breathe a sigh of relief that he's going to let it go.

Nine

On Saturday Henry picks me up in our spot at six o'clock. I made sure that I'd done all of my chores very well and very quickly. I was still trying to figure out how to sneak out when my parents started fighting, giving me my chance to escape. I'd gone up the stairs as if going to my room, as I knew they would expect, then pulled Henry's jacket on (which he's kept insisting I keep for another day each time I try to return it to him) and climbed out my window. I run all the way to our meeting spot, keeping to the shadows in case they see me in the dusk.

I arrive just as he's pulling to the curb. I don't wait for him to get out and open my door, just pull it open myself and jump in.

"Hey!" he complains.

"Go!" I command, sliding down in the seat as I slam the door behind me.

"Is someone chasing you?" His body is taut with alarm.

"Not yet. Just go."

He doesn't question me again, just hits the gas and peels away from the curb. When I feel the car complete the u-turn, I peek up over the back of my seat. I don't see my parents or their car. With a sigh of relief, I sit all the way up and smile at him.

He's looking at me oddly.

"That has to be the strangest way I've ever picked anyone up."

"Sorry." I know I don't sound sorry; I'm exultant. I've gotten away!

We drive about three blocks, then turn left and go another two blocks. He turns left again onto a side street and pulls into the driveway of the third house up. He puts the car in park, and shuts it off.

"Don't even think about touching that door handle," he warns.

He didn't need to bother, I don't think I could move if my life depended on it.

I'm staring out the car window with dismay at the large, red brick house that rises in front of me. It's *huge*. I know people who live in houses like these—people like Jessica. People who wear jeans that cost more for one pair than my entire wardrobe cost. People who drive expensive cars and drink expensive wine and who spit on poor families like mine.

Henry opens my door. After a minute, he leans down and peers in at me.

"Did you want to come in, or should I bring your dinner out here?" he teases.

I'm glad it's getting dark enough that he can't read the alarm on my face or see the tears that shine in my eyes. I climb out of the car, keeping my eyes down.

"You live *here*?" I ask and hope he can't hear the quaver in my voice.

"Yeahhh," comes his drawn out answer, hesitant, ending on an upswing like a question.

I look at the manicured lawn with its groomed flowerbeds and bright landscape lighting and feel my stomach sink. There is stamped, colored cement covering the wide driveway beneath my feet, a four-car garage up ahead with obviously expensive custom doors. A rather large building stands behind the house.

Probably a stable, I think cynically.

I should have known. He'd told me his dad was a veterinarian, I should have known he had money but he's so *nice* that I never pictured it. I look at him now and it seems so obvious. His clothes are clearly nicer than average, his shoes the overpriced kind, even the way he holds himself with an unassuming confidence screams money. His jacket that I now wear is thick, good quality. I feel sick at my stupidity. Jessica was right—I don't belong with him, not even as a friend.

"I should go home," I tell him, my words saturated with dejection.

He pulls my hands into his.

"Kate, have I done something wrong? What's the matter?"

"You're rich," I accuse.

"Actually no, I'm not. My *father* is rich; I myself am poor and am living on his good graces," he teases, an unsure grin on his face. That's something only someone raised with a lot of money can say, I grumble to myself.

I look down and see my shabby shoes next to his neat, clean ones. "I don't belong here."

He laughs and gives me a hug.

"Of course you do. Listen, my family is going to love you, just like—" He stops mid-sentence, noticing the look on my face. "Please, my mom is really looking forward to this. *I'm* looking forward to this."

My resolve crumbles in the face of his pleading tone. I let him pull me forward, feeling like Daniel going into the lion's den. *Well,* I think, *I'll just stay through dinner and then make my escape. I can survive the snobbery and disdain they will surely have for me for that long—for Henry.*

He keeps hold of my hand as we go through the luxurious front door, into a foyer that's like pictures I've seen of grand hotels; marble floor, curving staircase with stairs of hardwood, dark wood table next to the perfectly painted wall with a large vase of arranged flowers. To the left stands a living room with formal, uncomfortable looking furniture. To the right is a dining room with a long table surrounded by heavy chairs.

My stomach clenches tighter if that's possible.

We walk down a short hallway toward the back of the house, and I can hear people laughing and talking. As we go through the archway into the family room, the house changes. This room is full of comfortable, overstuffed furniture, the kind meant for curling your feet up on.

There's a large TV, which is playing a Halloween cartoon. In front of the TV sits a small girl with wispy blonde hair, an open book on her lap that she's looking at with absolute concentration, ignoring the noise around her.

The family room is open to the kitchen, which is putting forth smells that make my mouth water, smells of comfort. There are four people in the kitchen, the ones making all the noise, seeming to be tripping over each other in their proximity.

I stand for a moment, taking it all in. It's not the quiet, elevator-music-playing scene I had pictured moments before. It's the scene I dream of sometimes, of how a family should be. The tiny girl reading turns and sees us standing there.

"Henry," she squeals, scrambling to her feet, climbing up on and leaping over the back of one of the couches. She runs, jumping at Henry. He catches her up and she wraps her arms around his neck.

"You know, I just saw you ten minutes ago," he tells her with a tickle in her ribs that sends her into a fit of giggles. He plants a kiss on her cheek. Her noises have caught the attention of the rest of the family, and they all come over to where we stand.

He shifts the little girl so that he holds her with one arm, and puts the other around my shoulder.

"These are my parents, Paul and Emma, and my sisters Claire and Amy. And this one," he says, shifting the little one higher in his arm, "is Christine." He smiles down at me.

"Everyone, this is Kate."

His dad reaches out and shakes my hand. He looks very similar to Henry, only with laugh lines around his eyes, a little gray sprinkling his hair, which lays flat instead of spiky like Henry's, and stands maybe an inch shorter than his son.

"It's good to finally meet you," he tells me.

His mother steps forward and instead of shaking my hand she gives me a hug, releasing me quickly before I have a chance to respond or be discomfited. She keeps her hands on my shoulders though, smiling into my face.

"All we ever hear about is Kate, Kate, Kate, so I can't begin to tell you how glad I am to meet you and see that you are a real girl."

My mouth drops open at this, and Henry's dad pulls her away with a laugh. "Okay, sweetie, that's enough embarrassing the girl for now."

"My turn, my turn," calls Amy, who's ten. She also gives me a hug.

Claire pushes her out of the way. This is his sister who is thirteen I know, but she looks sixteen. She's as tall as me, she's absolutely beautiful—and I'm intimidated by her immediately.

"Sorry they're all such a bunch of dorks," she says. There's no malice behind the words, though. She puts her arm around my shoulders, shoving Henry's off and maneuvering me further into the room.

Christine scrambles out of Henry's arms and returns to her book by the TV. He catches up to us and tells me, "Let me just apologize now for this one," he jerks a thumb towards Claire, who looks at me and rolls her eyes.

"*Whatever,*" she says sarcastically, and then in the same breath, "Cool jacket."

"It's not mine. It's Henry's."

"Huh," she eyes me. "He must really like you, because if *I* borrow anything of his he goes *ballistic*. You have really awesome hair."

I jerk a little at the sudden change in subject. I reach up to touch my unremarkable hair.

"Can I touch it?" she asks, then does so without waiting for permission. "That's what I thought. It's so soft. It looks like those commercials, you know, for shampoo or whatever, where they always have this perfect, shiny, glossy hair that you know is only that way because someone brushed it for hours. You must brush yours a lot! I'd love to get my hands on it, see how it looks curly."

"Claire," Mrs. Jamison says warningly, "Kate is not one of your makeover guinea pigs. Try to restrain yourself."

"Sure, Mom, whatever." I'm stunned at the sarcastic tone she uses with her mother, which only earns her a wry look, rather than a smack or kick.

Mrs. Jamison comes over to where we stand.

"Can I take your jacket?" she asks politely, giving Henry a pointed stare.

"Oh, sorry," he says. I'm not sure if his apology is for me or her. "I've just kind of gotten used to seeing it on you."

I unzip it, and try not to show my surprise when he helps me take it off. I've seen chivalry in old movies where men always did things like that for the women, but not in real life, much less be the recipient of it.

An informal table stands off to the side in a nook, already set and decorated with a plethora of autumn and

Halloween decorations. Even the dishes are shaped and colored like fall leaves. It looks like something out of a magazine—kinda like the front part of the house.

"The table looks great," I tell Mrs. Jamison.

Claire beams with pride.

"I did it. My mom told me I could help once I was a teenager, and this year I am thirteen—*officially* a teenager—so she let me do it myself."

I'm impressed, and tell her so.

"You shouldn't encourage her," Henry tells me, "She doesn't need any help with her ego." This is said with an indulgent smile towards her.

"I hope you like pumpkin," she tells me.

"I don't know," I say, "I haven't ever tasted it."

"Really? Who hasn't tasted pumpkin?" she asks with nose wrinkled. "Oh well, you'll like it. No one makes pumpkin soup like my mom."

"If you don't like it, sweetie, you just tell me and we'll get you something else," Mrs. Jamison says.

Soon we're seated at the table, after a little fuss from Christine who wants to finish her book. A promise from Henry to read her a bedtime story later solves that. It's obvious that she and Henry are crazy about each other as she insists on him sitting next to her.

I sit on his other side and look around at them, all smiling and laughing and talking over top of one another with an organized kind of chaos, and I feel the world shift again. I didn't know that this kind of family really exists. I watch the way his parents look at each other, with a deep understanding and security in their love for each other. His sisters bicker somewhat, but there's obvious love there as well, both for each other and for Henry. They include me in as if I belong.

They all take for granted the pumpkin soup served in hollowed out pumpkins, the homemade rolls in a wicker basket lined with a cloth napkin, the sautéed squash, the whole atmosphere, things that, to me, are like a fairy tale. When Henry's mom rises to go to the kitchen to retrieve the pumpkin cookies she's made for dessert, my eyes follow her. As she disappears through the open doorway my gaze comes to rest on Henry, who's watching me closely. I watch his eyes darken as they do whenever he's feeling strongly about something. He seems to read something on my face, but he doesn't question it, simply reaches under the table and takes hold of my hand, giving me a secure anchor to hold on to.

After dinner, Mrs. Jamison won't let me help clean up as I'm the guest, no matter how persistent I am.

"Take her out to see the clinic," she tells Henry.

I'm not sure what the clinic is, but I'm okay with being alone with Henry so I happily go along. He grabs his jacket for me to put on. We step out through an impressive pair of French doors onto a deck that's larger than my bedroom. We cross an expanse of lawn that's still green in spite of the fact that it should be going into hibernation. He takes my hand and leads me toward the big building I had seen earlier.

Turns out I wasn't so far off when I thought it was a stable—no horses since his father doesn't specialize in large animals, as Henry explains, but it's the clinic where he treats animals. He opens the door and turns on the overhead fluorescent lights, revealing a clean, sterile room which, he tells me, is the operating room. He leads me in, showing me the individual treatment rooms, the recovery room, and the waiting room which has large windows looking out the opposite side of the building from the house. I can see the parking lot out there and realize that it's accessible from the main road.

"Your dad works at home?" I ask.

"Pretty much, yeah."

"Your mom is okay with that?" I ask, thinking about how much my own mom hates it when my dad's home. When he is home all they do is fight anyway.

He laughs. "Weird, huh? My parents are still embarrassingly in love. She spends most of her time out here when he's working."

We're standing in the doorway that separates the waiting room from the rest of the clinic; I look around at the comfortable waiting room which is more welcoming than my own home and I feel tears sting my eyes at the glaring differences between my life and his.

"I don't deserve you," I whisper, immediately flushed with embarrassment at having voiced the thought.

"You don't have any idea how I feel about you, do you?" he asks.

I look up at him. He stands with both hands buried in his front pockets, shoulders hunched slightly forward, leaning against the doorframe opposite the side I lean on. We hadn't turned on the lights in the waiting room; the only light is coming from the streetlights gleaming through the windows, and from a huge fish tank that glows in the corner. The lights from the hallway behind shine brightly, shadowing his face in darkness so that I can't make his expression out.

I shake my head.

He cocks his head. "Have you ever had a boyfriend?"

I choke out a laugh.

"Hardly. You've seen...well, you've seen how it is at school. I don't even have a *friend*."

"You do now," he says, quietly.

"I don't know why you want to be, but you *are* my friend. My only friend. You're my *best* friend."

He laughs softly, "I'm glad about that." His tone is low and husky with a concentration I haven't heard him use before. Slowly, he leans toward me, bringing his face close to mine. He stops inches from my face. "But I've been trying really hard to be more."

My breath catches in my throat at his nearness.

"Ever been kissed?" he whispers, with a grin.

Only by you, I think. If he doesn't remember, I'm not going to bring it up. I shake my head, ducking a little in awkwardness.

He kisses me then, his lips warm and soft on mine. I'm stunned, my wide eyes staring at his closed ones. I kiss him back, instinctively, innocently, awash in the sensation of feeling. There's no movement in the room, no sound but our breathing, my heart pounding in my ears. He's not touching me anywhere but with his lips on mine.

It's the best moment of my life, even better than swinging.

"Ew, gross," Claire comes in behind us, without us hearing her approach—or at least, I didn't hear her over the thrumming in my ears. I jerk instinctively, but Henry presses closer, bringing one hand up to the back of my neck, trapping me. He doesn't remove his mouth from mine, though he does open his eyes to find me still staring at him. He feels the tension in me, and whispers, "relax," against my mouth. He reaches out to his left and gives Claire a light shove backwards.

"Hey!" she calls out.

"Go away," he grumbles, mouth still pressed to mine. He pulls the door closed, shutting us into the darkened waiting room. I smile against his mouth, and he meets it with a smile of his own, pulling back slightly. I look down, reluctant to meet his gaze in the raw emotions of the aftermath of the kiss. It was more than I could have dreamed of, even more amazing than when he holds my hand. I didn't think anything could be better than that, the simple human contact that I haven't experienced since I was young.

He brings both his hands up, bracing my neck on both sides, thumbs skimming lightly over my cheeks, forcing me to look up. The smile drops from his face as he brings his mouth back to mine. This time I close my eyes, letting the sensations flow through me.

Ten

"So, Wednesday is Halloween," Henry says as we walk to school Monday morning. We're enjoying a late Indian summer this year, chilled air in the mornings and late evenings but seventy-five degrees during the day. So we've decided to walk to school every day until we no longer can. He holds my hand as we walk, carrying my loose books in his other arm.

"Yeah, I know."

He looks down at the books in his arm. "Don't you have a locker?" His change of subject makes me laugh. Sometimes conversation with Henry is as schizophrenic as conversation with his sister, Claire.

"No, I haven't had a locker for years." I'm not about to tell him that I discovered early that lockers are nothing more than a torture device. It was bad enough finding all manner of disgusting garbage left in there that I had to clean out, or finding a destroyed text book that I couldn't begin to afford to replace and the accompanying visit to the principal's office where only my genuine tears got me off the hook for that. The last straw was when I had been shoved and locked into it; I decided that was my cue to never step near one again. Therefore I carry everything to and from school.

"You can share mine," he says.

I imagine him opening the locker to see a moldy sandwich smeared on his stuff, and shake my head.

"That's okay. I don't mind carrying them."

"Especially since you don't carry them," he says, shrugging them higher in suggestion. I feel my cheeks flush.

"You don't have to carry them for me, you know," I mutter.

He laughs and leans down to give me a quick kiss, surprising and warming me at the same time.

"You really have to learn not to take everything so seriously."

"Says someone who comes from the family that laughs all the time."

"They were just putting on a front for you."

I look at him, eyebrows raised sardonically.

"Okay, so they *are* annoyingly cheerful," he says. "They liked you. Especially Claire. She really wants you to come back so she can play with your hair."

I laugh. "I really liked them, too. And I just might come by some time and let her do that."

"You don't know what you're saying," he warns mockingly. "I've seen the damage she can do. She's done it to me!"

"What? She's done your hair? Your hair seems pretty short for that."

"Why do you think I cut it this way? It used to be longer."

"She have pictures of this?" I ask, laughing when the pained look he shoots me says, yes, she does.

"So about Halloween. You doing anything?"

Yeah, I think, *the usual; making a sign for the door that says "no candy," so that I don't get blamed for kids knocking on the door, wanting candy we don't have. Then I'll get up extra early the next morning to clean up the eggs and pumpkins that have been thrown at the house because of that sign before* she *sees them.*

"Because there's a group of kids going to the corn maze, and I thought it might be fun," he continues.

"Oh, well, yeah." I feel a stinging jealousy that he'll be having fun without me. I know he has a life, that he doesn't hibernate in his room when he isn't with me, but I haven't really thought consciously of it. "Sounds like fun. Who are you going with?"

He looks at me, shaking his head. "No, Kate, I'm *asking* because I want *us* to go."

"Oh," I feel both stupid and elated at my misunderstanding. Of course, I can't go, there's no way. "Sure, I think I could do that," I say.

"Great." He squeezes my hand and leans down to kiss me again. *I could* so *get used to that,* I think.

"Do you have a costume?"

My face falls. "No." And no way to get one, either.

"That's okay. You're about the same size as my sister. Think how thrilled she would be if you let her lend you one. It would probably make her *year* if you let her dress you up."

I laugh at that, wanting to deny it, but knowing it's probably the truth.

As we come within sight of the school, I pull my hand out of Henry's. He glances at me questioningly.

"It's bad enough for you that we're friends. It could be really bad if people thought…." I can't say the words, not sure what they really are. His eyes cloud, stormy, as he clenches his jaw. I reach up and smooth my hand along the tensed muscle, reveling in the fact that I can do that and not have him cringe from me with disgust.

"Please?" I ask, thinking that Jessica isn't the only one who might want to hurt me if they see him holding my hand or, worse, kissing me. He places his hand over mine, holding it tight against his face, eyes softening.

"How can I say no to you?" he asks. "Okay, I will keep my distance. *For now*," he qualifies.

"Thank you," I say, hesitating, then standing up on my tiptoes to kiss him. He growls against my mouth, and I jump a little, wondering if it's rejection of my boldness, but he's grinning at me.

"What was that for?" I ask, trying to keep the nervousness out of my voice.

"I must be *insane* for agreeing to this."

Wednesday is a crazy day at school. Kids are allowed to wear costumes as long as they're "tasteful" and don't involve a mask. It's drizzling a little as we pull into the parking lot; a group of girls walk by dressed as a nurse, a witch and a corpse bride—but not really looking like what they are supposed to be.

Henry watches them walk by, then looks at me, eyebrows raised.

"When exactly did Halloween become an excuse to dress like a hooker?" he asks.

"You're telling me you don't like it?"

He gives a short snarl then says, "If Claire tries to put anything like that on you, I'll shoot her."

I try to picture myself dressed like that, walking with confidence, and nearly choke at the image. I turn to pull open the door handle, knowing he'll protest, but instead he grabs my hand.

"Hey, I need to tell you something."

I turn back. "Okay."

"Tonight, when we go to the corn maze, I'm going to hold your hand, and probably kiss you too." His jaw is stubbornly jutted, daring me to argue.

"Oh...um, okay," I say with a smile, enjoying the stunned look on his face. "See you at lunch."

As he drops me off after school, though, I feel the familiar cramps beginning in my stomach. I'd been pressing my luck the two times before when I had gotten away. However, it's a week night, which means my father won't be home to fight with, and there won't be any miraculous dinner parties.

Henry lets me out, pulling me close to kiss me thoroughly, and for a few minutes, my dilemma disappears from conscious thought. This kiss is definitely more intense than the others he's given me.

"So I'll pick you up at six?" Henry asks, smiling at the unfocused look in my eyes.

"What? Oh, yeah, sure."

He kisses me again, then begins to walk around to his side of the car. The loss of his warmth brings me back to the world.

"Wait, Henry..." I intend to tell him I can't come, but he's walking back toward me, an oddly intent look on his face, eyes dark. His look stills me, his hand sliding along the side of my neck to tip my face up for his kiss. He pulls back, looking into my eyes.

"That's the first time you've said my name."

"It...it is?" It's hard to think clearly with him looking at me like this.

One corner of his mouth turns up in a smile, and his gaze drops to my mouth, following the path of his thumb that brushes lightly across my bottom lip.

"I like the way it sounds on your lips."

"Oh," I breathe, as he leans to replace his thumb with his mouth. When he finally steps back, I'm weak in the knees. I didn't know that was actually possible—I thought it was only something that happens in novels or movies.

"If I don't go now..." he doesn't finish. He takes a deep breath. "Okay, I'm going now. I'll see you soon."

I watch him walk away, climbing into his car and turning around to head back home. I watch until he's out of sight, and it isn't until he's gone that I realize I hadn't finished what I started to tell him. And, of course, I have no way to call him. With dread in my heart, I know how angry he's going to be when I don't show up.

I walk in the door, seeing my mother asleep on the couch. I stand and watch her for a minute, comparing her to Mrs. Jamison. I wonder, if things hadn't gone bad, if my baby brother had lived, if she would have been more like her.

I put my books away, doing my chores without much enthusiasm, and without trying to be silent as I usually am when she's sleeping. There isn't anything that will change my fate today, so why try?

"John?" I hear her call, and wonder briefly why she'd be calling for my father with concern in her voice.

"No, mom, it's me."

Silence, then she calls for me to come to her. She's slurring her words, so I know she's been taking too many of her pills again. I walk in and stand next to her, waiting.

"How was school?" she asks. I stare, mouth hanging open. I haven't heard those words from her for years...if ever.

She clucks her tongue at me with disgust. "Close your mouth, you look like an imbecile."

I almost smile; that's more like her.

"It was fine," I answer, then suddenly an idea comes to me. "But I need to go to the library to study tonight." I hate lying, even to her, but I'm willing to lie to get to see Henry.

"Why can't you study here?" Her words are garbled as she reaches with hooded eyes for her glass of water and a bottle of pills. "I need you."

"I need to use the internet. I won't be gone long. I'll make you dinner first." I try to keep the desperation out of my voice.

She waves me away as she tips her glass up to swallow her pill. I make my escape to the kitchen, pulling out the items I need to make her dinner. For once, I'm not even jealous of her food, don't try to sneak any of it.

When I finish, she's lying back on the couch, eyes hooded. I bring her a plate of food and set it on the table next to her.

"I'm going now." She looks up at me, eyes drifting lazily. "I'll be back as soon as I can," I tell her, rushing out the door before she can stop me. It's far too early for Henry to be waiting for me, and I have no desire to stand on the street where anyone might see me. I decide that walking to his house is a better plan.

There's an overgrown field that forms a shortcut between our houses. It has not been developed yet because it's filled with large quaking aspens and pine trees, surrounding a little pond of water where the geese flock each summer. That makes the area protected, but also neglected. I've been in the grove many times before, because it's a good hiding place.

I walk through, making my way to Henry's street in less than fifteen minutes. I walk up toward his house; when I get to his driveway, I see that his car isn't here. I stop, stymied in my intention. I'm unsure what to do. I suppose I could just go wait in the trees until I see his car turn up the street.

Claire makes the decision for me when she walks out the front door and sees me standing there.

"Kate, hey!" she calls, jogging down the driveway and pulling me into a hug. I feel that same intimidation and wonder how I can be so unsettled by a thirteen year old.

"Henry told me you'd be coming over. He said you needed a costume? I have all kinds. Plus, I can do your hair for you if you want. You guys are going to the corn maze, right? It might get cold. Did you bring a jacket? Never mind, we'll just do a costume that will keep you warm." This non-stop speech is going on as she links arms with me and practically drags me up to the house.

"Henry's not home yet?" I ask.

"No, he went to find a costume. Didn't he call you?"

"We don't have a phone," I admit.

"Bummer," she says, as if it isn't embarrassing at all. "Well, I'll call him and tell him you're here already. I'm not going to tell him what costume we're putting you in. That's going to be a surprise."

When she calls him from her cell phone on the front steps, she's silent while he talks, rolling her eyes at me. "Okay, fine," she sighs, frustrated.

"He says they're doing this medieval theme thing at the corn maze, and he happens to know I have a costume that will work for that. Can't wait to see what *he's* wearing, probably some tights or something hideous like that, when I could have made him something *cool*," she grumbles. Immediately, she brightens, "You will look so cool, though. And I can put beads in your hair."

I try to picture myself with beads in my hair, imagining long rows of braids ending in brightly colored plastic orbs, and can picture how ridiculous that would be. There are girls who could probably pull that look off—I'm not one of them.

She leads me into the museum part of the house, passing through into the homey part that I prefer. Mrs.

Jamison is sitting on the couch with Christine cuddled on her lap, watching Elmo talk about colors. I feel a pang of longing as I watch her absently smoothing Christine's hair. She glances up when we enter and stands, picking Christine up with her.

"Well, hi, Kate." Her tone is warm and welcoming; she follows that with a hug that encompasses me and Christine, who is still in her arms. I'm not sure I'll ever get used to that; how they all hug one another and me—a virtual stranger—as if it's the most natural thing in the world.

"Hi, Mrs. Jamison. Hi, Christine."

Christine waves shyly, tucking her head into her mom's neck but keeping her eyes and smile on me. She's such a cute little thing, with dark eyes that are the same as Henry's.

"Can I ask a favor, Kate? I'd like you to call me Emma. Mrs. Jamison is my mother-in-law."

"Sure, okay."

"Guess what, mom?" Claire's excitement is palpable. "Kate's going to borrow one of my costumes. And I get to do her hair."

"Oh yeah? And did Kate agree to let you do her hair, or did you just push that on her?" Emma looks at me with a smiling question.

"Well...." Claire trails off.

"It's okay," I jump to her defense, not wanting to get her into trouble. "I don't mind." That's only another half-lie.

"Alright, well you girls have fun. If she gets too pushy, Kate, you just tell her to back off," She says gruffly, accompanying the words with an affectionate ruffle of Claire's hair. "She means well; she just gets a little...enthusiastic."

Claire rolls her eyes at me, then grabs my hand and hauls me up a second set of stairs in the family room. She's talking animatedly the whole time we're walking, which is good because I'm speechless. The second floor is more homey than formal, but it's big. There are several rooms off a hallway that forms an L, but most of the doors are closed, so I don't know what kind of rooms they are.

Claire's bedroom is amazing. The floor has thick pink carpeting, the bed covered by a white and pink patch quilt, which is neatly made and covered with a variety of pillows in pink, white and green. A netted canopy sewn with pearl beads hang from the ceiling to surround part of the bed. It's definitely a girly-girl room, but the most amazing thing is the walls.

Instead of posters of the latest bands or movie stars, it's covered with fashion photos cut out of magazines, and hand drawn pictures that look like they could also have been pictures cut out of magazines—they are that well drawn. I look at a grouping of them, when the name in the bottom right corner catches my eye.

I turn to look at Claire, who is currently in her walk-in closet that's almost as large as my whole room.

"Did you draw these?" I ask.

She leans around the door jamb, looking at the drawings.

"Yeah. Those are my originals. Someday they will be real clothes—I mean clothes that other people can wear."

"You made these up? They aren't copies?"

She steps all the way into the room, carrying a pile of dark red material.

"No. I'm going to be a fashion designer some day. I just play around right now. I draw them and my mom buys me the material and helps me make a pattern and sew some of them. Sometimes she wears them herself."

I look at them. As unaware as I am of fashion I can tell they are good.

"These are really great. I think you're a fashion designer *now*."

Claire beams at the compliment.

"Thanks, but I still have a lot to learn. I'm going to go to college to learn more about fashion, but also to learn how to be a business woman because I want to run my own place."

I wonder what it would be like to be so young and so sure of your future, with not only a plan in place, but also the talent to back it up. I'm about to graduate and have no idea what I'm going to do. How depressing.

"Anyway, I'm glad you like them, because this is one I made," she says, holding up the pile of material by the hanger, which reveals it to be an elaborate dress. "This is the costume I was telling you about. It will work good, I think, because it kind of looks medieval and it's heavy so it will keep you warm. And, oh!" She throws the dress across her bed and runs back into the closet. She comes back out carrying a pile of black material. "This cape will look really cool with it, in case it's too cold without a jacket."

"This is really nice of you," I tell her. I walk over to the bed, running my hand across the rich ruby velvet. "I don't think I should wear this to the corn maze though. It will probably get dirty and might get torn or something."

She waves her hand, "No biggie. I can fix it. Here, come sit," she indicates a chair in front of a beautiful vanity with a tri-fold mirror. The back edge of the vanity is neatly organized and holds a dizzying array of makeup and hair products. I sit obediently and she begins brushing my hair.

"What I wouldn't give to have your hair. You're so lucky."

I look in the mirror, trying to see what she sees that I don't. My hair grows so straight that I only wash and comb it and let it air dry. I don't even own a hair dryer or curling iron. Maybe all those years of having done nothing harsh to my hair helps it to seem healthy. To me it only looks plain, blonde and straight, hanging halfway down my back.

"I have an idea. If you don't like it we can take it out and do something different, okay?"

It actually feels good to have someone brushing my hair. Even the gentle tugging as she starts pulling pieces up feels good. I close my eyes and pretend that I'm a normal girl, sitting at her vanity, her mother or sister doing her hair.

I try to remember if my mother has ever done my hair. She must have when I was a little girl, but I can't call up a single remembrance of it. Instead of feeling sad like I usually do, I felt a little spark of anger.

"There, how's that?" Claire asks. I open my eyes and can only stare. She's wrapped the front of my hair into a sort of natural head band, interlaced with strings of red beads that look striking against my light hair. The back falls in soft ringlets. Fear sinks through me—I can't go out like this. I feel exposed with my shield pulled away. I can't disappoint Claire, though. She looks pretty pleased with herself.

"It looks good," I tell her, my voice wavering. But in her youth she doesn't notice.

"Cool. You want some makeup on?" Before I can gather my horrified thoughts to tell her no, she answers herself. "No, I think you're really pretty without it. You don't need it."

Pretty? I don't think so.

"Okay, let's get the dress on and see how it all looks." She glances at the clock on her bed stand. "Right about on time, too."

She steps out while I undress and pull the dress on, but it has a long row of hooks on the back that I can't reach, so she has to help me do those. I'm self-conscious about having her do that since no one has ever seen me in any state of undress. She's so matter-of-fact about it that I can't feel too embarrassed. Once those are hooked, she adjusts the ties on the lace-up front, pulling the velvet around the white silk beneath, leaving just a hint showing, to make it fit just right.

"Perfect!" she announces. "Look." She turns me toward a full length cheval mirror that stands in the corner. I have to admit, I look different, like someone who has stepped out of a time past. The dress also has lace-up sleeves, which expose the white silk panel she has sewn beneath. The bodice is tight and the skirt is full, the silk panel theme repeated down the front of the skirt. It's an amazing dress—it would transform anyone who wore it.

"This is great," I tell her, wrapping one arm around her shoulders. It's only half-a-hug, but it's more than I might have thought I was capable of a few weeks ago. She smiles at me.

"*You* look great. Now, wait here. I want to see if Henry is home yet so you can make an entrance."

She doesn't wait for an answer, hurrying out of the room and closing the door behind her. I sit nervously waiting, until I hear her footsteps coming back down the hallway.

"Okay, he's here, but we just have to wait a minute while Mom gets her camera."

"Camera?" I squeak.

"Oh, yeah, get used to it. If you're gonna be Henry's girlfriend, plan on having your picture taken for, like, every event imaginable. My mom's the queen of picture taking."

I barely hear the last part because my mind is stuck on the other word she said—the same one Jessica used.

"You think I'm Henry's girlfriend?" I ask.

"Well, duh! I saw you guys kissing, remember?"

The shock on my face slowly gives way to a smile. *Girlfriend.* I'm someone's girlfriend! Not just someone—*Henry's* girlfriend. At least, that's what his sister thinks. She probably knows more about these things than I do.

I don't know what Henry thinks, maybe that we're just friends, but maybe not. Maybe *he* thinks of me as his girlfriend as well. The thought sends a shaft of light through me.

Claire leads me out of her room, this time in the opposite direction, toward the stairs at the front of the house.

"Okay everyone, get ready. Here she comes."

I'm still grinning, but my mouth drops open when I start down the steps and see Henry. He has on a white, loose shirt that also laces up the front and some kind of black pants tucked into boots. It's at best a loose interpretation of a medieval costume, but that doesn't matter, because he looks amazing. Like a hero or knight stepped out of some distant time, waiting at the bottom of the stairs for *me*.

"Oh, honey, you look like a princess," Emma sighs. I glance at her and she snaps a picture. My eyes are drawn back to Henry. He's staring up at me; the look on his face intensely powerful. As I look back at him, he slowly smiles, melting my knees again.

Emma keeps snapping pictures as I walk down, and when I place my hand into Henry's outstretched one, she takes a photo. She turns the camera toward me to show me the last shot. I'm looking up at Henry while he gazes down at me, both of us with half-smiles on our faces, looking as if we feel we're the last two people on the earth.

Henry grins at the picture, then leans down to kiss me. Before he can, Amy speaks up.

"Did you make that one, Claire?"

"Yup."

"Wow, it looks really good on her."

"Pretty," Christine echoes.

I smile at them all.

"Okay, okay, stand by each other so I can take your picture. Put your jacket on, Henry."

His jacket turns out to be a black and gold velvet doublet with slashed sleeves. I didn't think he could look any better than he did, but then he puts the jacket on. He reaches out, wrapping his arm around my waist and pulling me in against his side, still not taking his gaze from me. Emma takes a few more pictures, followed by a round of hugs for me and Henry.

They all follow us out to the car to wave as we drive away. Henry grins deprecatingly at me as he waves back at them. When we've driven up the street and turn the corner, he suddenly pulls over to the side of the street, putting the car in park. Without a word, he leans over, pulls my face to his and kisses me deeply.

After a few minutes, he pulls back and smiles.

"Hi," he says.

I laugh.

"Hello."

"You look great," he says, eyes skimming me, touching my hair first with his eyes, then lightly with his hand. "I'm gonna have to do something really great to thank the little squirt."

"You don't look so bad yourself," I tell him.

He kisses me again, and I lose a little of the guilt over lying to be with him.

Eleven

At the corn maze, we meet Ian and Kaden, and another of our lunch buddies, Brock, with their dates. Their dates are dressed predictably in the prostitute-version of different things, and they're all freezing. The guys are a vampire, werewolf, and a doctor of all things. The girls ooh and ahh about my dress, which Henry informs them his sister designed. But even while they are admiring the dress, they're looking at me askance, and at Henry with desire.

"Okay, here's the plan," Ian says. "We all have to figure out all of the clues in the maze. There are thirty numbered clues you have to find. Each post has a stamp for your paper." He hands each couple a small piece of paper, numbered from one to thirty. "All the losers have to buy ice cream for the winners. No cheating; I know the guy who works the ticket booth and he'll 'fess up if someone gets the answers from him.

"You two start at number one," he says, pointing to Brock. "You two start at number fifteen and go backwards," he indicates Kaden. "Henry you start at fifteen and go up in numbers, and we will start at thirty and go backward. First couple out with all the answers wins." I'm completely confused, but no one else is, so I pretend like I understand as well.

Henry takes the cape that he holds over his arm, and places it over my shoulders as we head into the maze. He keeps his arm around my shoulder once it's in place. I hear the girl who's walking with us sigh, and I glance at her to see her watching Henry with longing. I look at Henry and for the first time feel a tickle of fear in my throat.

For whatever reason he's chosen to be my friend, and though he likes to kiss me and touch me, he hasn't *said* that we're anything more than that. I have no rights to him—he could be kissing other girls as well. Ice shoots down my spine at the image that thought brings to mind. On the other hand, he could get tired of me and walk away without looking back. My stomach lurches.

Henry glances at me; I had grabbed my stomach unthinkingly.

"Are you alright?" he asks.

I nod, wrapping my arm around his waist. Just in case he starts to wonder himself why he's wasting his time with me, I decide I better make as much of what time I can.

We find marker fifteen, and take the paper and pencil they had given us when we entered and write down the answer to the first clue. The other couple head right to find the next marker and we head left.

We're hunting for the next marker; I'm studying the map in the dim light when I realize Henry is no longer with me. I stop, turning in a full circle.

"Henry?"

Where did he go? I feel a hint of fear—has he abandoned me? Is *this* the prank I've been waiting for him to pull all along? It's elaborate; I have to give him that. Tears prick the back of my eyelids, but I bite my lip to stop them. I *won't* give them that.

Then his hand shoots out of a cluster of stalks and he grabs my arm, pulling my into a private haven created by the corn.

"Henry, wha—?"

Then his mouth is on mine, cutting off my words and coherent thought. He wraps his arms around my waist under the cloak. I put my arms on his shoulders, dragging the edges of the cloak up with it, forming a cocoon around us.

He draws back, bringing one hand up and using his thumb to wipe away the tear that escaped and is running down my cheek.

"Did I hurt you?" he asks, concerned.

I shake my head.

"I made you cry, though."

"No, just scared me a little."

"I'm sorry." His apology is full of remorse.

I shake my head again.

"It doesn't matter."

"Of course it does, I would never purposely do anything to make you cry."

Afraid his words will make me cry more, I tilt my head up for another kiss, to which he obliges. We're sheltered by the corn stalks, but we can still hear others walking by, laughing or talking.

"Come on, we'd better get going."

With reluctance, we leave the cove and continue on our way. This time I keep my hand firmly in Henry's so he can't disappear again. We make occasional stops in various private pockets in the stalks whenever we can find them, which makes it difficult to solve the clues with my thoughts all muddled. For that matter, the stops make it hard to even *care* about solving the riddles—free ice cream or not.

As we get closer to the thirtieth marker though, I start to notice some disturbing sounds. Creaking and groaning, something that sounds like a chain saw, but the worst is the screaming. I look at Henry and he doesn't seem to notice anything, so I decide maybe it's my imagination.

When I hear another scream and jump, drawing closer to Henry, he glances down at me and smiles. I try to smile back, but my heart is pounding. We walk through an archway and find ourselves in a foggy, nearly dark area. The creaking and groaning are louder now; we walk around the corner there's a girl lying on a table, screaming for help while some man with wild, gray hair in a blood smeared apron stands over her with a knife dripping red, getting ready to hack into her bleeding abdomen.

My feet freeze in place. I looked at Henry with panic and see to my shock that he's looking at them with a smile. Just then someone else in a white mask and blue jumpsuit jumps out at me with the chainsaw I'd heard earlier.

I cringe against Henry, ready to flee, panic filling my head. He glances down at me with a laugh, holding me tightly in place. *Henry wants to kill me?* I think with horror. *That's what this is about?* Then his face changes from laughter to a panic nearly reflective of my own.

"Are you okay?" he asks.

I can't answer. It feels as though all the blood has drained to my feet and I couldn't move if my life depended on it—which it does when the boy with the knife starts towards us. Henry grabs my shoulders and shakes me a little.

"Kate!"

And then he's scooping me up into his arms, striding back the way we had come, all the way out the entrance until we're in the parking lot. He sits down on a hay bale with me in his lap.

"Is she okay?" I hear someone ask.

"Get her some water," someone else says.

I never take my eyes from Henry's face, which is alarmed, and he never takes his eyes from my face, even when someone gives him a cup of water, which he presses to my lips.

I pull his head down, placing my mouth next to his ear. "You have to get someone to help that girl," I whisper urgently.

He pulls back to look at me. "What girl?"

"You saw her—that guy was hurting her!"

"What? You mean—" He breaks off, letting out a relieved laugh. He pulls me close, hugging me tightly.

"No, Henry, you have to—"

"It's not real." He says this low so that no one else can hear.

"What?"

"It's not real, Kate. It's fake. Haven't you ever been to a haunted house before?"

I shake my head slowly, realization dawning of what he's telling me.

"You mean, they're just...?"

"Just pretending, Kate. It's not real. You thought...?"

As his words sink in, my face flames with mortification.

"Not...real?"

He smiles, relief evident on his face. I glance to the side, seeing the crowd there, curious, concerned looks on their faces. Henry follows my look.

"Hey, can you guys just back up a little? She just needs some air," he calls out.

"She okay?" someone asks.

He looks back down at me, and I'm glad to see there isn't any mockery on his face.

"Yeah, she just got a little sick, a little faint."

"Scared, huh?" one of the workers asks. "We get at least one a night."

I bury my face in Henry's shirtfront, and he hugs me tighter. Everyone loses interest when they see that there isn't anything exciting happening, and eventually they leave.

"I'm so embarrassed," I mumble into him.

He laughs softly. "You scared *me* to death!" I just burrow in deeper. "You really haven't ever been to a haunted house or anything like that before?"

"No."

"I'm sorry. If I would have known I would have warned you. I can only imagine what that must have looked like..."

I picture it again and shudder.

"You know you'll make those actors happy, right?"

I peek up at him. "Why?"

"That's what they work for, to scare people. Yours was probably the best reaction they've had all night."

"Is that supposed to make me feel better?"

He shrugs. "Think of it as a charitable act."

I sit up a little more, looking at him questioningly, a wry smile in place.

"Sure," he says, "they don't make squat for working here; their only reward is in the reactions they get from people. So you gave them what they wanted. Charitable."

"That's warped," I tell him, smiling.

"I do what I can." He smiles back. "Do you want to go home, or should we wait and get ice cream with the others?"

"Let's wait."

It's some time before the others return. I move to sit next to Henry on the hay bale, and we sit there talking, waiting.

"So, why don't you play football?" I ask him.

He looks at me, surprised at the question.

"I mean, you're big, built like the rest of them."

He shrugs, "I missed tryouts. They were done when we moved back."

"You played before?"

"A little," he says, and I get the impression it was more

than a little. I'm glad he's not—otherwise he'd probably be dating a cheer leader and not hanging out with me.

We obviously lose since we didn't even finish, but everyone comes back laughing and out of breath from running from the chain saw guy. I'm glad to see that fright is normal, though I suspect their fear is put on, rather than real, as mine had been.

We go to the Ice Castles Ice Cream Parlor. It's fun pretending to be normal, though I don't say much, mostly just sit quietly and observe. I have to watch Brock's date watch Henry, but also have the joy of being the center of his attention so completely that by the end of the night she's alternately pouting and glaring daggers at me.

When Henry finally drops me off, it's much later than I had planned, and I walk home with the familiar dread. I sneak in my bedroom window, unsure if my mom's asleep or awake, but I'd seen the glow of the TV through the window. I decide my story will be that she'd been sleeping when I came home, which is entirely feasible, and so I had gone to bed. I'll probably get a smack or two, or maybe an insult, but she won't have much proof otherwise, and won't be able to recall clearly if she'd seen me come in or not.

I guess there's one advantage to having a mom gorked on drugs.

Twelve

Since that night, Henry's thrown out my ruling about not letting anyone see us together. He always either holds my hand or has his arm around me, walking me to classes and kissing me when dropping me off. And I no longer care to try to get him to stop—no matter the threat from Jessica.

Most weekends I'm able to get away one night to see Henry, and sometimes during the week as well. At home, I'm as beyond reproach as much as possible, though *she* still manages to find fault; but since her dinner date with my dad, there's a slight change in her.

She isn't ideal by any means, but sometimes she tries a little bit, by asking about school or even allowing me some dinner. She and my dad aren't fighting quite so much; I haven't seen a bruise or fat lip on her since their dinner date.

October rolls into November, and snow begins to fall.

At first, it only lasts a day or two and then melts, but the week before Thanksgiving a heavy snow falls that seems determined to stay for a while.

Because of how happy I am in my life with Henry, and because of the calmer atmosphere at home, I become somewhat content and hopeful—hopeful that there might be a chance for us to become a real family—maybe not as good as the Jamison's, but at least a shadow of them.

I decide to make us a traditional Thanksgiving dinner. Usually Thanksgiving passes unnoticed as do most holidays. In the past, I would pathetically prowl the streets to watch families gather in their homes. Not this year. This year I'm determined that *our* family be the one having a happy, laughing meal together. Maybe the laughing, happy part won't happen, but I'll settle for together.

I know of a place where I can go get food provided by the food bank. I've been there a few times previously out of desperation when there was seriously no food in the cupboards at home, and no money to buy any. Of course, I have to tell my mother that the money came from the pitifully thin grocery funds she places in a can. She hates charity.

They provide a small turkey, some potatoes and dressing, some noodles, two cans of veggies and a can of cranberry jelly—all expired, but at least still edible. It's not the elaborate layout I'm sure they'll be having at Henry's house, but it'll have to do. It's better than we usually have.

Thanksgiving morning I get up early to start the turkey cooking. I follow the directions on the box and stuff the turkey. After it's cooked a few hours, and the house is filling with the mouthwatering aroma, I go into the kitchen to start the potatoes.

By four o'clock the mini-feast is ready. I've set the table for three as fancy as I can with what we have, including a few late fall leaves I'd found on the back porch under the eave, miraculously not completely dried out. I have to say, I'm pretty proud of myself—it's nothing like Claire's table, but not bad.

My father had come home quite late last night, and I heard him get into the shower twenty minutes earlier. I sit at the table, waiting for him to come down the stairs, and then I'll go into the living room and bring them in for my surprise.

I hear his footsteps on the stairs, and almost immediately my mother starts in on him about having been out all night. He begins yelling and within minutes it escalates into a screaming match. I sit at the kitchen table, hands vainly over my ears, tears running down my face as my plan unravels. Then I hear the tell-tale sound of fist meeting jaw—a sound I know better than most sounds—then his car pulling quickly away.

I don't move, looking at what I've done. What a fool I am.

"What the hell is this?"

I look up at my mother, hulking in the doorway. Her face is filled with rage above her swelling jaw.

"It's Thanksgiving," I tell her lamely.

"Where did all of this come from?" she screams.

"I got it," I murmur, fear threading its way through my veins.

She takes a step toward the table, looks at the perfectly cooked turkey, lying on the plate, waiting to be carved.

"Did you steal from me again, or is it charity?" her voice is low, more of a warning than her screaming. I blanch. She knows I steal from her? I can't answer, frozen in my terror.

She touches the turkey, then in a quick movement picks it up, plate and all, and hurls it at my head. I duck too late, the heavy glass platter glancing off my eyebrow. Immediately blood begins spilling down my face from the cut it leaves there. I dive sideways off the chair, cowering where I fall. She strides over, kicking me in the ribs. I try to protect myself, but this only angers her further, and the kicks come more frequently and harder. That isn't enough to vent her anger, so she picks up the chair. She swings it down towards me, and I put my arm up in unthinking defense. I feel my wrist snap as the wooden spindles break.

With an enraged shriek, she reaches down and gathers my shirt in one fist, pulling me up into a half-sitting position, using the other to pummel my face. With only one good arm for protection now, she has the advantage. She takes turns raining blows on my face and kicking my screaming ribs. I feel when she starts to tire, which is a good thing since consciousness is fading.

But she isn't done. She releases me and I fall back to the floor. Then she's on me, straddling me, both hands wrapped around my throat as she cuts my airway off. She's shouting again, but I can't hear her words above the ringing in my ears. The world fades around the edges, and the last thing I see is her face, contorted and purple with rage before blackness blissfully finds me. My final thought as I give in to the pull of the darkness is: *this time, she'll kill me*.

When I come to, I'm still lying on the kitchen floor where she left me. I'm lying in something sticky. The juice from the turkey?

I roll onto my side, crying out at the pain in my ribs, stopping and gasping for painful breath. I concentrate on my breathing, getting it under control, knowing from experience that this is the only way to ease the pain somewhat. I push myself up with my good arm, leaning against the wall and taking slow deep breaths again when the world begins to spin. When I feel a little better, I look down at the floor and realize the stickiness I had been laying in was my own blood. Nausea rolls through me.

I use the edge of the table to pull myself up onto my knees with one arm, then onto my feet, fighting the new round of nausea and dizziness that comes with that. I look at the table, which is just as I had left it, minus the turkey. It sits there contemptuously, mocking my efforts. I stand unsteadily, trying to catch my breath enough to get upstairs and clean myself up. When I finally move, I go instead to the back door.

I look at my swing hanging there, blowing softly in the cold breeze—and make a decision.

I leave my house, moving slowly and carefully around to the front. I don't know if she'll be able to see me, but I'm not going to give her the chance. Once I'm down the street, undetected by her or any of the neighbors, I cut across to the field and eventually make my way through the trees to the other side.

I fall several times, each time taking longer than the time before to get back up. I know what I have to do—I have to get to *him*. His face keeps me going, pulling me up out of the snow each time I fall and red stains the untainted white.

I finally make it to his house, unsure of how much time has passed. It's beginning to get dusky, so I figure it's been a while.

What now? I ask myself. I limp up the drive, but instead of going to the front door, I make my way around back and collapse again near the clinic. I try to get up, but I'm unable to push myself up. I give up. I lay in the snow there for I don't know how long, when a miracle happens.

"Henry, the cherry and apple pies are on the top shelf, but the banana cream and pumpkin are on the bottom, so don't forget them," I hear Emma calling as the back door opens, light and warmth spilling from his house.

"Okay, Mom," Henry calls back, stepping out onto the deck and letting the door fall closed behind him. "As if that isn't where they are every year," he grumbles to himself as he walks, zipping his coat. "I haven't forgotten them yet, have I?"

He's clearly been sent out to fetch some pies from out of the clinic. His low grumbling continues. "You store them out here every year. It's not, like, a surprise, or anything." He doesn't see me lying there, intent on his purpose so that he can get in out of the cold.

"Henry," I call weakly, lifting my hand. He starts and looks my way, not recognizing me beneath my swollen and bloodied face. He approaches cautiously, not getting too near.

"Who's there?" he says.

"Henry," I say again, and see the change in his face as he hears my voice.

"Kate!" He rushes to my side, dropping in the snow, hands everywhere and nowhere, since he doesn't seem to be sure of where to touch me not to hurt me.

"What happened? How did you...I can't...I've got to get my dad," he says frantically.

"No!" It takes all my strength of will to get the word out forcefully enough to stop him in his rising motion. He drops back to the snow.

"Promise..." I rasp, breaths coming painfully too fast, but it's important to get his word. "No cops...no parents...promise."

"Okay, okay," each promise coming on a gasping breath, and I realize with shock that he's crying.

"Help me," I beg him.

"How?" he's distraught.

"Help me...up."

He leans down and gently rolls me onto my back. I gasp at the pain.

"I'm sorry," he moans.

"Don't be...sorry."

He slides one arm behind my back and another under my knees, standing slowly and carefully, holding me steadily in his arms.

"I'm...cold." I say.

"Okay, I'll get you inside."

"No...not house.... You promised."

He nods unhappily, tears still running down his cheeks. He carries me instead into the clinic. It's intended for animals, but the bed in the exam room is just long enough to fit me on, my heels hanging over the end. He lays me down, carefully placing my arms across my belly, jerking as I cry out when he moves my obviously broken arm.

"Wait here, I'll get some blankets."

I try to smile, though it probably looks like a ghastly grimace with the swelling and blood.

"Not...going...anywhere."

He gives a half-sob, half-laugh at that, leaning to kiss me softly on the forehead. He's only gone half a minute when he returns with a stack of blankets. None of them are long enough to cover me, so he piles them down my body.

"What happened?" he asks again.

I shake my head, not wanting to tell him just yet. The door opens behind him.

"Henry, your mother sent me to see..."

His father trails off when he sees me lying there. Henry jumps up and places himself defensively in front of me.

"What in the world.... What's going on Henry? Is that...Kate, is that you?"

I close my eyes.

"I found her, dad, just now, outside the clinic."

His dad comes over and moves Henry impatiently out of the way. He takes one look at my face, then pulls the blankets down. He takes one look at my wrist lying across my chest and blows a breath out between clenched teeth. I start shivering and he pulls the blankets back up over me.

"Call 9-1-1," he commands Henry. He moves away and starts opening cabinet doors.

"No," I grab Henry's arm with my good hand. "No, you promised. Please, you promised."

Dr. Jamison turns back at that, lifting his brows at Henry who shakes his head.

"No, Dad, I promised her I wouldn't do that."

Dr. Jamison looks at me, and finally sighs, coming to a decision.

"Alright, but we at least need to call her parents."

"No!" My protest is even more vehement. That's worse! I struggle to sit up, pulling against Henry's arm for support. "No…no…I'll go…. Please, *no.*"

"Dad…" Henry's plea matches my own.

Dr. Jamison is immediately at my side, hands trying to keep me from rising.

"Kate, calm down. I won't call anyone, okay? Calm down before you hurt yourself further."

I fall back onto the bed, ribs screaming in agony, trying to catch a breath as tears stream down my face. Henry leans down, putting his forehead against mine, agony in his dark eyes shining with tears.

Dr. Jamison sighs again.

"I'm a vet, Kate, not a doctor. I don't know if I can help you."

"No help…just rest."

"I don't think that will help you now. You obviously have a broken wrist and you need stitches. And that's just what I can see. You might have internal damage. I can't leave you untreated."

I reach out and grab his hand. He has to understand how urgently important this is.

"No cops…no parents…or she will kill me." My voice is hoarse from the choking, but he understands clearly enough. If I didn't look so bad, he might not have believed me, but my injuries make my claim absolutely legitimate.

He clenches his jaw, something I've watched Henry do countless times when he's upset.

"Okay." He sounds unwillingly resigned. "I'll do what I can to help you." I relax at his words, letting go of his hand.

"I'm going to have to tell your mother," he tells Henry. "She'll wonder what's taking so long and it's better if she knows rather than send one of the girls out here to find us."

He looks at me for approval. I don't want to be the cause of distress for any of his sisters, so I have no choice but to nod my consent. He instructs Henry to hold some gauze against the cut on my brow and leaves to return to the house to tell Emma.

Henry pulls a rolling stool over and sits at my side, smoothing my hair back, holding the gauze gently over the oozing cut. His tears have stopped, but the expression on his face alternates between grief and anger. He doesn't talk, and finally, I let my eyes drift closed. I'm not sleeping, but resting, peaceful and safe for the moment, the pain a thrumming background against my relief, as long as I'm still.

Soon Dr Jamison returns with some clean quilts. Emma had told everyone that he had an emergency, and since that isn't uncommon, they don't question it. He pulls out a suture kit and sets to work on my laceration, after getting my assurances that I know he isn't a doctor, and that it will probably scar.

He stitches me up swiftly, then has Henry get some wet cloths to clean my face. He decides the cut on my lip doesn't need sutures, but that I definitely need x-rays. Henry lifts me up carefully, though it still causes me pain, and carries me into the x-ray room. He lays me on the table, and leaves while Dr. Jamison takes the pictures, having to take more than usual because the x-ray films aren't as large as needed.

He tells me I have three broken ribs and two cracked. My wrist is broken, but it's simple, though painful, for him to set it. He does that, and I watch him and Henry wince as I cry out. As soon as he's finished, my arm feels better. He x-rays it again, splints it, and explains that it will need a couple of days for the swelling to go down before casting it.

He sends Henry to the house to get Emma to help wrap my ribs, as it requires my clothing to be removed, and he wants to protect my modesty. When she comes and sees me, she gasps and immediately starts crying, which nearly sets me off, that this woman would cry over the injuries that had been *caused* by my own mother. Between the two of them, I'm soon bandaged, and wrapped in one of the quilts. Dr. Jamison says lying in the cold snow had probably helped my injuries. It had been like laying on a large icepack.

"She can't go home," Dr. Jamison tells Emma meaningfully, and though I see the curiosity in her face, she keeps her questions inside, ordering Henry to carry me into the house and put me in the guest room.

"I'll distract the others for now so she can go in privately. Take her through the front door."

Henry again lifts me, pulling me close without hurting me, tucking me under his chin, caressing his jaw against my hair. He carries me into a guest room that's just off of the entry way behind the formal living room—another room I hadn't noticed before.

Henry and his father settle me carefully into the bed. Dr. Jamison checks my temperature, which is still a little low, piling a few more blankets on me, helping me to swallow a pain pill.

"Come on, Henry; let's get back to the family and let Kate rest."

"I'm not leaving her," Henry says, eyes on mine.

Dr. Jamison sighs again.

"Somehow I knew you were going to say that. Alright, but let her sleep. She needs sleep more than anything right now."

Henry nods, pulling a chair up next to the bed and tucking his arm under the blankets to hold my good hand.

"You're going to be fine, Kate," he says, and it sounds like a command.

I want to assure him, to thank him, but already my eyes are drifting closed. I've never been so tired in my life.

* * *

When I open my eyes again it's dark in the room. For a minute I don't know where I am, but when I try to move, my body immediately reminds me. The day's events come rushing back, and I groan in pain.

"Kate?" Henry is immediately next to me, hands soothing my head.

"Henry," I whisper, all my throat can manage.

He reaches over and turns on the bedside lamp, and I watch him flinch at the sight of my face. Humiliated, I turn my face away. He grasps my chin lightly and turns me back toward him. He leans down and kisses me lightly on the undamaged corner of my mouth.

"Who did this to you?" his own whisper is ravaged.

I shake my head, tears falling from the corners of my eyes.

"I'm not a violent person—mostly—but I would happily kill whoever did this to you." My eyes widen at this. He's absolutely serious.

"Was it Frank?" I have to think for a minute of who he means, remembering that he had stopped Frank from bullying me at lunch.

"No." My answer is a croak.

"Then who?" he asks. I can't tell him.

I'm saved from having to answer when Dr. Jamison and Emma come into the room. They'd seen all their guests out and had left Claire in charge of the two younger girls.

Emma hurries over to my side, cooing and soothing, something only a real mother knows how to do. Dr. Jamison is looking at me watchfully, as if deciding something in his head.

"Okay, you two, I need to examine Kate. Leave us alone for a few minutes."

"Dad, I'm not—"

Dr. Jamison lays his hand on Henry's shoulder, cutting him off.

"Henry, it's only a few minutes. Go get showered and then you can come back and stay with her tonight."

Henry's reluctant, but nods his agreement. He kisses me again and leaves.

"Emma, she could use some ice packs, maybe some broth?"

Emma nods, tears in her eyes as she looks at me. And then she does an amazing thing—she leans over and kisses my forehead. It's the strongest maternal love I've received in as long as I can remember.

When we're alone, Dr. Jamison checks my wrist and the binding on my ribs, taking my temperature again and looking at the stitches. I feel like he's just fussing, finding something to do. Finally, he sighs and sits in Henry's chair.

"I don't suppose you'll tell me what happened?" He looks at me, but I can see in his face that he already knows the answer even before I shake my head.

"I'm better at taking care of animals than people, of course, but I can read an x-ray." He glances up at me, holding my gaze with eyes so like Henry's. "There were a lot of old, healed injuries. This isn't the first time you've been hurt."

My eyes drop.

"There is a reason you didn't want to go home."

I don't answer.

He clears his throat. "Does Henry know?"

I could ask him what he's talking about, pretend nothing untoward is going on at home, but the truth hangs in the air between us.

"No."

"There are people who can help you, places you can go…"

I meet his gaze again.

"Dr. Jamison, I'm seventeen years old, almost eighteen. What happens, the state puts me in foster care? Who takes in a seventeen year old?" My injured throat pushes the words out. "Someone who's in it for the money, maybe. Or, I don't know, someone who wants to get something out of it. Those who want to get a family out if it adopt babies. You think things would be different for me somewhere else? At least this way I know what to expect."

His head drops into his hands as he acknowledges the truth of my words. "I don't like this," he mutters, probably not meaning for me to hear. Then he looked up at me again. "You're pretty badly injured. Has it been this bad before?"

I think of the other times I've been beaten, but I have to admit, this is the worst. I shake my head.

"What if it gets worse? Worse could mean dead."

I know that. I sharply remember thinking she would kill me this time. She hadn't, though. Something had stopped her. Would something stop her next time?

"I can try to help you."

"No," my throat is on fire, talking painful. It's imperative I make him understand. "I couldn't live with it if Henry knew. I couldn't stand it if he pitied me. He's my friend. That would change if he knew."

Dr. Jamison shakes his head. "You don't give him enough credit."

"*Please*," I beg.

"This isn't about Henry, or what he thinks. It's about you."

"Right. And I'm asking you to let it go. If it makes it hard for you—legally, I mean—I'll leave. I'll find somewhere else to go for a few days."

He doesn't answer, asking instead, "What will happen if you don't show up at home for a few days?"

I glance out the window, as if the answers are there in the stars.

"She won't contact the police. She won't want them investigating. She probably wonders if she killed me," I rasp, remembering the pool of blood on the kitchen floor at the foot of my failed Thanksgiving dinner.

Dr. Jamison jerks in surprise—whether at my admission, or the fact that I said *she* instead of *he*, I don't know. He blows out a breath full of uneasy resignation.

"Okay, well, you need to rest for a few days. Broken ribs can be dangerous, and if you puncture a lung you would *have* to go to the hospital to live."

"I'll stay down," I promise.

He walks to the door, taking a breath without turning to look back at me, hand on the knob.

"She should be in prison for this."

Thirteen

Because it's Fall Recess, we don't have to return to school until the Wednesday following Thanksgiving. I spend those days recovering in the Jamison's home. The girls had been let in on my being there, told I'd been in an accident. They don't question why I'm staying at their place instead of my own. They're just happy to have me here.

After a couple of days, I'm allowed to be up more, and spend time with them in their family room area, eating leftover turkey sandwiches, which are far better than the turkey sandwiches they have at school. The whole family has taken it upon themselves to try to outdo one another as my caretaker. It's become a kind of game to them, to see who can do the most for me.

Mostly, I revel in being near Henry, all day, every day. I try to get him to take a break from me, but he won't hear of it. Except for when he's showering he's with me;

even at night he sleeps in the chair next to me.

Dr. Jamison casts my wrist, and allows me to have my ribs unwrapped temporarily for a shower myself. They even bring a plastic chair in for me to sit on in the shower.

I could have lived in this fantasy world forever, but inexorably, Tuesday comes. School is back in session tomorrow, and I can't afford to miss it and have attention fall on me.

"Stay one more night," Henry pleads. "I'll take you home tomorrow after school."

So I stay. I only have my torn and bloodied clothes which had been taken that first day—thrown away, I suppose—and have been wearing a pair of Claire's pajamas. She brings me a pair of jeans and a top to borrow for school tomorrow, since we improbably wear the same size. They are the nicest clothes I have ever worn, but in a very girly and vain way, I'm glad that Henry gets to see me at least once in something that isn't shapeless and ugly.

I awake the next morning, binding my ribs extra tight, not an easy task with one wrist in a cast. I'm still very sore, but I know I can make it. I looked at myself in the mirror, my face mottled with purple and yellow bruises. Most of the swelling has gone down though. My lip is only a little swollen, the biggest drawback to this being that it hurts when Henry kisses me, so he's done very little of that.

We ride to school in a lightly falling snow. Henry has given me his coat against my protests, since his jacket is still at my house. I'm happy he insisted, because his jacket has long since lost the scent of him, but his coat is filled with it. He's already spread the word among some of his friends about my "car accident", knowing word would get around school.

He's still frustrated with me because I won't tell him exactly what happened.

I find that my "accident" makes me the recipient of some sympathy—probably more because of how my face looks than anything. Not only does no one try to hurt me or trip me, they actually hold doors for me and help me to carry my books—which had luckily been left at Henry's—when I'm not with him. Mostly, this is carried out by Henry's friends, which I'm grateful for when I pass Jessica in the halls and see not only a lack of sympathy in her eyes, but anger instead.

After school Henry argues with me, trying to get me to come back to his house. I want to do just that, take the easy way and hide as long as I can. He makes it so much harder when he looks at me with desperate appeal in the dark depths of his eyes. I don't know what he knows, but I think maybe he suspects the truth, or something close to it.

Finally, he relents when I hold my ground. "At least let me take you to your house. You shouldn't be walking so far."

This starts a new argument, but I find Henry is as stubborn as I am. We compromise that he won't drop me in front of my house, but in front of the house next door, and that he will let me make my way home alone.

He helps me out of the car, pulling me close for a gentle hug, dropping kisses on my face and lightly on my mouth. He presses something into my hand and I look down to see a cell phone there.

"No," I protest, my voice still a little rough.

"It's not from me. It's from my dad." When I start to hand it back he wraps his hand around mine, trapping the phone there. "It belonged to one of his employees who no longer work's for him. My dad pays each month for it to sit in a drawer. He's worried that you don't have a phone. It's a loan. Take it."

"I can't..."

"Please. For me. It has all of our phone numbers programmed in it. All you have to do is call and I will come; I'll be here before you finish dialing."

"Henry..."

"It's just a loan." He sees my hesitation. "If you don't take it, I'll throw you back in my car right now and hold you hostage at my house until you agree."

I smile up at him. "Where's the threat in that?"

He laughs, kissing me lightly.

"Please, take it. My mom will not let me back in the house if you don't."

I capitulate.

"Well, we can't have that, can we?"

He shows me how to use the phone, since I've never owned a cell phone myself. He has, of course, programmed himself as the first speed dial.

He kisses me again, then holds me firmly. I relax into him, already dreading the time to go until I can see him again.

"I'll miss you tonight," I tell him.

He looks down at me.

"Call me before you go to bed."

"Okay." He releases me and I turn toward my house, frightened of going in, but knowing it's time. He waits until I've arrived at my front door before turning away and getting back into his car.

Mom is sitting on the couch, but instead of being asleep or watching TV, she's sitting, head in her hands, arms propped on her knees. She looks up as I close the door behind me. Relief floods her face at the sight of me. I walk over to stand before her and her eyes skim down me, taking in the cast on my arm, and my stitched brow before coming to rest on mine. She holds my gaze for a minute, then looks away.

"I was...I thought...I didn't know where you were," she stammers, and if I didn't know better I might believe there is concern in her voice.

"You mean, you didn't know if I were alive or not," I say, fear twisting through my stomach at the thought of what she might do to me for talking to her that way.

She looks up at me again and her face is contorted with guilt. I feel a moment's compassion for her, but that disappears when I take a deep breath and my ribs throb in protest.

"I'm alive and I'm back, and I need to rest to recover fully." I move past her toward the stairs, glancing into the kitchen. She's cleaned up the mess, scrubbed the wall and floor so that no evidence remains. So much for her concern for me personally—it seems she was more concerned about whether she might get caught. I take a step up the first stair, and then turn to face her again, heart pounding. She watches me closely.

"You can't do that to me again. You can't hurt me anymore." She doesn't say anything, so I turn and walk up the stairs. In my room I lay down on my bed, dizzy from the effort it took to stand up to her.

A smile crosses my face.

A new kind of life begins again. Because it's my right wrist that's broken, it requires help with my work both at school—for which I oddly have plenty of volunteers, again mostly Henry's guy friends, but also from several of the "losers" who share our lunch table—and with my homework after school. I tell my mother this, amazed she doesn't argue. So after school I go home with Henry and stay the afternoon and into the evening each day.

Emma seems happy about this, and makes sure I have dinner each night before leaving. I recover quickly, probably because my body is receiving more nutrition than it's ever had. I find myself fitting into a family, and I like how it feels.

Claire makes sure to show me plenty of embarrassing pictures of Henry—especially ones of her doing his hair when it was longer. I'm bribed to see these ones by allowing her to do *my* hair. I'm shown a picture of extended family members, including the Grandpa Henry was named for, and that brings back a clear memory of Henry as a boy.

The first day of school, he had announced his name in front of the class, telling everyone he had been named for his Grandpa Henry, and for the next few years, each time he introduced himself to someone new, he would repeat the same story. By the time we were in fourth grade, everyone was well aware of where his name had come from.

I laugh at the memory and tell his sisters about it, who find it to be a great thing to tease him with. They start calling him "Henry-who's-named-for-his-Grandpa," like it's one long name.

Each night when I return home, I clean up the kitchen and living room, though it isn't as hard as before, because my mom is making something of an effort as well. I clean my bathroom as I get ready for bed, then call Henry as soon as I'm in bed, and we talk until one or both of us fall asleep.

As the weather turns colder, sometimes dipping down below zero at night and struggling to rise to the mid-teens during the day, Henry starts picking me up and dropping me off in front of my house. He ignores my protests that I've been walking in weather like this for years, and when there doesn't seem to be any fallout from Mom, I quit objecting.

One night we're alone at his house. We're sitting in the living room on the floor, doing math homework. This is my favorite place to be because of all of the holiday decorations. A mishmash of ornaments, made by the Jamison kids throughout the years, adorns their huge Christmas tree, along with store bought ones that have been picked by the kids. Each one is carefully marked with their name and the year the ornament was made or acquired. Somehow, Emma has made it look elegant and homey all at once.

Dr. Jamison told me I needed to wear the cast until the New Year, so I'm still unable to write. We aren't getting much accomplished, though, since Henry keeps distracting me by kissing me since the swelling in my lip is gone and it no longer hurts. Also, I *way* preferred kissing him to math, so I'm not really protesting much.

"I want to ask you a favor," he says between kisses. He's watching my mouth, long thick lashes hiding his eyes, so I'm having a particularly hard time thinking straight.

"Anything," I breathe, kissing him back. He smiles, then looks into my eyes, his gaze darkly intent.

"I want you to tell me something,"

"Okay," I agree, ready to tell him anything.

He lifts his hand, brushing his thumb across the fading scar above my brow, following the movement with his eyes. The laceration had run along the line of my eyebrow, so it really isn't very noticeable now that the stitches have been removed, and will eventually be almost unnoticeable.

His eyes come back to mine, and softly, sounding off-handed, he says, "I want you to tell me who did this to you."

I freeze beneath his touch. His gaze doesn't waver. I drop my eyes and sit up, moving away from him.

"Don't ask me that," my own voice is low.

"Don't you trust me?" he asks. I turn to him, shocked. He's looking down, drawing patterns on the floor.

"Of *course* I trust you, Henry. I lo—" I catch myself,

but his eyes come to mine, stillness settling over his body. I think about the words I'd almost said; words that can't be spoken aloud. So I tell him the next truth.

I drop my eyes, take a breath then look at him steadily again. "I mean, you're my best friend. I trust you more than anyone else. I'm asking *you* to trust *me* when I say I can't tell you."

He still hasn't moved a muscle, watching me, waiting. When I don't say anything else, he releases a breath, looking away. Finally he nods.

"I can accept that." He moves then, coming up onto his knees, pulling me up with him onto my own knees and into his arms. "I don't like it, but I can accept it." He keeps one arm about my waist, bringing his other hand up to rest alongside my neck, thumb tracing my jaw. "Can I ask you something else though?"

A little wary now, I nod.

"Is that all we are? Friends?"

"Uh..." my thoughts scatter again.

"Because I thought we were more." He tips his head down toward mine. When his eyes are just inches from my own, he asks, "How many friends do this?" Then his mouth is on mine.

Heat flows through me as it always does when we're this close, as if I'm on fire. Tonight it's more intense with the realization I've come to about my love for him. I'd been about to tell him I *loved* him before, and I think he knows it. As soon as I thought the words, I knew it was the truth—that it will always be true. I can't tell him that though, knowing that what we have now is only for now, that as soon as we graduate he'll be going away to school. By the time he comes back, his life will have moved on, probably with someone else. Jealousy shoots through me.

We hear the garage door open, and pull apart as the door flies open, spilling his family in. They all come running over to kiss Henry and hug me, even his parents. With them here, the atmosphere is lively and vivid, intimacy gone. But still, while we do our work, Henry keeps his hand entwined with mine, his thumb tracing across the pad of my hand, turning my thoughts to mush. It's only when he glances up at me from under his lashes with a secret smile that I realize he knows exactly what it's doing to me. I think of pulling my hand away to wipe the smugness from his face, but then I'll be without his touch. I'm not dumb enough to torture myself just to prove a point.

Later, as we're leaving for Henry to take me home, Emma walks with us to the door. "Did Henry tell you we are going to Florida for the holidays?" she asks.

My eyes fly to Henry's. He's leaving? My horror must show on my face, because he answers for me.

"No, Mom, I haven't told her yet."

"Oh," Emma's answer is casual, as if she hasn't just told me I'll be spending two weeks in misery. Henry squeezes my hand.

"Well, actually, I know it's Christmas, which is really a family holiday..." *Hah,* I think, *not where I come from—it's just another day.* "...but we'd really like you to come with us, if you think it would be okay with your parents."

I look at her, stunned. They want me to come with them on their family vacation?

"Paul's parents live there, so we're going down to spend some time with them."

"You want me to come with you?" I'm not sure I've heard her right.

"Well, I know it's a little odd, to ask your parents if you can go on a trip with your boyfriend's family..."

I look at Henry at the word *boyfriend*, and he simply smiles back cockily, eyebrow raised, daring me to dispute her use of the word.

"It's not so much that," I begin, every fiber of my being wanting to scream yes, "Christmas not being an especially big holiday at our house," *understatement of the year,* "It's more, um..." I'm embarrassed at having to tell her there's no possible way I can afford it. She waits. "It's not that I wouldn't like to, I'd *love* to, but, uh...."

"You think about it," she says, noticing my discomfort and letting me off the hook. "Talk to your parents and let Henry know. We'd love to have you come."

She has no idea how tortuous her words are. I'd give my good left arm to go—and the broken right one as well—but since I don't think there's a place to sell my arms, I know it's only fantasy.

We ride home mostly in silence. When we stop in front of my house, he turns the car off and turns toward me.

"I can't believe you didn't tell me you were leaving," I say.

"Mom wanted to ask you to come herself, and it would have been torture for me to tell you I was going and not be able to ask you to come. If you can't come, I'm going to stage a mutiny and stay home."

"And miss out on Grandpa Henry?" I'm teasing, but I

can see the disappointment that passes across his face at the thought.

"I can't come, Henry."

His jaw clenches, but his voice is resigned.

"Parents wouldn't let you, huh?"

I try to picture myself even asking my parents, but can't even imagine it getting to that point. "No, it's not that. It's...well, look." I sweep my hand towards my little dilapidated house in my rundown neighborhood. He looks, then looks back at me, brows furrowed in confusion.

"So?"

"Henry, look at my clothes." He does. "If they could afford to send me to Florida for Christmas, they could afford to buy me at least one outfit that wasn't secondhand," I tell him, shamed at admitting this.

Henry's face clears. "That's the hold up? Money?"

"Spoken like one who has plenty to spare," I grumble.

"Kate, when my mom asked you to come, she knew you couldn't afford it."

"Then, why..." my thoughts immediately turn to wondering why she would do something so cruel, teasing me like that.

"They intend to pay for you."

"No! Henry, no. I can't accept that. I'm not a charity case," I lie, knowing that's exactly what I am.

"Kate, sweetheart," my heart skips a beat at the endearment, the first from his lips, "they wouldn't offer if they didn't want to. My whole family happens to be crazy about you. It's embarrassing to admit but you *know* that they can afford it."

"That doesn't mean I would feel right taking it."

"You would let your pride stop you from spending the holidays with me and my family?"

I know he's trying any tact, even shame, to get me to change my mind. The problem is, it's working a little.

"Don't do that."

"What?" He's genuinely curious.

"Don't make it seem like it's my pride keeping this from being a reality. It's a matter of right and wrong. And it's wrong to let someone spend so much on me."

"It's not so much. It won't change the cost of the place we're staying at, or most of the meals that we'll be eating there, since we'll be eating mostly at the beach house we're renting. It's something they really want to do. You'll break my mom's heart if you say no." It's starting to sound like a painful possibility—painful because it *isn't* possible—is it? Then he says the thing that makes me crack a little.

"It'll break *my* heart if you don't come."

I sigh. "I'm pretty sure *she* won't let me come anyway," I say, jerking my thumb toward my house.

His sudden smile is brilliant, victorious.

"But you'll ask?" He's triumphant.

I can't remain strong in the presence of his joy. I smile, "I'll ask."

"Yes!" He shoots a fist up in the air like he's just scored a touchdown. He kisses me enthusiastically. "When?"

"When what?" I ask.

"When will you ask?"

"Oh. Uh, I don't know. When the time is right, I guess."

He's only slightly deflated.

"Okay. But don't wait too long. It's only two weeks away."

The next Saturday I arise early and set to cleaning the house quietly but thoroughly. I've been taking advantage of my mom's guilt and slacking in my servant duties. Today I need her nice because today I ask about Florida.

I clean and scrub and organize, and I make sure when I hear her get up that she has a nice lunch waiting. I'm quiet, staying out from underfoot but available if she needs me. By the time I have her dinner cooked, served and cleaned up, I'm exhausted. I really want to go be with Henry.

I walk into the living room, where she sits looking at an old magazine—probably pilfered from her last drug-searching doctor visit. I sit next to her, and she looks at me with a guarded expression.

"Mom, I was wondering if I could talk to you."

She sets her magazine to the side—a first—and turns her attention to me.

"I have something to ask you." I swallow nervously.

She reaches out toward me, and instinctively I flinch away. She stops abruptly, her hand frozen in the air between us. Something like sadness shadows her eyes. She holds her hand there until the panic leaves my face and I nervously sit up straight. She touches my cheek, with gentleness.

"I haven't been much of a mother to you, have I?"

I'm sure my mouth falls open, but I'm not about to agree with her and set her off.

"I'm sorry about that. I wish we could wind back time..." she looks away, dropping her hand. "What did you want to ask?"

I take a breath. "I have a friend," I almost smile at the word, thinking of Henry's face when I called him a *friend*, "and my friend's family invited me to go on a trip with them during school vacation."

"You have school vacation coming up?"

"Yeah, Mom, for Christmas."

"Oh."

I hold my breath. She hasn't said no yet, nor gotten angry.

"You want to go away for Christmas?" She looks at me, stunned.

I nod.

She lets out a breath.

"But what will I do without you here?"

"It's only two weeks. Then I'll be home again."

She shakes her head, and I feel a stinging disappointment.

"Well, I suppose it's the least I can give you now."

I stare at her. Is she saying...? She looks at me.

"I can go?" I dare ask.

"I guess," she sighs.

A wide grin splits my face. I feel like I'm soaring—higher than I've ever been able to get on my swing. I stand up, controlling my reaction so she won't have reason to take it away. On a whim, I lean down and kiss her cheek.

"Thank you," I tell her. I hurry up the stairs to my room, closing myself in before falling on my bed in ecstasy, laughing at my good fortune. It's so much more than I could have hoped for.

That night I dream.

The sky is gray and overcast. I hurry out to swing first thing in the morning, my first time after having it delivered and cemented in by the big delivery men. It's the quiet time of day; there isn't any yelling going on yet. I know there will be a lot of yelling today, because Dad had come home really late again last night, stumbling and cursing loudly as he banged against the walls.

The cursing and stumbling had started two days earlier when Dad had come home too early from work, announcing that he had lost his job. He smelled funny, and his words were slurred.

There's never been any cursing in our house, and Dad had never been drunk before. I only knew he was drunk because Mom had called him that that first day. He had stormed out of the house, slamming the door and that was when her tears had started. That night when he came home the yelling had begun. It continued the next afternoon when he had finally stumbled out of bed, and was followed by another door-slamming-storm-out, then more yelling again that night when he came home drunk again.

I know it will be the same today because there's a new pattern forming in our family.

Mom is crying a lot. She has a new, pinched look around her mouth that I've never seen before. I'm scared. I don't like it. It makes me feel vulnerable. So I stay in my room, hiding, only coming out when Mom comes to get me for lunch or dinner.

On this, the third day, I know the cement is dry, and I want to swing. So I do, without even asking for permission first. I grab the chains on both sides of the middle swing and hop up with a push of my feet. As I begin to swing, I feel my world right itself a little bit. Even though I'm a young girl, I can recognize the normalcy of the activity, a kid out on her swing with no yelling coming from her house.

As I push myself a little higher I feel a tightening in my abdomen with each drop back towards the earth. Soon, I'm going pretty high, almost high enough to see over into the neighbor's backyard.

I don't know how long I've been swinging when I hear my dad call for my mom. She answers, with a yell of her own, and then they both started arguing in earnest, their voices getting louder.

I swing higher.

The wind whistles past my ears, blurring the sound somewhat, so I push higher. I don't get off the swing when Dad starts calling her names that I would definitely get my mouth washed out for saying. I don't get off when she screams back. I don't get off when I heard what sounds like someone getting smacked on the cheek, or when the pitiful crying starts, or when I hear Dad slam out of the front door, his tires squealing as he speeds away. I don't even get off when the quiet returns, and time passes and my stomach growls with hunger.

I figure the swinging has to be a good thing—it dries the tears no one else will.

Then, the familiar dream—a memory really—changes. I'm still swinging, but I'm not alone. Henry sits next to me, holding my hand. Instead of the terrifying noises coming from my house, I hear laughter. Suddenly, the rest of Henry's family comes out of the back door to join us. They are the source of the laughter. Most surprising of all, they are followed by my own parents—not as they are now, but as they had been before. Young and happy, smiling at each other and at me.

I jerk awake, feel the tears sliding down my cheeks. I smile at the new turn in my dream, but my smile fades as I realize the impossibility of it. My tears become a self-pitying torrent as I bury my face in my pillow, praying for a dreamless sleep to take me away.

I wait until I'm at Henry's for dinner on Sunday to break the news. I tell all of them at dinner, and am pleasantly amazed at their response. Emma claps, Christine squeals, and Claire and Amy jump up in joy, rounding the table to hug me joyously. Dr. Jamison reaches across to squeeze my hand. The best reaction is from Henry. He doesn't say anything, just leans his jaw against his fist. But his face is alight with happiness, the smile on his face and the look in his eyes just for me, satisfaction radiating from him.

Fourteen

I come home from school the day before we're scheduled to leave and find an old suitcase sitting on my bed. I open it and inside lays a one-hundred-dollar bill, tacked to a note that simply reads, "Merry Christmas." I know what this cost them, and feel tears start at the kindness behind it.

It doesn't take me long to pack, since I really don't own many clothes, throwing my personal items into grocery bags and putting those in the suitcase. I have an old swimsuit because it had been required the year before for gym class, so I throw that in, not knowing if I'll need it or not. Lastly, I throw in my tattered pajamas, hoping Henry will not have occasion to ever see me in them.

I tell Henry I should probably stay home tonight, since I'll be gone for so long. It terrifies me, though, that *she* might come in and take this away from me at the last minute. I know his family will have preparation themselves and probably don't need me underfoot, so no matter how much I want to be with him, I stay home.

I look at the money as I slip it into my pocket, and suddenly, decide to do something. I need help though. I call Henry and ask him if he can help me. I take the money that had been left in the suitcase, and hurry downstairs, out the front door.

He drives me first to the mall. I make him promise to wait for me where he won't be able to see what I'm doing. I go to one of the kiosks that sell knick-knacks and pick out a sterling silver ornament for my parents. I pick up a few other things for Henry and his family, and a roll of Christmas wrapping paper. I buy a small tabletop pre-decorated plastic Christmas tree from a discount store. It isn't anything like Emma's large pine tree covered with beautiful things, but it's more than we currently have—which is no tree at all.

I wait until I know my parents are in bed before going back downstairs to set the tree up, placing the wrapped gift underneath. I go back to bed and sleep fitfully until my alarm sounds at five a.m. Hurrying to get dressed, I grab my suitcase and run down the stairs to find Henry already waiting for me there in the pre-dawn darkness.

He drives me back to his house, where we transfer my suitcase into their already packed family SUV. We drive to the airport, butterflies in my stomach at the thought of my first flight. Christine is tired, having been dragged out of bed so early and not really caring about the excitement of a trip. She insists that Henry carry her and won't let anyone else touch her. So he carries her in one arm, and keeps the other around me.

The flight is amazing. How many times have I been on my swing, pushing myself higher to try to get the sensation of flying? Now here I am, really doing it. Henry lets me have the window seat so I can look out. I keep my hand clamped to Henry's, but my eyes outside, watching the sun begin to rise as we take off, amazed at the sight of clouds *below* me. Even if we had landed, turned around and went back home, I would have been happy.

We're staying in a small, white house not far from the airport. We pull into the garage, and unload our baggage from the rental van. There's a smell in the air that I can't quite place, but I like it. It smells clean and kind of salty.

We walk into the house, coming down a short hallway into a large living area. My feet skid to a halt and my suitcase drops from my hand, thudding loudly on the floor. Henry drops his own bag and sets Christine down, hurrying back to my side, a look of alarm on his face.

"Kate, what's wrong?"

He follows my gaze. I'm staring out the back of the house, which is made up entirely of glass windows that go ceiling to floor. But it isn't those extraordinary windows that have caused my reaction. It's the sight beyond it.

"Is that the ocean?" I ask, awed.

"Well, yeah. Haven't you ever seen it before?"

"No."

"Take her out and let her see it up close, Henry," Emma calls from another room.

Henry smiles at me, taking my hand and leading me out through the glass door. There's a deck attached to the back of the house, with three steps down to the sand.

"Wait," he says, kneeling down to roll my pant legs up and tug my shoes off. "You've gotta take your shoes off to get the full experience." Standing on the deck I realize that what I had smelled a little in the garage was stronger out here, and accompanied by the rhythmic sounds of the waves hitting shore and birds squawking overhead.

After Henry removes his own shoes, and rolls his pant legs up, we walk down to the shoreline, sand squishing between our toes, warm on the top, cool underneath. The blue water comes rushing up with a wave, washing over my feet. I squeal as the cold water hits me, leaping away from Henry and running up above the watermark. I turn back to see him standing in water up to his ankles. He's grinning ear to ear. The ocean makes a wide, beautiful, writhing backdrop behind him.

"Come on," he calls.

"It's cold!" I exclaim.

"Come on, wimp," he taunts.

The water is already back down the shore, his feet half-buried in the sand now. I walk back toward him, poised to run when it comes back. He grabs my hand and urges me closer to the water.

"No!" I laugh, standing firm as he pulls me toward the sea. He laughs and scoops me up into his arms, walking purposefully as the water again rushes at us.

"Put me down," I cry, still laughing.

Instead of answering, he pulls me closer to him, planting his mouth firmly on mine. All of my protests are forgotten in the warmth of his lips. Slowly he releases my legs, letting me slide down the length of his body as the water swirls around his ankles. My feet touch the water, and I start to pull away, but he holds me tight, deepening the kiss.

It's an amazing sensation, heat flooding through my body, icy coldness at my feet—ice colliding with fire. My eyes pop open in surprise and I see him watching me intently. That look alone is enough to douse the ice with the flames and I give my struggle up, rather enjoying myself even as the ocean recedes.

After a few minutes, he lessens the strength of his embrace, but doesn't relinquish his hold on me. The water is once again swirling about our ankles, and I look down, surprised.

"It doesn't feel cold anymore."

"Yeah, it just takes a few minutes for your body to get used to it." He's scrutinizing my expression, then he grins mischievously.

"Wanna go in?" he asks.

My own eyes widen in astonishment.

"Now?"

"Now," he confirms.

"But...we're dressed."

"So?" he shrugs.

"What about my arm?" I lift it, indicating the broken wrist which Dr. Jamison has removed the cast from, replacing it with a splint, which I can remove to shower, but not for any length of time—and probably not to play in the ocean.

"When we get back, we'll take it off and I'll dry it for you."

I look at the water, then back at him with a smile.

"Okay."

He seems slightly surprised at my answer, but doesn't comment on it, just turns, keeping his arm around my shoulder as we walk to the point where the water has receded to.

At the first wave I draw my breath in with the cold that comes up to my knees with the wave, and nearly fall over when the water begins to withdraw again, sand drawing back against my ankles and trying to suck my feet in. It's powerful! Henry keeps a firm hold, laughing with me.

We keep walking in until we've passed where the waves are breaking, Henry now holding my hand and showing me how to jump as the waves come, jumping over the crest so that it doesn't push us back into shore. Then we're in water up to my chest, jumping as the waves roll over us. Henry turns, wrapping his arms around my waist and pulling me close. I wrap my arms around his shoulders, Henry lifting me weightlessly in the water to hold me tight against him, keeping my head level with his.

He kisses me again and I taste the salt and cold on his lips. I laugh as a big wave comes unheeded and pours over our heads, knocking us off our feet and separating us. Henry grabs my hand quickly as he regains his footing, pulling me back to him, smiling.

"I'm glad you came," he says.

"Me, too," I smile at him.

"I love you," he says. I stare at him, stunned. Before I can begin to fully process his words, another wave washes over our heads, pulling us apart. This time, Henry manages to keep hold of my hand.

"Wanna try something fun?" he asks.

"Sure," I say hesitantly, my mind still whirling from his words, wondering now if I heard him correctly. When I had dared dream of it, I had imagined that any proclamation of love between us would come with…I don't know, candles and violins, I guess—not thrown out casually in the ocean. I *had* to have heard him wrong.

"When the next big wave comes, lift up your feet and let it take you into shore."

I lift my eyebrows doubtfully, and he laughs at me.

"It'll be fun, I promise. I won't let you go," his words have a serious undertone, and I cock my head slightly. He turns to look toward the waves, and I follow his gaze.

"Not this one," he pronounces. "It needs to be just right."

"And how do you decide which one is 'just right'?" I ask, looking at his profile.

"You just know," he says, turning his dark gaze back on me, underlying meaning in his words again, a meaning I think I understand but am afraid to hope is true. He looks back at the ocean, then grins at me.

"This one," he says. I look and see a wave larger than the others rolling toward us. I glance back at him, and he must see the panic on my face because he leans close, planting a salty kiss on my lips.

"Trust me," he urges lowly.

I nod.

We turn to face the shore.

"When I say so, give a jump and let the water pick you up. Keep your feet up."

I swallow loudly, gripping his hands beneath the water. The water begins to get deeper as the wave rolls in.

"Now!" he yells, and I jump. The water catches us and propels us to the top crest of the wave, shooting us inexorably forward.

This feels like flying in the water, I think, laughing and getting a mouthful of sea. Henry is further ahead than me, but still he holds my hand. The wave launches us into the shore, our knees scraping along the bottom. Almost immediately it starts pulling us back out, and I feel a moments panic at the power of the pull. Henry has gained his feet and turns to grab my other arm above the splint, hauling me clumsily up.

"That was fun!" I exclaim, the words out before I realize how childish they sound. Henry only laughs, kissing me quickly. I shiver, and he pulls me against him. His skin is cold, but I can still feel the heat of his "internal furnace" beneath the surface.

"Gets a little cold when you're out of the water, huh?" he asks. *That's not exactly why I shivered,* I think, but then my body breaks out in goose bumps, belying any protest I might make.

"Let's get back and get changed and help unpack."

I look back longingly at the water, and he smiles.

"We'll have plenty of time for body surfing," he tells me. "It's less constricting and not so cold when you get out if you're in a swim suit anyway."

We walk back up the beach, quite a ways further down the beach than when we had entered the water. The beach house has a shower cabana behind it. There are two towels and two thick terry bathrobes waiting on the bench inside.

"My mom," Henry smiles. "She probably knew I

wouldn't be able to resist getting in. Go ahead and shower and put the robe on, then you can go inside and get dressed."

I walk in, closing the door behind me. It's a little strange, showering here. It feels like I'm outside even though it's an enclosed structure, and I feel vulnerable once I have my clothes off. I can't believe how much wet sand there is inside my clothes and still stuck to my body.

I shower quickly, washing the sand out of my hair, amazed at the amount of sand that washes off me and swirls down the drain. I wrap up in the robe that's luxurious and soft.

I open the door shyly, feeling exposed again, even though the robe covers me from neck to mid-calf, and to my fingertips.

Henry turns toward me, eyes sweeping over me, an intensity lighting his eyes as they return to mine.

"Kate, just leave your clothes in that sink," Emma calls from the back door. Henry and I both start at the sound of her voice, Henry's face oddly flushed with guilt. I look at Emma to see she's pointing toward a sink that hangs from the side of the cabana. I drop them in, a little embarrassed to be putting my underclothes in there.

"Later we'll come back out and rinse the sea water out of them," Henry explains. He looks at me for a moment longer, then turns and goes into the cabana himself with a muttered, "Man, I need a shower—a cold one, I think."

What an odd thing to say, I think, as I follow Emma into the house.

"You are sharing a room with Claire and Amy, if that's okay," Emma tells me. Like I have grounds to complain if

I don't like it, but I wouldn't have complained anyway. I'm pretty fond of the two of them.

"That's great. And thanks, Emma, for bringing me."

She turns and hugs me. This time it isn't so surprising or unexpected, and I manage to hug her back before she lets go.

"You're welcome, sweetie. I'm really happy you were able to come." She releases me. "Did you like the ocean?"

I laugh.

"Yeah, it was amazing. Henry taught me to body surf. I hope it's okay we got our clothes wet."

She smiles indulgently.

"That's what washers and dryers were made for."

I think of my own mother, at what her reaction would be in the same circumstances and shudder. Oh well, I don't have to worry about that or her for two glorious weeks. I smile in pleasure at the thought as I enter my designated shared room, where I'm received with great joy by Henry's sisters, as if I've been gone a week, rather than half an hour.

Oh yeah, I reflect, *it's going to be a great Christmas!*

Fifteen

The next day, we go to visit the infamous Grandpa Henry. He and his wife, Grandma June live in a forest, which surprises me, because I didn't think there were any forests in Florida. They live in a small cabin on the edge of a river. Grandpa Henry doesn't look much like Henry and his father, except for his eyes, which are almost exactly the same as Henry's.

Grandpa Henry and Grandma June spend some time hugging and kissing the family members while I stand back and watch. Grandpa Henry pulls some large silver coins out of his pocket and gives one to each of the kids, Henry included. Then he sees me standing there. He walks over with a big smile.

"You must be Kate. I've heard a lot about you."

He hugs me, something that no longer surprises me coming from anyone in this family. He slips a coin into my hand also. Grandma June hugs me, then Grandpa Henry tucks my hand into his arm.

"Let's walk," he says.

"Henry, let the child alone. She hardly knows you," Grandma June chides.

"I just want to walk with her, get to know her a little," he says, steering me toward the back door.

"I don't mind," I say to my Henry, who's watching with clear intent to interfere if I want him to.

"June, honey, why don't you get the kids something to eat while Kate and I talk?"

He doesn't wait for an answer, just takes me out the back door, closing it firmly behind himself, a clear indication that we aren't to be followed. He leads me down the steps and onto a path that leads along the river.

"So, you're my Henry's girlfriend, eh?" he asks, grinning mischievously.

I shrug, "I guess so."

"You guess so? Don't you know?"

"There hasn't really been anything..." I search for a word, "*formal* declared by either of us." Even as I say it I remember Henry's words the day before as we played in the ocean. *I love you.* At least, that's what I thought I had heard.

"Huh," he's lost in thought. "Odd," he finally declares.

"What's odd?"

"I talk to Henry several times a week," he tells me, something I hadn't known. "And all that boy talks about is you. I think I can say with certainty that that boy is head over heels with you." I duck my head, embarrassed but also extremely pleased at his words.

"Well," I mumble, "the feeling is entirely mutual."

Grandpa Henry laughs, directing me over to a bench that sits facing the river.

"Let's sit here a bit."

"It is really beautiful here," I tell him, admiring the lush green pine trees that are thick and deep around us. The clear water gushes by.

"It is, isn't it? June and I have lived here, oh, I guess it would be about ten years now, and we plan to die here."

I nod. "I can see why. I'd like to die here, myself."

He looks at me, and I realize what I said, how foolish it sounded. My cheeks pinken in chagrin.

"What I meant was, if I *were* going to die, this would be an idyllic place to do it."

Grandpa Henry laughs.

"Well, let's hope you don't have to worry about that for some time." He eyes my splinted wrist. "What happened there?"

My stomach tightens at the question. I find myself very much *not* wanting to lie to this man, but also not wanting to admit the truth. I struggle with my answer, while he waits patiently, watching the river flow by. Maybe it's the calming influence of the river, or the way he seems to inspire confidence with his presence—another trait shared by his son and grandson—or just the fact that his eyes are so like my Henry's, but I find myself blurting the truth.

"My mother did it." As soon as the words are out, I want to recall them, but instead of gasping with shock or looking at me with censure, he simply nods, keeping his eyes on the river.

"I've been told I'm a pretty good listener." Now he does turn toward me. "I'm also good at keeping secrets."

And like that, I find myself telling him everything.

"When I was young, my life was pretty normal, I think. I don't have any bad or traumatic memories anyway. Then when I was nine my dad lost his job. I don't know why that should have been such a big deal, since he goes through about a job a year now. But it changed everything."

I tell him how my mother had changed after losing the baby, all the way up until the last beating, leaving out the worst details of the frequency and severity of the beatings, but I think he fills in the blanks anyway. He watches the river, not commenting or interrupting. At some point during my story, he had reached out and gently took hold of my hand. His weathered, wrinkled, calloused hand over mine has a calming effect, and rather than tell the story with tears or anger, I simply state the facts. When I finish, he squeezes my hand then releases it.

"Does Henry know about this?"

I shake my head. "No. I think he might suspect a little, but he can't really imagine it, coming from the family he does."

"No, I don't imagine he can. My son knows?"

"He knows some. He's the one who fixed me up after the last...time. He saw some old injuries on my x-rays and asked me."

"He's a good boy."

I smile at his description of Dr. Jamison as a *boy*. I can hardly think of Henry as a boy, let alone his father.

"Yes, he is," I agree. "They are all good people. They have become my ideal of what a family should be. I never imagined that there were really families out there like that, where everyone was so nice, and loved each other so much."

"My son did well in choosing Emma for his wife. She reminds me very much of my June." He eyes me sideways. "Looks like Henry has the same propensity for picking a good girl to love."

I smile at him, warmed by the compliment.

"You shouldn't go back home," he tells me, deadly serious. "It sounds like it keeps getting worse. What happens next time?"

I swallow. I've had those same thoughts myself, many times.

"She seems to be trying now. She has been nice to me since the last time, and she allowed me to come here. She even gave me a little money, which was a big sacrifice for her."

"Does she know you came with Henry?"

"No," I look away, feeling guilty. "She doesn't even know Henry. I just told her I was going with a friend, which wasn't a lie. Henry is my best friend."

We hear leaves crunching against the ground behind us and turn to see Henry coming toward us. I look at Grandpa Henry, stress tightening my eyes at the thought that he'll tell my secret. He glances at me and shakes his head, indicating his confidentiality.

"There you two are," Henry says, glancing at his grandpa with a loving smile, then turning his gaze on me, concern in his expression. I smile and he visibly relaxes.

"We're just sitting here, admiring the river." Grandpa Henry tells him. "Wanted to make sure this girl was good enough for you." His tone is light and teasing, but I have a feeling that underneath it all he's a little serious about that.

"And?" Henry asks, smiling. I look toward Grandpa Henry, also awaiting his response.

"And I think now that I have to wonder if *you're* good enough for *her*!" They both laugh while I shake my head at them.

"Well," Henry says, "if I'm not, I'm going to try really hard to make myself worthy." Henry reaches us and leans down to pull my hand up into his.

Grandpa Henry stands, and I hurry to follow suit. He pats me on the shoulder, keeping me in place.

"I think you will do just fine," he tells Henry.

"And what do you think of Grandpa?" Henry asks me.

"I think I know where you get your charm from."

Grandpa Henry bursts out laughing at that.

"Good answer," he tells me. Then he looks at Henry. "I'm going back up to the house. You two kids just come along when you're ready."

Henry sits next to me on the bench where his grandpa had been and strings his arm around my shoulder. I happily lean into him, wrapping my arm around his waist. We sit that way for some time, watching the river in comfortable silence.

My time in Florida is rejuvenating to my soul. I'm not required to do anything under threat of violence, there isn't anyone torturing me or teasing me in anything but a loving manner.

Henry's family takes me to an amusement park, and I'm as excited as Christine by all of the characters and rides. Claire and Amy try to pretend indifference, but they soon drop all pretenses and become as excited as me about it all.

Henry takes me on roller coasters that drop my stomach with thrilling fear, and on rides that amaze me with the creativity in each one. Best of all, he takes me on a huge swing that pulls us high into the sky and, when Henry tugs a cord, drops us 150 feet toward the earth at a speed that has me laughing and crying all at once. It takes me as high as I've *tried* to go on my own swing-set, but which I haven't been able to do, since it doesn't have the height of this one. It's exhilarating.

We eat popcorn and caramel apples and cotton candy until we're sick. Emma takes hundreds of pictures.

We go to the swamps and see real live alligators on an airboat, then eat at a restaurant on the shore of the swamp and eat "gator bites," which to my horror are *real* alligator. We go to the theater and see a movie, another first for me.

We spend many days with Grandpa Henry and Grandma June, sometimes at their house, sometimes at the beach house. Those are my favorite times, surrounded by this loving family where there's always laughter. We barbecue steaks and hamburgers, which I've never had before. Dr. Jamison laughs at my insistence on watching him do this so I can learn how.

I always help Emma in the kitchen if I'm there, even

though she protests that I'm a guest. One night after a busy day, Claire, Amy and I kick her out of the kitchen and the three of us make a bit of a feast for the family. All my years of having to create meals out of what was available comes in handy. We set the table formally, Claire taking charge of that and showing me how to properly place the utensils. I have to push back the memories of the last time I'd attempted such a thing, stomach tightening with nerves when we let the family in. But Emma's overjoyed reaction and the appreciation of the rest of the family sweep that memory away and replace it with this new, good memory.

Christmas Eve and Christmas day are spent at Grandpa Henry and Grandma June's. After a delicious Christmas Eve dinner, made by Grandma June, Henry takes me out to the bench by the river so we can exchange gifts. He insists on opening mine first.

Now that it's time for him to open it, I feel doubtful about it. It hadn't cost much. At the time I had bought it, I'd wanted to give him something to tell him how I feel about him, but now that I'm unsure of his words that day in the ocean, I'm a little afraid he'll think it's too forward.

He un-wraps it, opening the box to reveal the small crystal square with a heart laser-engraved in the center of it.

"It's not much I know. It's just...I wanted.... It means..." I trail off, not sure what to tell him.

He looks at me, and I see something like hope in his eyes.

"Why did you give me this?" he asks softly, not demanding, just wanting to know what it means.

I sigh and looked away, embarrassed.

"Because I wanted you to know how I feel about you."

He tugs my chin up until my eyes meet his.

"And how do you feel about me, Kate? Besides being your best friend," he quickly qualifies.

I swallowed loudly, glancing down, afraid to speak the words now. Then I decide to tell him anyway, and hope that he won't think I'm a silly girl. I look him directly in the eyes and take a breath.

"You know...that I love you," I tell him.

He smiles, a smile that lights up his face, pulling me into his arms and kissing me deeply.

"Finally!" he exclaims.

"Finally?" I echo.

"I was beginning to wonder, Kate. It's been almost a week since I told you that I love you, and you haven't said anything. I was starting to worry that you didn't and I've been wondering what I could do to make you love me."

"You *want* me to love you?" I ask, stunned.

"Kate, I've loved you for years. I mean, I know twelve-year-olds don't know what love is, so I guess I should say I've really *liked* you for years. But when I saw you this year, I knew. I knew we should be together. I just didn't know how hard you were going to make me work to get you to even *like* me. So, yeah, of course I want you to love me back."

I smile.

"Well, I *do* love you. More than I thought I could, more than I should. But I don't care. I don't care if it makes other people mad, or if I don't deserve you and I don't care if you don't like it because I do love you and I am going to forever, no matter what."

Henry laughs at my speech, kissing me again.

"Okay, give me my present now," I demand jokingly when I can catch my breath.

He bought me a silver chain with an open heart pendant hanging from it. "Same theory behind my gift," he tells me, shrugging. I kiss him. "I thought about giving you a jacket," he smiles wryly, "but I like seeing you in mine."

"Thank you. It's the best gift I have ever received."

Later, Emma asks me and Henry to help play Santa Claus and lay out the girls' gifts. I haven't had a Christmas morning since I was a young girl. I'd forgotten how much fun it can be, all the excitement and anticipation.

Christmas morning begins early with Christine's excited squeals. I watch her and the other two girls as they excitedly tear into their gifts. Claire is aware of just who Santa Claus really is, of course, but she plays along for the sake of her two younger sisters.

After they finish, Claire digs under the tree, pulling out the family gifts there. I'm surprised and a little self-conscious when she produces gifts for me from each member of the family, Grandpa Henry and Grandma June included.

I'm glad I'd taken the time before we came to get them each a small gift, which I'd placed under the tree the night before. I had gotten Grandpa Henry and Grandma June gifts at the flea market on the beach a few days earlier.

I'm overwhelmed at the love and acceptance I feel, and grateful for all of their gifts. I finger the silver heart hanging from the chain around my neck and know that the greatest gift any of them have given me is Henry himself.

New Years Eve is a day I'll remember always. Before dark falls we drag blankets and chairs down the beach to the water's edge. We haul coolers and bins full of food and drinks. Then we carry bundles of wood, and a stereo with a stack of CD's, which we play the entire time we're out here. The batteries even grow dim at one point and have to be replaced.

We light a fire and roast hot dogs on sticks. Emma makes potato and macaroni salads that we eat with the hot dogs.

Then we make s'mores. I've never even eaten a roasted marshmallow, which is like heaven in itself. But when Henry makes me a s'more and holds it up for me to take a bite of, I melt in delight.

There are fireworks over the ocean at midnight, lighting the sky and the water with brilliant colors, better than the ones I had seen from my swing on previous 4th of July's from home—especially since I watch these with Henry's arms wrapped around me.

After the fireworks, Dr. Jamison stands up to dance with Claire and Amy. Christine has fallen asleep in Emma's arms. I sit on a log, with Henry sitting in front of me, his hands holding my arms, which are wrapped around him, my chin resting on his head.

I watch Dr. Jamison, the man who has so much compassion that he'd helped and taken care of me when I was a virtual stranger, who had offered his help and kept my secret. He is who I wish my own father was—a man who will roll up his pants and dance in the sand with his daughters even if he thinks he might look silly.

I look at Claire, the girl with excellent fashion sense and immense talent who has befriended me and made the differences in our ages unimportant. And Amy, the shy girl who sometimes comes up next to me and slips her hand into mine timidly, or will sit next to me, content to sit quietly.

I turn to Emma, watching her rub her chin lightly over Christine's head, watching her husband and daughters with love shining from her eyes. The woman who has raised my Henry to obsess over being a gentleman at all times, just so that he won't disappoint her.

Grandpa Henry and Grandma June are sitting together in a folding loveseat. They have also accepted me and love me unconditionally; especially Grandpa Henry, who knows everything about the horror that is my life and has kept it to himself, and has not treated me any differently for it.

I squeeze Henry, who turns to smile at me before turning back to watch his sisters. He has given me these people that I have come to love so strongly. I'd be content to just have him, but he has given me so much more. I feel a peace and contentment that I don't think I will ever be able to duplicate, but I know I'll always have this memory.

Sixteen

We fly home on Saturday night, so that we will have a day to relax before returning to school on Monday morning. I'm reluctant to return to my house, feeling the familiar anxiousness in my stomach as soon as the plane lands.

We first go to Henry's house, where we transfer my suitcase and extra bag that I had to get to bring home all of the gifts and souvenirs I have received to Henry's car. I have even brought my parents home a bottle filled with sand and some carefully chosen seashells from the beach.

I receive hugs from everyone, and am made to promise that I'll spend more time at their house, since they will miss me, which is going to be a difficult promise to keep since I already spend most of my time here.

Henry opens my door and as I climb in, I place a hand in my jacket pocket and feel the other secret that is now between Grandpa Henry and me.

Guilt floods me as my fingers touched the thick envelope, stuffed with ten one-hundred dollar bills. He insisted I take it for, as he called it, an "emergency fund."

"You don't have to use it. But I would feel better if I knew you had it, so that if you need an out, quickly, you have an option," he told me.

I argued, but he had insisted, and somehow I'd found myself boarding the plane with the money in my pocket. I plan to bury it deep in a drawer and when I move out of my house, I'll send it back to him.

Henry drives me to my house, the trip all too short. He parks and helps me unload my baggage, then pulls me into his arms, which are warm against the cold night air.

"How am I going to stand not seeing you all day, every day?" he asks, hugging me.

I don't answer, wanting to cry at the thought of returning to my dismal life, knowing I have to wait until Monday morning to see him again.

"Are you sure I can't help you carry your stuff inside?" We've had this argument many times before, and I can hear in his tone that he already knows the answer. "I really should meet your parents. It seems wrong to hide us from them."

"Henry, it's complicated. You know that. The day will come when you can meet them," I say, having a hard time imagining when that time might be. "But not yet. Please."

He sighs, giving in. He kisses me, then climbs back into his car and leaves. I feel the cold seep into my skin at the loss of his contact, and with both dread and a little hope, turn toward my house.

I wonder what the chances are that her good mood has lasted.

My father's car is not parked in the driveway—not unusual for a Saturday night. I drag my luggage up the front steps. I pull the money-stuffed envelope from my pocket and push it into one of the suitcases before opening the door. I have to pull one suitcase in while holding the door open, and then turn back for the other. Before I can retrieve the second one, though, I hear her call my name.

"Kathryn! That you?"

My heart sinks like a stone. I know that tone only all too well. A lifetime of training to obey turns me toward her, leaving my second bag on the porch. I see immediately that her eyes are hooded and glassy, pupils dilated. I want to walk away, but my feet moved toward her, seemingly of their own volition. She sits on the couch in the dim light of the lamp.

"Where the *hell* have you been?" she demands, deadly quiet.

"I...I went to Florida, remember?"

I see a flicker of remembrance in her eyes, but she pushes it away, intent on her anger.

"Who said you could do that?"

You, I think, but don't dare say it aloud, well trained in my responses. It's then that I notice the house—it's a disaster. Trash litters the floor; old plates of food are on the table and floor. It smells like some of it has probably been here the entire time I've been gone.

She follows the trail of my eyes, and her eyes flare in response.

"Do you see this mess?" her voice is getting higher now, her words coming faster. "You made this mess, then left to go on some *vacation*," she spits the word out, "leaving this here for me to clean up!"

Because I'm still staring around me in revulsion, already picturing the hours of hard work it's going to take to clean it up, I almost don't see her next move. With one fast motion that I didn't know she was capable of, she has risen from the couch, a metal baseball bat in hand, swinging toward my head.

I throw my newly un-splinted arm up instinctively. The bat smashes into my weakened arm, continuing its arc to slam against the side of my head. I fall to the ground, the pain from my shattered arm the only thing keeping me conscious as I gasp. Self-preservation has me scrambling to my knees to get away from her even as she swings the bat down again, the hard metal rocking forceful pain through my spine as it makes contact, stealing my breath away.

I'm on the floor again, rolling away as the bat comes down again, this time missing my head by inches. This enrages her and she lets out an animalistic screech that scares me more than any screaming she has ever done before.

The wall is next to me and I push my throbbing back against it, using it as leverage with my good arm to push myself into a standing position as the bat comes hurtling again, this time making violent contact with my stomach. I double over involuntarily and she swings again, bringing it down across my upper back. That propels me forward. It's the end table that breaks my fall, knocking the lamp to the floor, the light bulb popping and leaving us in inky darkness. The only light shines in the window from the street lamp. I roll across the table onto the couch, using that as a temporary barrier to gain my feet.

She swings toward my face, catching me on the cheek with shattering pain as the world swims temporarily out of focus. I fight to keep consciousness as I look at her, see her face contorted in horrible rage, and know that she will kill me if I don't get away. A picture of Henry flashes into my head, and with it I find a reserve of strength from somewhere inside. I stumble toward the kitchen, but she anticipates me and comes around the couch from the other side, beating me to the door.

She swings the bat up again and my good hand intuitively comes up in defense. The end of the bat slams into my palm and I close my hand around the bat, my injured hand coming up to lend strength to my grip. Before I have time to think, acting on survival instinct, I shove it toward her, the handle thrusting into her chest with enough force to propel her backwards. She doesn't expect that and so she isn't prepared. The force sends her reeling backwards. Without time to try to break her fall, still clutching the bat that I quickly release, she falls to the tile floor. I hear her head hit with a sickeningly loud thud.

The force of it also sends me stumbling backwards, and I land on my battered back with crushing hurt that takes my little remaining breath away. I lay still, gasping, knowing I have to move before she gets up again.

Painfully, I roll onto my stomach and start to push myself forward with my feet, unable to rise, crawling as the world undulates around me. I have to get away. I can feel blood pooling beneath me, smearing with each forward push. I only move a few feet before I can't go anymore. My head is reeling, consciousness a barely held onto thing. Finally I lay still, waiting for her to return, to finish what she started.

Henry.

His name runs through my head, memories and thoughts incoherently jumbled together. I'm not sure how long I've been lying here, painfully trying to breathe, before I realize I haven't heard her move.

Oh please, I pray, *let her be unconscious.*

At the thought that I might still get away, I push myself forward again, but the effort and pain cause the room to spin precariously, so I stop.

Henry, I think again, and as if my thought has summoned him, the borrowed cell phone in my front pocket begins ringing. I manage to painfully lift my hip up enough to reach in and pull it out, my bloody fingers slipping the first time. I finally wriggle it out, pushing it along the floor near my face, knowing without looking that it's him. I push it open and try to say his name.

"Hey, Kate, I know I said I wouldn't call yet, but I couldn't wait. I wanted to talk to you *now*," I hear his voice coming from the speaker. I take a ragged breath.

"Henry," it comes out a whisper.

"Kate? Are you there?"

Please, please, I plead silently.

"Hello? Kate?"

"Henry," I gasp again. This time he hears, and in the ragged words hears that there is something wrong.

"Kate? What's wrong?" There's an edge of panic in his voice now.

"Police...call police," my voice is wet and torn.

"Kate! Katy, hold on." I can hear Henry talking frantically to his father, who immediately guesses what has happened. He takes the phone from Henry.

"Kate? Are you still at home?" his voice is calm and authoritative.

"Help...me," I whisper.

"Get the police on the phone, Henry, and give them Kate's address," I can hear him telling Henry.

"Kate, are you hurt?" he says into the phone to me, his voice concerned but strong.

"Help me," I whisper again.

"Kate, help is on the way. Try to get into a closet or somewhere safe if you can," I can hear the worry beginning to creep into his words.

His words are fading. I want to tell him to tell Henry that I love him, that I will miss him. Because I'm dying—I can feel it. But there aren't any words left. A soft, warm darkness enfolds me and I give myself to it.

Seventeen

There's white all around me as I slowly blink my eyes open. *Well,* I think foggily, *everyone talks about the white light.* There's also a steady beeping sound, and a rhythmic whoosh of air with a clicking sound. Something is pulling heavily on one side of my mouth, and I feel bound, as if I couldn't move if I tried.

"Well, well, look who finally woke up."

A woman comes into view with a kind face, and I'm surprised that angels dress like...nurses? I try to speak and am unable to form any words, only making sounds in my throat.

"You won't be able to speak, sweetie. You have a tube down your throat that's helping you to breathe." I have to breathe in heaven? I move an arm and feel pain shoot up into my shoulder. I wince, beginning to suspect that I'm not in heaven at all; which means either I'm in hell, or I'm not dead at all—neither one a pleasant prospect.

"I can give you something for the pain if you'd like," she tells me. "But it will probably make you sleep again, and there's someone here who would like to see you."

She looks meaningfully across me, and I turn my head slightly. There's Henry, sitting in an uncomfortable looking chair in the corner, asleep. His face is unshaven, several days worth of whisker growth there, making him look older. I realize I've never seen him any way but clean shaven.

Tears form in my eyes and run from the corners of my eyes at the sight of him there. I look back at the nurse, who looks concerned that I'm in too much pain, but she sees something else in my eyes and smiles.

"He hasn't moved the whole time you've been here. It's been all we could do to get him to leave the room while we were doing the things we needed to. Even then, he only went outside the door. Quite a devoted young man you have there."

She walks across the room, which I now recognize as a hospital room that is inexplicably filled with flowers. She shakes him gently on the shoulder, calling his name.

"Henry, there's something you should see."

Henry shoots straight up, body tense as if he's expecting something bad, eyes immediately flying to me. I stare back at him, and confusion passes across his face as he sees my eyes, then disbelief. He looks at the nurse, and she nods. His eyes come back to mine as he stands. He slowly walks toward me, as if afraid that any fast movement will change what he thinks he's seeing.

He comes near, his own eyes shiny with tears as he reaches out a finger, catching my tears on his fingertip.

He rubs his thumb and fingertip together as if to reassure himself that the tears are real.

"Kate?" My name is a question. His hand caresses my cheek and I lean into it. He bends down, laying his forehead against mine, his eyes inches from mine.

"Kate," he breathes, relief evident in his voice. He closes his eyes and swallows loudly. "Please be okay," he whispers, opening his eyes to look into mine again, and there I see love mixed with the relief, and something else, too. Guilt?

"I'll just go call the doctor, let him know you're awake," the nurse says. We both hear her but neither of us looks away, absorbed in each other.

"I didn't think...I thought you might not ever wake up, Katy." He swallows, blinking as he reaches down blindly for my hand with his free hand, enfolding it in his own, gently. "I would have died." I try to shake my head fiercely at the thought of Henry dead, impeded by the tube in my throat. I can't begin to imagine him dead—beautiful, vibrant, kind, caring, very *alive* Henry.

The nurse comes back into the room, trailed by a respiratory therapist, and the doctor who had just been coming in to see me anyway. Henry stands up, stepping slightly back, but keeping hold of my hand.

"You gave us quite a scare, young lady," the doctor tells me. I don't know him, have never seen him before, wonder if he's as good a doctor as Dr. Jamison, though he probably wouldn't appreciate being compared to a veterinarian.

"Let's try to get that tube out of your throat, huh?" I nod, wanting to talk to Henry. "We'll pull it out, but you've been dependent on it for a while so it might be difficult for your body to breathe on its own. We might have to put it back in," he warns.

He and the nurse step forward, forcing Henry to step back. He moves to the end of the bed where he can see me. They pull the tube out, me coughing and gagging at the sensation. The respiratory therapist steps forward and places a mask over my face, pumping a big bulbous thing on the end, forcing air into my lungs. For a moment I feel as if I'm suffocating, then my body's instincts kick in and my lungs pull in a small breath of air on their own, then another and another.

The three medical people beam, looking like proud parents. A canula is placed in my nose and oxygen begins flowing.

"Henry," my voice comes out thick and raspy, barely above a whisper. Henry smiles his wide smile that I love so much.

"It's going to take a few days for your voice to work right," the nurse tells me.

Henry comes back to my side, leaning down to kiss me softly on my freed lips.

"I love you," I mouth.

"I love you so much," he returns.

It's a slow, painful recovery to even get to the point that I can get out of bed. I have respiratory and physical therapists every day. My lungs seem well on their way to recovery. I'm informed that one lung had been punctured by a broken rib and the other collapsed when it filled with fluid. My body is weak from disuse, so the physical therapy is harder, especially since I still have many broken bones.

It was two weeks from the time of the attack to when I woke from the coma. There are scans and tests performed by an occupational therapist that determine there's no obvious brain damage.

Henry never leaves my side.

His parents, Claire and Amy have all come in to see me, Emma and Claire crying when they see me. Claire promises to make me a special outfit to wear when I leave the hospital, and Amy silently slips a four-leaf clover into my hand. Emma later tells me she had found it the year before and has been keeping it for luck. I'm touched that she would want me to have it; I need all the luck I can get.

I see the way Emma looks at Henry, concern etched in her face.

"Henry," my voice is still scratchy, but he hurries to my side when I call. "Go home, Henry. Take a real shower and shave," I reach up, no small accomplishment, rubbing my hand on his bristly cheek. "Get a good night's sleep in your own bed. I'm not going anywhere; I'll still be here in the morning."

Emma joins her voice with mine.

"Go, honey, I'll stay here."

He looks about to protest, but then he nods his head wearily. I can see the toll it's taking on him to be here all the time. He agrees to go shower and shave, but insists on coming back later this evening.

* * *

A week later I'm going stir crazy. I want some privacy from all of the doctors, nurses and therapists that are constantly in the room. I'm also afraid, because I can't go home.

I haven't asked yet about my mother. Neither she, nor my father, has been in to see me. It's gotten to the point where the not knowing is worse than asking, so when Henry and I have a rare few minutes alone together, in the deep of the night while he sits in his chair and tries to get comfortable next to my bed, I ask.

"What happened to my mother, Henry?"

He stills where he's sitting, looking down at his feet. Finally he exhales a loud breath and looks up at me.

"I'm not sure it's my place to tell you, Kate."

I laugh scornfully.

"You're the *only* one who should tell me, Henry."

He doesn't say anything.

"Are you mad at me, Henry? For not telling you, I mean."

He looks at me, confused.

"For not telling me what?"

"About...*her*. You know, for not telling you what was going on at home."

He comes over and takes my hand, pressing it to his mouth.

"Of course not."

I look up at him. "Not at all?" I ask.

He shrugs and grins sadly.

"Maybe a little, because I could have helped, maybe.

Because I hoped you trusted me enough to know that you could tell me anything."

"I do trust you, Henry, more than anyone. It wasn't that at all."

"What was it then?"

"I couldn't have stood it if you pitied me. I knew you did a little anyway, because of the kids at school. But if you had known about her, I would always have wondered if you really loved me, or if it was sympathy."

"How could you wonder that? Don't you know how much I love you?"

I smile at him. "It's a little hard to fathom, because if there's one thing I know, it's that I don't deserve you."

"Don't say that," he looks pained at my words. "*I* don't deserve *you*, especially now." The last two words are muttered low.

"What do you mean, 'especially now'?"

His face is anguished as he squeezes my hand.

"This is my fault," he says, his hand sweeping the length of my body, which has been mostly freed from its various tubes and straps.

"What? Henry, by what stretch of the imagination do you think this is your fault?"

"Because I took you home. I had the feeling that I needed to come in with you, but I let you talk me out of it. If I had come in..." he breaks off, tormented.

"Henry, look at me," I say, waiting until his eyes meet mine. "If it hadn't been then, it would have been later, after you left. Or the next day. Or the next week. It's not your fault, and for the first time in my life, I know it wasn't mine either. I won't let you blame yourself.

Besides that, it's over. I won't ever let her touch me again."

He looks away at my words.

"Thanksgiving? Was that her?" he asks.

"Yes."

"And all the other times, when you had black eyes, or other bruises?"

"Yes."

"I should have known, should have *guessed*," he says miserably.

"No you shouldn't have, Henry. I was good at the hiding game."

He doesn't look convinced by this.

"Is she in jail?" I ask.

He doesn't answer, holding his breath with dread and I know that she isn't.

"If she's not in jail where she should be, if she's still at home, I'll have to find somewhere else to go. I can't go back there."

If possible, Henry looks even worse than before.

"What is it, Henry?" I'm starting to feel afraid now at the look on his face. "Is she at home?"

Henry shakes his head, and I feel a little relief. But he still looks miserable. Now I'm afraid *and* confused.

"Henry?"

"Kate, there's something you need to know. About your mom." He blows out a resigned breath. "Kate, she's dead."

Eighteen

On that day I become a murderer. She died as a result of hitting her head against the tile floor, a rare but fatal injury separating her brain from her brain stem. She'd died immediately—there would have been no saving her even if anyone had been there to try.

It explains one thing I've been wondering about; why my father hasn't been to the hospital to see me. He must hate me, I think.

The police want to speak to me as soon as the doctors feel I'm able; the only thing keeping them away thus far is the fact that I've been unaware of her death.

With the knowledge of her death I become despondent, numb, and they bring in a psychiatrist to speak to me, the only condition being that a police psychologist is allowed to listen in.

I really don't want to talk about it, though. I tell the police everything I remember, but I don't want to share with a psychiatrist. I don't want to share with anyone. Henry tries to get me to talk about it, but I can't even look at him. I can't imagine him wanting to be with a murderer; how will he ever look at me the same again?

I'm told there will be an investigation—there always is when a violent death occurs—but it will wait until I'm out of the hospital and feeling stronger.

I continue to improve physically, eventually getting to the point where I'm no longer attached to any machines nor have any tubes in me. I also continue my physical therapy until I can walk mostly unaided. The doctors decide I can go home and continue my therapy on an outpatient basis. This brings up a new fear—where will I go when I do leave the hospital?

Henry, Emma and even Dr. Jamison all try to convince me to come to their house, but I adamantly refuse. I will not do that to them, bring a murderer into their house, with them, and with Claire, and Amy and Christine.

The day before I'm to be released, my father comes to see me. I've just finished physical therapy and I'm tired, ready to sleep for a while when he walks in. Henry is sitting in his chair, working on homework that Emma has started to bring to him from school. They're being more lenient with me, waiting until I'm released before they send a teacher with my own homework.

Henry looks up as he walks in, and stands.

"Hey, Mr. Mosley," he says to my father.

"Hi Henry," my father returns. I look between them, stunned. When did they meet?

Henry walks over to me, leaning down to give me a kiss.

"I'm going to go to the cafeteria to get a drink. I'll be back in a little bit," he tells me. I grab his hand, imploring him with my eyes to stay. He just squeezes my hand, trying to reassure me, before turning to leave. I watch him go, panicked at being left alone with this man who is my father, but who's more of a stranger to me than even the doctor or nurses who care for me.

He stands in the doorway, seeming as reluctant as me to see Henry go. He's wearing a baseball cap which he removes, twisting it in his hands. I can see he's made some effort to look presentable, wearing a button down shirt that's wrinkled but clean, and freshly shaven—that given away by the piece of tissue that's still stuck to his chin.

I study him, and realize that some time in the last ten years he has aged. I remember him as young and handsome, but now he looks old and ragged, gray streaking his hair, wrinkles on his face, and heavy bags under his eyes.

He clears his throat and takes a single step closer.

"You look better," he says.

"You've been here before?" I ask, surprised.

"I came at first, but then it didn't seem that you would wake up and so..." he trails off, lifting a hand as if that explains his absence.

"I've been awake for almost two weeks now."

He looks away, guiltily.

"I know," he says, "Paul—Dr. Jamison—came by on the day you did to let me know. He offered me a ride, but I didn't want to face you."

Guilt nearly smothers me at his words. Of course he

didn't want to face me; I killed his wife. I nod, tears pricking my eyes as I look away.

He takes another step closer.

"The thing is...I failed you, Kate."

I look at him, staggered by his words. *He* failed *me*?

He shakes his head, stepping closer and I can see he's struggling with his own emotions.

"I could stand here and say I didn't know, but..." he releases a heavy breath, and even from where I lay I can smell the alcohol; not strong, but there nonetheless. "I think I did. I guess I *know* I did. I just didn't know how bad it was." He glances at me to gauge my reaction. I'm open-mouthed. Is he saying he knew of the abuse? That he's known all along?

"I didn't know she would hurt you so badly." A sob escapes him, which he sucks back in. "I swear I didn't know *that*."

"I killed her," I tell him, wanting him to hate me.

"I know. It was self defense though, right? I think that she wouldn't have stopped. If you had seen yourself—" he breaks off at some memory that crumples his face. I turn away, not sure how to deal with this stranger who suddenly is giving off some mixed-signal paternal indications.

"They told me there might be a trial," I tell him. He nods, moving another step closer so that he's only a few feet from my bed now.

"They said you can come home tomorrow," he abruptly changes the subject.

"Can I?" I ask, and he looks questioningly at me. "Can I come home, I mean?"

Realization clears his face, then his mouth turns down.

"Of course you can. It's your home. Where else would you go?"

I think of Henry's home, of the life and laughter and *light* that is there, of the love and care and comfort I know I'll get if I go there. I think of my own house, how dark and dismal and lifeless it is in comparison.

That's where I belong.

"Will you come pick me up, or...?"

He looks away, guilty again.

"I came in tonight to sign the papers. They said you could ride home with Henry."

I feel a catch in my throat. So, he hasn't come to see me after all, has just come to sign the papers pushing responsibility for me off on someone else. Things are back to normal, at least where he's concerned.

Henry comes back then, and the tension leaves the room at his appearance. He's carrying his drink, eyes on me to determine if I'm upset or not. I am, but try not to show it.

"So, I guess I'll go now," my father says. "You'll bring her home tomorrow then, Henry?"

"Of course. I'll stay with her until you get home. I think my mom was planning to bring some dinner over."

My father nods.

"That's nice of her. Tell her I said thanks."

"Sure thing, Mr. Mosley." Henry, ever the gentleman is being polite, but I know him well enough that I can hear the tension below the surface.

"Well, goodbye then," he says to Henry, looks toward me with a nod, and leaves. We both watch him go.

"You didn't tell me he had been here," I say to him.

"You didn't ask." I throw a condemning look his way and he shrugs, sipping his drink and setting it on the table next to my bed. He sits on the edge of my bed, stroking up and down my arm with his hand.

"I thought it might upset you. I wasn't sure if he was part of the..." he grimaces painfully, then forces the word between his teeth, "...*abuse* that you were being subjected to."

I gasp. "You thought he was abusing me also, but you left me here alone with him?"

"No, I don't think that; not anymore. But to be honest, I was outside your room the whole time, watching." He smirks with charming guilt. "I asked one of the candy stripers to go grab me a drink."

I smile, then recall his words.

"Why don't you think that anymore? That he was part of it?" I ask.

"Because I watched his face when he was here. He cried a lot and seemed really guilty, but not the kind of guilt that someone who was capable of this would have." He glances up at me. "Am I wrong?"

"No."

"But he didn't stop it from happening either, did he?" His voice is low with controlled fury.

"No." My eyes fill with tears again and I wipe them angrily away.

"I would have. I would have found a way to stop it." His eyes are boring into mine, intent clear as he speaks. "If I had known...." He looks down. "I *should* have known. I should have seen—"

"Don't," I tell him stiffly. "Don't do that. Don't make this something for you to be guilty about. That is *not* what it is."

He looks back up at me, torment in every line of his face.

"I can't stop thinking of it. I can't stop imagining what it must have been like for you, every day. All that time I thought you didn't want me to come to your house because you were embarrassed by it, or by your parents, or even by me. It *never* crossed my mind that it could be *this*."

"Henry..." the tears are running down my cheeks now.

"When you came to my house on Thanksgiving...I thought...someone else...but I didn't think it was your *mother*." His head drops next to my arm on the bed.

"Henry," I pull his face up. "Of course you couldn't imagine it. Look at *your* mother." Guilt flashes through his eyes again.

"No!" I tell him. "You are *not* going to feel guilty for having a great family."

"But I brought you home, waved them in front of your face when all the time you had to go home to face...*that*."

"Yes, and thank you for doing that," I say sincerely. His eyes widen a little at my words. "I didn't know there could be a family like that. You brought me in and showed me how it is supposed to be. And your whole family...they showed me love and kindness, whether I deserved it or not. I *love* them, Henry."

He pulls me into his arms, his body trembling with the force of his emotions as he processes my words and tries to let go of his own guilt.

"Are you going to be okay going back there?" he asks into my hair. "Because you know you can and *should* come to my house."

I hug him tighter, not wanting him to see the lie on my face.

"It's going to be fine. I want to go home." I force my voice to sound sure.

He releases a loud breath, giving in.

"Okay, but plan on me being there all the time, until you're sick of me."

I push back to smile at him.

"That isn't going to happen. No way would I ever be sick of you."

Nineteen

Henry takes me home in the morning. I'm glad there isn't anyone there but him and me. I expected it to be changed somehow, to look different. But it's the same; the couch and small TV in the same place, the wood floor still scuffed and marred, the kitchen still small and plain. The only physical difference is the missing lamp.

The unseen difference is where I falter. I look at the wall where I had fallen with the first swing of the bat, and imagine I can see the outline of my body there; the place on the wood floor where I had dragged myself forward, imagining I can still see a faint outline of the blood streaks I had dragged with me; the tile floor in the kitchen where I imagine I can see the circular outline of her head, the place that had taken her life by the force of my hand.

I shudder and turn my face into Henry's shoulder, his

arms coming up to surround me with safety. I take a deep breath, forcing strength into my mind. I know that if I give him the slightest provocation he'll sweep me up into his arms and carry me to his home. I ache with longing at the thought, then mentally shake my head to clear it of *that* yearning.

Emma soon comes with Christine to help me settle in. The other girls are in school but she's promised to bring them to see me later. I want to see them, but I'm ashamed to have them see my house; it's such a depressing place compared to their beautiful, bright home. I think that maybe it's good; maybe they should see me in my real world so they can understand how much I don't belong in theirs.

I sit on the couch—on the opposite end from *her* end—curled into Henry who sits next to me. It has exhausted me, the trip home, and soon I'm asleep.

When I awake, I'm lying on the couch with a pillow under my head and a blanket covering me. I can hear Henry in the kitchen, talking with Emma, the sounds of food preparation underway. Then I hear my father's voice, and stiffen.

"That seems like a fine way to go. Medical school has to be pretty pricey, huh?" I hear him question.

"Yeah, but I've already got some scholarships lined up to help with that," Henry says.

"You gonna be going to school around here?"

"Henry has applied to and been accepted at several schools," Emma announces proudly. "He's always wanted to go away to school, so I imagine I won't have him around much longer."

I can almost hear the shrug in Henry's voice as he responds.

"I might hang around awhile, go to school here."

"Oh?" I can hear the surprise in Emma's voice. "I didn't know you had even been thinking of that. Oh, excuse me," she says as her cell phone rings. There's silence in the kitchen with the exception of her responses.

"That was Paul," she tells them. "He and the girls are just leaving the house so they will be here soon. I hope you don't mind us taking over your house like this, John."

John? I try to picture my father as a person, with a name, rather than just as *my father*. I can't do it, but it doesn't surprise me that Emma can.

"I'm glad to have you. You have been a great help to me...and to my daughter."

What an amazing conversation. Seriously... *my daughter?*

"Well, we all love her. She's a good girl."

The doorbell rings and Henry comes into the living room to open it. He automatically looks my way, stopping when he sees my eyes open.

"Hey, you're awake," he says, changing course and coming to me. Emma must have heard him, because she follows right behind him, continuing on to open the door to admit Dr Jamison and the two girls. I wonder briefly where Christine is, then find myself speechless when my father walks into the room a moment later, carrying her.

Henry helps me to stand up so that I can hug the girls. And just like that it's my own house that's filled with the love and laughter that I'd thought possible only at Henry's.

There isn't room enough for us all to sit around our small kitchen table with its three chairs—the fourth had been smashed against me on Thanksgiving and never replaced—so Emma decides we should all sit in the family room, balancing plates laden with food on our knees. Henry carries the three chairs into the room, which barely fit around the perimeter, then stakes out his place on the floor next to my knees, knowing that if he leaves it will be taken by one of his sisters.

Much later, after everything has been cleaned up and all of the Jamison's have left except for Henry, my father says goodnight—the first time I ever remember him doing that.

"When do you start back at school?" I ask Henry. We had argued about him needing to be *in* school rather than sitting at the hospital all day, but we had finally agreed that once I was home he would go back. Emma and Dr. Jamison had adamantly taken my side on that.

"Tomorrow." He sounds put-out.

"You should go home, then. Go to bed."

He turns to me.

"I could stay here, and just leave in the morning."

"Henry..." my voice holds a warning.

"I'm not saying miss school. I'm just saying—"

I put my fingers on his mouth.

"Go home, Henry. Go to sleep. Come back after school."

He looks at me for a long minute, then finally nods, pressing my hand tighter to his mouth for a kiss.

"Okay, but you have the cell phone. You promise to call if you need *anything*?"

I raise my right hand. "Promise."

He spends some time kissing me goodnight, which I don't mind at all—in fact, rather enjoy—even though I know he's just stalling. He insists on helping me up to my room, but I don't let him in. I make him leave me at the door of my room, waiting until he has walked down the stairs, turning lights off as he goes, and hear him close the front door.

I walk into my room, small and plain, but organized and clean. It feels even less like home to me now than it had before. I lay down, pulling my covers over me, tears falling to soak the pillow beneath my head.

Three days later the police come by to formally charge me with my mother's death, and to read me my Miranda rights. I'm grateful it's during the day, my father still at work and Henry at school. Emma is here, as she is most days, standing pale and shaking while the Officer does his duty reluctantly. It's humiliating having Emma as a witness, but I'm also conversely glad of her support.

"Because of the extenuating circumstances of your health issues, the judge has agreed that once we take you to the station to be processed, we will immediately release you on your own recognizance. You will have an arraignment hearing within the next week or so, at which time you will be appointed a lawyer."

My mind reels at the words. What had been only a feeling of being a murderer has suddenly become reality. They don't handcuff me, but require me to ride in the back of their cruiser to the station. Emma follows behind in her car, stopping to drop Christine off with one of her neighbors. So when we arrive at the station, I'm truly alone.

The Officers are all kind to me, taking care with my injuries as they fingerprint and photograph me. I have to fill out some paperwork, trying to not notice the looks I'm getting from many of the other Officers, looks full of pity.

When I'm finished, I'm led out to a waiting room where Emma waits for me. I can see she has been crying and remorse washes over me, that I'm putting her and her family through this, just because they've shown me kindness.

By the time we arrive back at my house, I'm exhausted, emotionally and physically. I lay down on the couch and sleep solidly, not waking until after dark. I can hear Henry and my father in the kitchen, talking low. I can't make out their words, but just hearing Henry's voice comforts me. I struggle up, walking into the kitchen.

They both look up guiltily as I come in, obviously having been talking about me. My father looks oddly ashamed, and Henry looks furious. When he sees me, he tries to arrange his face into a pleasant expression, but it doesn't work, only serves to make him look constipated, which almost makes me laugh—except that I wonder what's made him so furious to begin with.

He stands and comes to me, wrapping me into his arms.

"It's about time you woke up," he teases, trying to mask the anger in his voice, and failing miserably.

"What's going on?" I ask suspiciously.

He steps back, looking toward my father.

"We heard about today," my father says.

"Oh." My face darkens with shame.

Henry hugs me against his side.

"I'm sorry I wasn't here," he says.

"It doesn't matter. It wasn't so bad." And other than the humiliation of it, it really hadn't been.

My father suddenly stands.

"I'm going out for a while."

I know what that means, but I can tell Henry has no idea, only seeming irritated that he'll be leaving when I've been through something so horrible that day. I feel my heart sink because my father has been sober for the last few days that I've been home, and "going out" has always meant coming home drunk.

Henry makes me recount for him every second of my time at the station, several times until I finally refuse to tell him again. He heats me up some soup that Emma had left earlier, along with some homemade bread. Then he holds me while we watch an old movie on TV that I can't concentrate on. My mind whirls with the implications of the day and what it could mean for me, but even more what it could mean for Henry.

Later, as I lay in bed, I hear my father come home; hear the tell-tale sounds of his stumbling up the stairs. I lay frozen as his footsteps came down the hall and stop in front of my door. My stomach tightens with a fear I've known only all too well in my life, but which I had hoped never to have to feel again.

I hold my breath, watching the door handle so intently I begin to imagine it turning when it isn't. Frightened, my temperature rises even as I pull my blanket up higher, over my cheek, leaving only my eyes out, as I if I'm invisible this way.

Finally, after what seems an eternity, he turns and stumbles back to his own room.

Ten days pass before the arraignment. I'm met at the door by a harried, agitated man who says he's my lawyer. He's wearing a brown corduroy suit, has brown, curly hair that looks as harried as he does, and round spectacles. He's juggling a folder jammed haphazardly with papers, walking quickly into the courtroom as if he's in a race, without waiting to see if I've even followed him. I look at Henry, who's holding my hand in support, then shrug and follow him. Henry looks as sick as I feel.

My father sits next to me, looking uncomfortable in a too-small wrinkled suit, tugging at the collar as if it's choking him.

My case is called and there are a lot of long legal words spouted by the prosecutor, my lawyer and then the judge. I'm trying to follow along, only really understanding the "not guilty" and "self-defense", but then the judge pounds his gavel, and suddenly my lawyer is hurrying back up the aisle into the hallway, motioning me to follow.

I follow him, Henry right behind me.

"Okay, so that was as expected," the lawyer says, pausing. Even in his relative stillness, he gives off the sensation of being in motion. "You're free to go; no bail. A trial date will be set. As soon as I know when that is I'll let you know." He digs in his jacket pocket and comes out with a slightly crumpled business card. "Here's my card in case you have questions. I'll talk to you soon." And then he's gone.

I look at Henry; give a strangled sound, somewhere between a sob and a laugh.

"*What* was that?"

Henry's face is taut with strain as his eyes follow the man who is practically running down the hallway. His eyes come back to mine and I can see the agonized look there. I don't like being the cause of that unnatural expression on his face.

"It'll be okay," he tells me, but it sounds more like he's trying to convince himself.

A week later another man comes to my door. He's tall, dark hair combed neatly, in an expensive looking pin-striped suit.

"Kate Mosley?" he asks, when I open the door.

"Yes?"

He holds out a hand.

"My name is Rufus Cain. I have been given your case to handle." When I just stand there, he says, "I'm your new lawyer."

"Do you always make house calls?" I ask, distrusting him.

"Not always, no. But sometimes yes. I knew you'd been injured so I didn't want to ask you to come to my office."

I'm home alone. I've made Emma reduce the amount of time she's spending at my house waiting on me since I'm now able to get around somewhat easier. She's only coming three times a week, in the afternoons, which is still too often, I think. It's the least amount of time I can get her to compromise to.

Henry turns up the street just then. I can't see him, but I've learned to listen for the sound of his engine so well I can now pick it out above all others. Rufus Cain turns at the sound of the car pulling to a stop in front of my house. He watches with me as Henry climbs out of his car, and I'm grateful for Henry's broad shoulders and height that can be intimidating.

"A friend of yours?" Rufus Cain asks.

"Yes."

"Do you mind talking in front of him or shall I make an appointment to return when he's not here?"

"No," I shake my head. "He knows everything. I want him here."

Henry comes up to the porch, eyeing the lawyer suspiciously. But Rufus introduces himself and I can see Henry relax. I have to admit, this man does inspire more confidence than the previous lawyer.

He comes in and we sit around the kitchen table, Rufus pulling out a notepad and pen, as well as a tape recorder.

"This is so that I make sure my notes are correct later," he says, indicating the recorder.

We go over some basic facts; name, parent's names, and birth date. Henry jerks in surprise when he hears that; I have never told him when my birthday is. It is, in fact, only a few days away, on February 23.

"Okay, I'm not sure how much you understood of the arraignment," he begins. "That was just a formality for you to enter a plea, which was..." he flips through some papers, making sure he's correct. "Not guilty by reason of self-defense. Okay. Good. That's all right for now. Now, I'm not sure how aggressive the prosecutor will be in your case. You've been charged with involuntary manslaughter," I feel the world tilt as he speaks the words, "but I want to have the charges dropped. That's what we will be going for."

Henry reaches over and takes my hand. I turn my hand in his, interlocking fingers and holding on tight.

"I know this is going to be difficult, but we need to go over everything that happened that night, in as much detail as you can remember. Then we need to go back over past offenses committed by your mother on you."

I don't want Henry to hear *this*, to know the entire depth of my shame and humiliation, but somehow I can't find the courage to let him go. So I tell my new lawyer everything, while he records my indignity, and Henry sits next to me, still as a statue except for the slight trembling that shakes him as he listens to the horror that has been my life.

Twenty

I came home from Florida, from a vacation I had taken with the Jamison's," I begin.

"I assume you were given permission to go?" Rufus questions without looking at me, writing on the yellow legal pad.

"Of course. I really didn't think she would say yes, really wasn't even planning on asking." I shoot an apologetic look at Henry, but he isn't looking my way.

"She was actually being nice, something that's rare. I think she was feeling guilty about how badly she'd hurt me on Thanksgiving." Rufus glances up, but doesn't interrupt, going back to his note taking. "Up until that last night—" I stumble, clear my throat and continue, "Well, up until then, the worst she'd hurt me was on Thanksgiving. I think she knew she'd gone too far.

"Long story, short, she said yes. Maybe out of guilt. So

I went. I guess while I was gone, she took enough pills to forget where I was."

"Pills?" Rufus interrupts.

"Um, yeah, she had a problem with pills."

"What do you mean by 'problem'?"

I refuse to look at Henry as I confess this new humiliation in front of Henry. "She took a lot. Too many. It was the only way she could cope."

"Were these pills prescription, or..." He doesn't speak the words, lets the question hang.

"Prescription, as far as I know. At least, they were always in prescription bottles."

Rufus is scribbling madly. I wait.

"Okay, so she was angry that you'd been gone."

"Yes, but..." I trail off, remembering. "She came at me almost immediately with the bat."

Henry winces, and Rufus looks up again.

"She had the bat with her? And this was unusual?"

"Yeah, I mean, I'm not even sure where it came from. Somewhere in the garage, I guess. But always before, if she's hit me with something, it's been a weapon of convenience, you know? Like a chair, or broom or something that was handy."

Henry shudders, and once again the thought flits through my head that I should tell him to go. I'm just selfish enough to ignore the thought.

"So that was weird—*different*, I guess. I don't remember a lot of detail, just her coming at me again and again with the bat. I honestly thought she was trying to kill me."

Henry squeezes my hand tighter.

"I grabbed the bat once when she came at me with it, and shoved. She fell. I heard her hit her head." I swallow loudly, realizing that must have been the moment of her death. I remember the sick fear that had choked me, trying to get away before she could get up and finish what she'd started. I take a deep breath. "I was on the floor, Henry called, and that's all I remember," I gush out on a single breath, "That, and crawling through the blood, to get away."

"Okay, Kate, that's fine." Rufus reaches out, as if to take my hand, then pulls back and clears his throat. "I know this isn't easy, but we need to talk about past abuse. Do you remember when it started?"

"When my brother died," I tell him. He looks startled.

"You had a brother?"

"Kind of, I guess. My mom was pregnant, and they knew it was a boy. But she and my dad had a fight, and she lost the baby. I was nine."

I look at Henry, pleading with him for...what? I don't even know.

"It wasn't always like this. There was a time when we were a normal family, when they loved me. But my dad...he lost his job, and everything changed. He started drinking, but she would still try to protect me. She loved me.

"But when she went to the hospital, and came home alone, she changed too. I think I must have been too strong a reminder of what she'd lost. I was the one who found her and got help. Maybe I wasn't fast enough, or I waited too long. I don't know...maybe it was my fault."

"No, Kate, no," Henry murmurs.

"She started taking the pills, to forget, I guess. And then she got angry, and took it out on me."

There is silence, stillness in the room. Henry looks at me, eyes wet with anguish, mouth tight, jaw clenched. I can't stand to see it, so I look at my new lawyer. He's suddenly searching for something in his briefcase, with some suspicious throat clearing going on. Finally, he looks up, and I pretend not to see the pity shining in his eyes. If there's one thing I hate, it's pity.

"Can you, uh...can you give some specific examples of some of the abuse?'

I laugh, but the sound holds no humor. My fingers are beginning to go numb from Henry's grip.

"Besides being starved, sometimes for days on end?" I ask, caustically. "Or do you mean other than being forced to stand in a corner for hours at a time? Or there's always the classic forcing me to sit in the closet for a few days, knowing that when she let me out I would be beaten, because it's impossible to go that long without going to the bathroom. Also, I don't suppose it's normal to get hit, pinched, slapped or kicked for breathing the wrong way."

In agitation, I throw myself backward, rising to my feet in the same motion as I jerk my hand from Henry's. I turn and stalk a few paces away, crossing my arms protectively. I've held the memories private for so long, it feels almost like a betrayal to let them go.

But a betrayal of whom?

"Did your father abuse you as well?" Rufus' question is almost too soft to hear.

"No," I say, hoping he didn't catch my slight hesitation.

"Was your father aware of the abuse?"

"He probably suspected," my voice is almost as low as his. "But we were pretty good at hiding it from him. And he was so rarely here, mostly just to sleep, that it was probably pretty easy for him to ignore."

"And do you feel the abuse increased over time?"

"It was pretty consistent after the first couple of years when she learned just how much she could get away with. But in the last year, yeah, it was getting much worse.

"I think after Thanksgiving, she knew she'd crossed a line. She lay off for a while, until I came home from Florida."

"Were there ever any hospital visits?"

"Sure, a few. But never so many there might be suspicion, and none at all for the past few years. I think the only reason she ever took me before was because she knew I would get a prescription for pain pills. Of course, I was never allowed to take the pills."

When I finish speaking, Rufus is leaning back in his chair, rubbing the bridge of his nose between his thumb and finger. He's silent, and in that silence I dare to glance at Henry. His face is pale, lips pulled tight. His eyes are staring straight ahead.

Finally, Rufus sighs and leans forward, pulling a folder out of his briefcase. I sit back down next to the icy, still Henry.

"I will be typing your statement up and presenting it to the prosecution," he says as he opens the folder on the table between us. "I will also be providing these photos, which were taken of you at the hospital."

He slides the folder across the table, turning it to face me as he does so. I look down and see a photo of something puffy and purple. I'm confused, then I look closer and realize it's *me*. I pass through picture after picture of myself, sickened and shocked at how I unrecognizable I had been. By the time I'd woken up from the coma, and been able to get up and near a mirror, most of the swelling had gone down and the bruises had begun to fade to a softer purple, ringed with yellow and green.

There are photos of me lying in the bed after I had been bandaged, with the monitors and tubes attached to me. I look like a movie version of someone who has been in a horrible accident, where the make-up artist has gone a little overboard in the dramatics.

I glance at Henry again and see that he's looking away from the table, refusing to look at the photos. With horror, I realize that he had actually seen me like this.

"Do we have to show these in public?" I ask softly, despondently.

"It's our best support of the self-defense theory. No one can look at these and not know you were in a fight for your life." A single tear rolls down my cheek, and I absently push it away. Rufus clears his throat. "Kate, this is your life we're fighting for now. I had been told there was some previous abuse..." he clears his throat again and I get the distinct feeling he's fighting some emotion of his own. "But after what you've told me, well, it's criminal the way you've been treated. This is one of the worst cases of abuse I have dealt with. You are the victim here, and we need to make the judge see that."

He looks uncomfortable, shifting in his chair. "I need to ask you a question that needs an honest answer, Kate."

I nod.

"Are you absolutely *certain* there has never been any abuse from your father?"

I think about the one time he *had* hit me, and about how he turned *his* abuse on my mother. I had seen her from time to time with her own black eye or puffy lip. I think about his footsteps outside my door and how I now sleep with a chair wedged under my door handle. Then I think about what might happen if he were arrested for the one time he did hit me: would that spark his anger, which he would then turn on me, now that she was no longer here for him to take his frustration out on? I don't know for sure, but I do know that I don't want to find out.

"No," I say. "Never."

Henry relaxes fractionally next to me and I realize he had been stiff with tension, waiting for my answer.

"Okay, just one more thing. Did you, with any forethought or intent, plan to kill your mother that night?"

"Of course not!" I explode, upset that he would even ask such a thing.

He holds up a hand, "Okay, I know you didn't. But you will probably be asked that very question." He reaches across the table and gathers the photos and folder back to himself, stuffing them back in the briefcase.

"All right, that's it then. I will let you know when to expect your trial." He passes a card across the table to me. "My office and cell phone numbers are on there. Call me at anytime if you have questions, concerns, or just have something else you need to tell me."

I look down at the card which is printed on expensive looking cardstock, with raised gold lettering, and I wondered how a public defender can afford such a luxury. He stands and shakes my hand—oddly formal after what I've just shared with him. He also shakes Henry's, then leaves.

As soon as he's gone, there's a stiff silence between Henry and me.

"How was school?" I finally ask—anything to break the strange spell.

He doesn't answer, just turns to me and opens his arms. I gladly go into them, though I'm surprised by the gesture. He just holds me, rubbing his hands lightly up and down my back in between tight, reassuring squeezes.

"I had no idea," he finally says.

"I know. No one did."

"Why did you keep it a secret?" he asks, tortured, "Why didn't you ask for help?"

I shake my head. "It's complicated. I was young when it all started, and I didn't know where to turn for help. I didn't have any friends, no adults who I trusted enough. By the time I thought to ask for help, I was embarrassed that I had let it go on so long. And I thought that she must have a good reason for it, that there must be something really wrong with me, or bad about me, to make her hate me so much."

Henry's arms tighten.

"I'm sorry," he says, sincerity in every line of his body and ringing in his voice. "I'm sorry you had to go through all of that alone. I'm sorry for everything you are going through now. But I promise you one thing." He leans back, taking my face between his hands and gazing intently into my eyes. "You will never be alone again."

Twenty-One

My trial date has been set for the end of May—just before graduation—which means I have more time to recover, but it also means I have to pretend to live again, to act as if I have a life that will continue past May.

I'm suffering from some pretty severe headaches, which I'm told will eventually ease, but it makes school work difficult. So for now I'm still excused from both attending school and from the bulk of my schoolwork. I remember not so long ago when I would have given almost anything to have been excused from school, now I would give almost the same to be able to *go* to school.

I miss my morning rides with Henry, sitting next to him at lunch and in photography. He still comes over as soon as school is over, only now we go to his house until ten or eleven each night when he'll then take me back home.

I dread home, because my father has returned to his old patterns, staying out drinking half the night and I worry that he'll be there when Henry drops me off. I haven't told him about the drinking and don't want him to witness it.

For my birthday Emma's planned a party, inviting my father to come to the Jamison's house for dinner. He comes, eyes bloodshot and haggard looking, but sober. He even brings me a gift. I realize sadly that it's the first birthday gift I've received from him since my swing set so many years before.

Emma and I talked a few days earlier about how it helps her during times of stress to write things down, and so Emma and Dr. Jamison give me a journal and pen set for my birthday. Amy gives me a framed picture of me with the whole Jamison clan taken in Florida. Christine gives me one of her books—those are her most prized possessions.

Claire is nearly leaping out of her seat as I open her present, which she made me save until last (except for Henry who, once again, is making me wait until we're alone later). By the size and weight of the box I know it's clothing, but when I open it, I'm stunned.

In the box lays a white dress made of the silkiest material I've ever felt. I pull it out and see that it's a dress--a gown really. The bodice is sleeveless, an intricately weaved pattern of the material covered with a sheer overlay of silver material that falls down the back of the dress, forming a sort of cape. The skirt flares out from the waist, again covered with the sheer material.

"Claire, it's beautiful," I tell her.

"It's for you to wear to prom," she says with a wide smile.

"Prom?" I look at her. She's beaming, and I don't have the heart to tell her that there is no way I'm going to prom. So I just hug her, telling her I love it, which I really do.

"You can try it on for me later, when you don't have your cast on anymore. Also, when Henry isn't around. I don't want him to see you in it before the big night."

I don't answer, just try to smile at her. I must look odd because Henry cocks his head questioningly at me, but doesn't say anything.

Emma brings out a cake that she made, and that the three girls helped her decorate. It's three tiers tall and she let each girl decorate a layer. The bottom layer is clearly Claire, very bright and covered with intricate swirls and flowers in pink and purple.

Amy took the middle layer and in her own quiet style had only put a few decorations—beauty in simplicity.

Christine did the top layer, which is mounded with all colors of frosting, messy and colorful, with one large candle sticking out the top.

It's the most beautiful cake I've ever seen.

They sing to me—another first for as long as I can remember—then we eat cake and homemade ice cream. My father leaves soon after that. As soon as the mess is cleaned up, Emma makes sure everyone has an errand or task which takes them to some other part of the house, leaving Henry and I alone. There's a fire blazing in the fireplace, and Henry pulls their oversized bean bag up in front of it so we can sit there together.

"You want your gift?" he teases.

"*This* is my gift, being here alone with you," I tell him.

"That's thanks to my mom, though."

"I know. I'll have to thank her for that."

Henry digs into his pocket and pulls out a small box. The last small box he gave me had been my necklace at Christmas, which I wear always. So I'm excited to open it and see what he gives me now.

My heart stops when I see what's inside.

"I know this isn't very romantic," he tells me with a grin, "and it isn't how I would really like to do it, but..." he shrugs, turning so he's facing me.

"I love you, Kate. I know we're really young, but I *know* I want to spend my life with you. I don't want to waste any time. I want to be with you every day, to wake up next to you every morning. I want to marry you, Kate."

I looked from his face to the ring nestled in the box. It's simple; a square cut solitaire with a plain silver band. It's perfect.

I look back at him, see the hope in his eyes.

"Henry.... We're too young, still in high school."

"I know that, Kate. I know what people will think of us getting married right out of high school, but I don't care. I'm not ever going to want anyone else; only you."

"Henry, I can't. *We* can't. There's so much—"

He cuts me off, pressing his mouth to mine.

"Don't say no," he whispers against my mouth. "Say maybe. *Please.*"

But I'm shaking my head. Henry's going away to college. As much as I hate the thought of that, dread it with horror and trepidation, I've known it all along. That's his destiny.

I'm realistic about his future which means at least eight to twelve years of school—or more—to obtain his dream of becoming a doctor, and that isn't going to happen if he's saddled with a wife, especially a wife who comes with my kind of baggage. Not to mention that realistically I might be in prison soon.

"I can't," my heart is breaking, the hated tears coming again.

"You can," he counters. "*We* can. You love me, right?"

I touch his face, "You know I do."

"Then what's the problem?"

"Henry, your life's path was laid out long before I came along. It would be wrong for it to change just because of me."

"Nothing will change. Except to be better, because *I'm* better when I'm with you."

"Henry, I—"

"Maybe," he interrupts me. "All I'm asking for is a maybe. Say you'll think about it; give me a chance to convince you."

I know the fair thing, the right thing, is to say no, to end it right here before I can hurt him further. There isn't even a remote possibility of a future between us. I'm also aware that Henry is a care-taker, and that this is nothing more than his way of trying to protect me.

However, I'm weak and can't imagine trying to get through the next few months alone, without him at my side. I'm selfish enough that I'll keep him for that long, that for every second I can I'll hold on to him, be with him. I imagine the wrenching pain of being without him, feel sick at the thought of it, and so I'll put it off as long as I can, even at the cost of leading him along, of being dishonest.

"Okay, *maybe,*" I say, crushing guilt consuming me at the look of happiness on his face, knowing my only true answer can be no. I push the box back into his hand. "But you have to keep this."

"You don't want to wear my ring?" he asks while looking down at the box, hurt in his voice.

If only he knew just how much I wanted to.

"Henry, there's so much going on right now. It just seems like one more complication—explaining a ring. Can't it just be our secret?"

He nods, but then looks at me teasingly.

"I kinda wanted you to wear it, so everyone would know you were mine."

I smile weakly, "Who wouldn't know that? They'd have to be completely blind to not know that."

He puts the box back into his pocket.

"What am I supposed to give you for your birthday then?" he asks, sulky. My heart is twisting violently in my chest, but I push the feeling away with practice born of years of hiding reality.

"I can think of something," I say lightly, pulling his face to mine, hiding the hurt behind my love for Henry.

Twenty-Two

I continue with my physical therapy twice a week, which Emma usually drives me to. I got my driver's license when I was sixteen and had taken drivers education through school, but as I have not driven since getting my license, I'm not sure I even remember how. Henry offers to leave his car with me so I can drive myself after I get my cast off, but I don't want to tell him I probably no longer know how to drive, so I just tell him I don't want to use his car.

The school administration has decided that based on my recovery period and my upcoming trial that I can have special tutoring, followed by taking tests to determine my eligibility to graduate with the rest of my classmates. No one says out loud what we're all thinking—that I might be in jail by the time graduation comes around and won't be attending graduation at all.

Senior prom is looming and Henry tries to convince me to go. He can't understand that I've had nightmares about those kinds of school functions for the last several years.

I made the mistake of attending one dance in middle school. It was toward the beginning of my seventh grade year, when the torture by my classmates led by Jessica had just begun and so was still in the less brutal stages. It was chaperoned by some of the faculty and a few parents, and yet Jessica still managed to make it a horrific day for me.

I had pilfered enough money from my parents to buy me a "new" outfit at the secondhand store. I purchased a really cute pair of white Capri's and a pink cashmere sweater. I spent some extra time doing my hair in curls and had even snuck into my mom's room to use a little of her makeup.

Jessica obviously spent some time thinking about how to humiliate me and set me up. She convinced Brad Johnson, one of the cutest, most popular kids in the school to help her out, as well as some of the other kids—both boys and girls. I'd had a little crush on Brad, as did ninety percent of the girls who went to school there. Not only was he cute, he was an *eighth* grader. Of course, Jessica was the prettiest girl in school, so I'm sure it didn't take much to enlist Brad's help.

The dance was going pretty well, lots of kids dancing. I, of course, was sitting by myself on the bleachers in the over-heated, sweat filled gym. I wanted to dance but didn't have the guts to ask anyone, or to dance by myself as many of the girls did. Then Brad came up to me.

He asked me to dance and I felt a surge of joy; Brad Johnson picked *me*. For a minute I felt a sense of justice—this would show Jessica and all those other girls. I followed him out to the crowded dance floor. It was a fast song and there were kids all over the place, bumping into one another, so it didn't occur to me to think there was anything unusual going on.

Brad grinned over my shoulder on occasion and I was stupid enough to think he was proud to be dancing with me, that he was smiling at his friends. But soon I became aware of laughter behind me, and then people pointing and whispering behind their hands to one another, the laughter spreading and getting louder. I looked behind me and didn't see anything that was funny.

Then I saw Mrs. Cowan, the gym coach, hurrying my way. She pulled me away from Brad, and walked me quickly toward the doors that lead to the locker room. I pulled back, asking her where she was taking me. I hadn't done anything wrong, had I?

"Let's go into the dressing room and we'll talk there," she told me urgently. I looked behind me and saw everyone now laughing and pointing my way. I saw Brad, arm around Jessica, also laughing—and Jessica smiling at me like the Cheshire cat. Once in the girls dressing area, Mrs. Cowan continued to lead me toward the restroom.

"What's going on?" I asked her, starting to feel a little afraid.

"Honey, I hate to tell you this, but it would appear that your menstruation has begun."

"What?" I was shocked, since my period had just finished the week previous.

"Do you have a pad with you?"

"No, I don't." My stomach began to ache with dread.

Mrs. Cowan hurried into the faculty office and came back, pressing the white bulk into my hand. I went into the bathroom stall with trepidation. Could my period have started again so soon?

When I got in there, it was obvious the blood was only on the outside of my pants—and had not in any way come from me.

My first thought was that someone was hurt and had bled on me. I reached out to open the door to inform Mrs. Cowan, but then my mind belatedly started to process information—the amount of blood on me would had to have come from someone severely injured. Even had it come from my menstruation, it could not have bled so profusely so quickly.

Then I remembered Brad's grins over my shoulder, all of the kids bumping into me, a feeling of damp on my backside which I had thought was maybe just sweat because of the heat. Mostly I remembered Jessica's grin. That was when I knew she had done this. I wasn't sure if it was real blood or something she had concocted, but it really didn't matter.

It was the humiliation that mattered—she had wanted it and made sure she accomplished it.

I've never forgotten the complete mortification of the laughter, followed by returning to school the next day and having kids pointing and laughing, having them throw pads and tampons at me as I walked down the halls, walking up to my locker which was plastered with pads stuck on the outside.

I'd sworn then that I'd never put myself in the position to be degraded like that again, which is why I have avoided all extra-curricular school activities—especially dances. I can't even think of going to a dance without remembering that day and reliving it.

It isn't a story I'm willing to share with Henry, especially on top of the knowledge he now has about the rest of my life. I know he's probably heard some of the stories about me from his friends, but only a girl can understand the complete humiliation of this one, so I doubt any of the boys really remember it.

Because I won't tell him the real reason and don't have a really good made-up reason not to go other than just to say I don't want to, he keeps asking me, trying to convince me.

"It's our only senior prom, we *have* to go," he tells me. I tell him he should go, but with someone else. He has no idea what it costs me to tell him to take someone else, jealousy eating me up, but he refuses anyway—to both my relief and chagrin.

"My mom will be disappointed if she doesn't have pictures of us for her scrapbook," he tells me, and I know she might be a little disappointed, but I also think that part of Emma instinctively feels why I don't want to go and so would never push it.

"Claire will be devastated if you don't wear her dress," he says, and I have to admit that that's the one argument that almost sways me. I don't want her to think I don't like her dress. Then I think about having her beautiful creation ruined in some prank, and my resolve is strengthened.

"I really, really want to go with *you*, and be with you that night," he tells me, and in the end we compromise.

I'll let Claire dress me up in the dress she made me, and do my hair, but Henry will take me somewhere else, away from anywhere the rest of the kids from school might be. Henry seems happy with that compromise, and soon he's scheming something secret for that night that he won't tell me about. Claire is told we're going to the prom and that makes her so happy that I feel guilty about the deception—but not guilty enough to capitulate.

Every day I have either tutoring or physical therapy, and I'm completely dependent on Henry and his family. My father has returned to his old ways, rarely coming home from work until he's already spent several hours at the bar drinking. I try to hide it from Henry and Emma especially, but since they're the two who spend the most time at my house or driving me around, it soon becomes pretty obvious.

One night, Henry's bringing me home, and as usual walks me in. We're saying goodnight when my father returns home, a little earlier than usual. He stumbles in, nearly falling as he passes us. Henry catches him.

"Whoa, Mr. Mosley, you okay?" he asks, dragging my father upright.

"Henry, you're a good boy," he says, words slurring, patting Henry sloppily on the cheek. Henry glances up at me and I feel my cheeks burning with shame.

"He's okay, he just needs to go to bed," I murmur,

hugging my arms around myself, wondering if the floor will open up so I can disappear inside.

"This happen often?" Henry asks, still steadying my father, who's now singing a raunchy song that makes my face flame brighter.

I shrug, not wanting to lie, but not wanting to admit it either.

"Are you safe here?" Henry asks, a fair question considering what he now knows about how my life had been, but I still feel mortified that he even has to think to ask it.

"'Course she is," my father interjects, breaking off in the middle of his song—a small blessing—and tries to stand a little taller. "I lock the doors myself."

I roll my eyes. Obviously that isn't what Henry is referring to.

"Yes, I am," I tell him. Henry eyes me dubiously, but then accepts what I say as truth.

"Okay." He grabs my father again, who's leaning precariously. "Mr. Mosley, let's get you up to bed."

"Oh, Henry, no," I step forward, hand outstretched, horrified at the thought of Henry having to help him like that. "I can do it."

"Really?" He sounds doubtful, eyeing my cast meaningfully.

"Sure," I try to sound confident, but fail. I've never helped him to bed before.

"Wait here," Henry says. "I'll be back."

I watch, dismayed, as Henry half-drags him up the stairs, listening intently to see if Henry is going to need help. Soon, he comes back down the stairs.

"He's undressed and in bed," he tells me nonchalantly, my shame at having him not only witness to this but actually part of it twisting my stomach. "I think he'll be okay."

"Henry, I'm so sorry."

"Why? You didn't take him out and pour drinks down his throat."

I can't say anything; my throat's jammed with words of apology.

He sees the look on my face, and pulls me close.

"Kate, why didn't you tell me this was a problem again?"

I shake my head against his chest, still unable to talk.

"You shouldn't be here," he scowls.

"I have to be. This is my home," I nearly choke on the word, automatically comparing my *home* to his home.

"I'm worried about you."

"I know." I take a deep breath and look at him. "But I promise it's okay. He doesn't hurt me. He just doesn't come home much, and sometimes when he does he's like *that*." I say, looking toward the stairs.

"I don't like leaving you here like this," his voice is urgent with concern. I hug him.

"It'll be okay," I promise him, not at all sure that anything will be okay ever again.

Twenty-Three

The day of Senior Prom inexorably comes. I have long since lost my cast and most of my limp, and am sporting a few new scars, but nothing extreme that indicates what happened four months earlier to change my life so drastically.

Claire is thrilled that I'll be wearing her dress to the prom, and I feel a little guilty again about my dishonesty—but as much as I love her, I'm still not going to give in on this one.

I let her do my hair in long ringlets, a process which takes almost two hours because she insists that each curl be just perfect. She talks the whole time, telling me all of the latest gossip with her and her friends. I can't help but compare her breathlessly exciting middle school experience with what had been my own horrifically terrifying experience.

I even let her put a little mascara and lip gloss on me—she insists I need it for the photos. She makes me promise to do the photos as soon as we arrive before Henry can "kiss your lip gloss off", as she says with a disgusted tone, while my own face heats in embarrassment. She's previously extracted a promise from Henry that he won't kiss me until after the pictures. My guilt mounts when I wonder how we will explain why there aren't any photos.

She positions everyone at the bottom of the stairs in the front foyer—my least favorite area of this house—before she lets me come out, adamant that I make an appearance, once again, coming down the stairs when they're all there, Emma with camera in hand. Claire stands at the top of the stairs so she can monitor everyone's reactions.

I'm learning that she has a flair for the dramatic—and I'm her favorite guinea pig.

I don't see anyone's reactions because once I came to the top of the stairs, my eyes go unerringly to Henry and I don't think I could look away if my life depended on it.

He stands at the bottom of the stairs, looking taller, broader and more gorgeous than I have ever seen him in his dark tuxedo. He's combed his hair down, but I know it won't be long before he mindlessly runs his fingers through it and it'll be standing up again. I smile and almost laugh as he does it just then, my heart melting at the familiar sight.

His eyes slowly travel down the length of the dress, then back up again and a slow smile crosses his face. I come to the bottom of the stairs, and he reaches for my hand, leaning down to kiss me like a magnet to steel, neither able to help it's attraction to the other.

"Henry, you promised!" Claire's screech reaches us as she hurries down the stairs.

"Oh, sorry," Henry murmurs, pulling away. But the smile on his face and the look in his eyes says he isn't really sorry at all. I smile back.

"Here," Claire says, armed with the lip gloss, as if she had expected Henry to break his word. She reapplies it, everyone laughing at her ire. "You can kiss her all you want later, Henry, but *not* 'til *after* pictures."

Henry holds up his hands in surrender, eyes still glued to mine. "Okay, okay, I promise for real this time. I just forgot for a minute."

"Eww," Claire and Amy groan together.

"Okay, you two, over here," Emma says, posing us after directing Henry to wipe my shiny gloss from his lips. Photos are taken, everyone telling us how good we look and giving us a hug, before we leave.

We get into Henry's car and I turn to him.

"How long do we need to occupy ourselves before it's safe to return do you think?"

"Don't worry; we'll be gone long enough."

"What do you have up your sleeve?" I ask suspiciously. He laughs and leans over to kiss me, pulling back before his lips touch mine. "Oops, I almost broke my promise again."

"Doesn't matter, does it? There won't *be* any photos."

He shrugs. "Maybe."

I look at him apprehensively. "Henry, you promised me. *No prom*."

"Don't worry," he repeats, "I won't break my promise to *you*. But I need you to close your eyes, and don't open them until I tell you."

"Henry..." I warn.

He reaches over and squeezes my hand.

"Trust me," he says, and because I do trust him, more than anyone I know, I close my eyes.

After a few minutes I feel the car turn off the road onto a dirt road. We don't drive far before he stops and shuts the engine off.

"Eyes closed?" he asks.

"Yes," I reply, curious now.

"Okay, stay there." He opens his door, climbs out and slams it closed. A few seconds later my door opens and he reaches in to help me out.

"Keep them closed until I say," he warns. "The ground is bumpy, but I won't let you fall."

He leads me across the uneven ground and I can sense the light changing a little behind my eyelids, getting brighter but not as bright as if we were indoors.

"Okay," he says, "You can open."

I open my eyes. In front of me is a scene out of a movie. Henry has led me to the clearing in the little forest that stands between our houses. He has built a fire—the source of the light—and has set up a table set for two, complete with candles and folded napkins. There are even clear Christmas lights twinkling from the trees. He walks away from me and pushes a button on the stereo, starting music—the same music they might be listening to at the prom right now.

He looks back at me, smiling, but I can read the

uncertainty in his face, unsure of my reaction. I walk over to him, reaching up to twine my arms around his neck and pull him down for a kiss.

"You made me my own prom!" I exclaim. "It's amazing. *You're* amazing."

"Claire's gonna be really ticked," he says with a smile, kissing me again, obliterating the gloss.

"What were you going to do? Take a picture of us in the trees and tell her it was a woodsy theme?" I tease.

"Even better," he says, leading me over to a backdrop half-hidden in the trees that I hadn't seen before. He flips a switch and a bright photographers light comes on, lighting it as well as if it were indoors.

"How in the world...?"

"Corey's girlfriend Amber painted the backdrop for the prom, so I asked her to do another for me."

"How did you get electricity in the middle of all these trees?" I ask, staring at the bright light.

"Generator down the hill there," he says, pointing.

"Clever," I murmur.

"And this way, Clair will never know that we were anywhere but the prom."

"Oh no," I laugh, placing my fingers over my now-bare lips. Henry grins, sticking his hand in his pocket and coming up with the tube of lip gloss.

"She knows us too well," he says, "So she put it into my pocket before we left."

"Then let's get that picture taken so we don't have to worry about it anymore." I laugh. "But who's going to take our picture?"

"I'll bet one of our waiters will do it," he says slyly.

"Waiters?" I question, brows furrowed in confusion. I hear another car pulling up and he smiles.

"There they are," he says. Emma and Dr. Jamison come into the clearing, dressed in jeans and white shirts and wearing aprons. I laugh at the sight.

Emma takes our picture, and I then wipe the gloss off, glad to have my lips unfettered again. Emma and Henry had spent the day making us a meal, which was packed in the Jamison's trunk and which they now serve to us at the candlelit table.

When we're finished eating, they clear away all of the food and dishes but leave the table set up for us. They also leave a box with all the makings of s'mores in it, and some beach chairs set around the fire. Emma tells Henry to leave everything and later they'll come back and clean it up. Then they leave us alone.

"Wanna dance?" Henry asks.

"I don't really know how," I tell him.

"Me neither. Let's fake it together."

"Okay," I smile, and he leads me out near the fire, wrapping his arms around me and pulling me close for a slow dance, even though the music isn't slow at all.

"You look really beautiful tonight," he tells me.

"This is a really great dress Claire made," I agree.

"Yeah, the dress is nice, too, but I meant *you*." He places his hand along the side of my face, caressing my cheek with his thumb. "But then, you always look beautiful to me."

And then he's kissing me as we move to a music of our own.

"Are you sure you don't mind this? Not going out in

public while you're all dressed up? Most girls want to be seen then."

"Maybe you haven't noticed; I'm not like most girls."

"I've noticed. That's what I like about you."

"Yeah?"

"Yeah. You don't ever play games, make me guess what it is you want, or what you're thinking. You're not afraid of getting dirty, you don't worry about if your hair looks just right, or get angry about having your prom in the woods."

"Oh." I'm not sure if those are good things are not. "Should I care about those things?"

"No," he laughs, "Please no. I love you just the way you are."

I lean my head against his chest, content to be here, just like this. Even if soon we we'll be apart—reality tries to intrude but I push it away. At least for tonight, I'm not going to think about anything else but just being here, with Henry, and feeling *happy*.

I hear another car pull up and feel Henry stiffen, but assuming it's just Emma and Dr. Jamison returning, I ignore it.

"Hey, Henry, you didn't tell us this was where the party is," a voice calls, and I feel my joy shatter. I turn and see Corey, Brock and Kaden with their dates coming through the trees. I relax again; these guys are alright, though I would have preferred being alone with Henry.

And then I see Jessica. She's with Ian, who's just now emerging from the dark. I freeze in horror, my insides turning to liquid fear at the sight, thoughts of my last dance with her rushing back. This is almost a duplicate of my last dance; from me being with the cutest, most popular boy in school, to the fact that I have brazenly worn makeup and have curls in my hair, and am dressed in white.

Henry feels the change in me and looks down, confusion in his eyes as they search my pale face. For one second, I felt a keen, crushing ache in my heart that Henry would be a part of Jessica's cruelty, that he would set all of this up to hurt me. Even as my body reacts to this hurt by pulling away from Henry, my mind is already rejecting it. I *trust* him.

"Are you alright?" he asks, tightening his hold on my waist. I let him pull me back in, pressing myself closer as I nod.

"I don't know how they found us, I didn't tell anyone—" Then his face falls. "It must have been Amber. She came here today to set up the backdrop. I'll make them go away." He starts to move away from me and I hold tighter. I know that Henry already spends too much time with me and not enough with his friends, and I don't want to be the cause of anymore of that.

"No, it's fine," I tell him. I try to smile, but know it doesn't look true when his expression darkens.

"I'll make them go away," he says, gruffly.

"No, let them stay." I keep him from walking away again. "Please. For me."

He looks at me oddly, and I can tell he wants to refuse, but he doesn't, nodding instead. The guys all come over, shaking his hand and smacking him on the back, each of them saying "hi" to me and telling me I look "good." The girls also say hello, but still are a little unsure of me, hanging back in their own circle.

Only Jessica stands away, by herself. She looks oddly uncomfortable, glancing at me then back at the ground. She seems even more anxious than me.

Huh.

I decide I'll just stay near Henry, secure in the knowledge that he won't let anything bad happen to me. The others decide they need a picture of just the guys, which leaves me standing to the side while Amber takes pictures. I feel exposed and vulnerable.

Jessica takes the opportunity to walk up to me, and instinctively I cower away. She sees this and her face falls in dismay.

"Can I talk to you?" she asks me, hesitantly.

I look at her, then back to where Henry stands with his friends, laughing as they goof around for the camera. There isn't really any way to call him to me without seeming like a complete coward. I consider calling him anyway.

"I promise I'm not going to do anything." She steps a few paces back from me. "Look, I'll stand here. I just want to tell you something, and then I'll go. I shouldn't have even come, but Ian wanted to stop, and I didn't know it was where you and Henry would be."

I keep silent, distrust running rampant through my veins.

"I know you have no reason to believe me," she says. "And I don't blame you for hating me. I have done some really awful things," her voice hitches and she looks away, guilt suffusing her face. "*Really* awful," she reiterates. "And I wish I could take them back, but I can't. I am *really* sorry, but that doesn't change those things, does it?" She glances at me, but I don't think she's expecting an answer, and I probably couldn't have given her one anyway, I'm so stunned by this odd speech.

"I've been so horrible to you. We were friends once, remember?" Again she glances at me, not wanting an answer. "I was stupid and petty and jealous and *cruel* and I have no excuse. I heard about, you know," she looks away, seeming embarrassed, "your mom and all, and all I could think was that you needed a friend. And when you needed a friend I was there making sure you didn't have one, that you didn't have anyone you could count on. And I'm really, *really* sorry, more sorry than you'll ever know. I wish I could make it up to you. I feel really bad, but I guess probably not as bad as I've made you feel for all these years."

I can't speak, wondering what's behind this amazing confession. I'm waiting for the punch line—or even just the punch—or the prank to cause me humiliation, or whatever it is she has planned.

"I just wanted you to know I'm sorry." She glances at me again. "Tell Ian that I went home, okay?" She turns to walk away. I look back at Henry, and then decide to take a chance.

"Jessica," I call. She stops and turns back toward me.

"Don't go," I say.

"What?"

"Stay." I shrug then wave vaguely toward the fire. "We're going to make s'mores."

She looks at me questioningly, taking a hesitant step

back toward me. "Are you sure?"

I'm not, but I nod anyway.

"Have you ever had a s'more?"

She smiles waveringly.

"Yeah, they're pretty good."

"They're *really* good. You should stay."

She walks back over toward me, stopping a few feet away.

"This is your night," she says. "I don't want to ruin it."

"So don't," I tell her. "Stay and have a s'more."

"Okay," she agrees with a small smile. I smile back, my uncertain smile matching hers. It would seem we have reached some kind of a truce, at least for tonight. I can live with that.

Twenty-Four

One week before graduation is my trial date. I borrow one of Claire's dresses, a modest, unassuming, light blue one. It's nicer than anything I own—even though the few clothes I have in my closet seem to be multiplying, somehow producing clothes nicer than my second-hand ones. Claire claims she was just going to throw them out anyway.

I'm a mass of nerves, hoping I won't have to go to prison for something that had been completely unintentional, at the same time believing absolutely that I deserve to be punished for causing the death of my mother.

My father has taken the day off work, and has managed to be sober and clear-eyed as he drives me to the courthouse. He's very quiet, and I know he's as nervous as I am, though I don't know why. It won't really change his life much if I'm home or in prison.

Rufus meets me at the courthouse, calm and soothing, a complete contrast to my previous courthouse experience with my first lawyer. We walk inside, and I see Henry waiting for me, sitting on the row behind where I will sit, with Emma and Dr. Jamison next to him. He reaches out as I pass and touches my hand, which nearly undoes me. I want to step into the protective shelter of his arms and hide there.

I move into my seat at the defense table, glancing back at him. Behind him I watch as Jessica comes in and sits on the back row. She smiles at me tentatively. I'm still unsure of her motives, not sure if she's here for support or to gloat.

Since the night of the prom, she's been marginally friendly to me at school. It's a bit awkward between us from all of the previous animosity. I don't think either of us are quite sure what to do with this truce.

The judge is announced and the woman walks in who is to decide my future. She's older, professional, face unreadable. She doesn't even glance my way as she takes her seat. The court is called to order, with my case announced and the prosecutor raises a hand, making an announcement I hadn't expected.

"Your honor, in light of the evidence and sworn testimony provided us by the defense, and the reports filed by police officers on the scene as well as the ME's report, the people move to dismiss the case against Kathryn Mosley at this time."

"I assume the defense has no quarrel with this?" the judge asks, sounding bored, as if she had expected no less. She peers at Rufus over the tops of her glasses.

"No, your Honor." He doesn't sound as stunned as I feel, but I can hear the relief in his voice nonetheless.

"Good." She removes her glasses and turns her gaze on me. "Ms. Mosley, I have reviewed your case, and I see no fault here on your part. I'm sorry for the trauma you have suffered. The system failed you; you should have been better protected. I believe the state owes you an apology for that.

"Case dismissed." Her tone has remained even throughout this speech, so when she pounds the gavel, I look at Rufus, confused. He's smiling at the prosecutor, shaking her hand and thanking her. I look back at Henry who's sitting behind me. He looks hesitantly hopeful. The judge rises along with the rest of us and leaves the room. This time she does look at me, and a slight smile lifts her mouth.

I look back at Rufus.

"What just happened?" I ask.

"I guess you could say we won. The charges have all been dropped."

"Dropped? Forever?"

He laughs. "Forever. They read your statement, saw the pictures. They knew they had no case; there was obviously never any malicious intent, only self-defense. I would have been surprised had they pursued this any further."

"So that's it?"

"That's it. You walk out of here free and clear. You don't ever have to think about this again." He shifts uncomfortably as he realizes how his words sound; how do you tell someone to forget their mother is dead by their hand, whether intentional or not? "I mean, as far as *legally* you don't have to worry about it anymore."

Henry understands before I do. He gives a whoop and scoops me up, right over the wooden divider, into his arms and twirls me around. He plants a kiss on my stunned lips, and then sets me down for Emma and Dr. Jamison to hug. My father walks over, in his slightly crumpled suit and stands before me, shifting nervously. I'm not sure what to say to him. We haven't spoken at all about what happened, and I'm not sure how he feels about the fact that his wife is dead because of me—and that I've just been given a get-out-of-jail-free card.

His eyes shift anxiously between all of us, including Rufus, who Henry belatedly introduces to my father. They shake hands, my father uncomfortable with his strange role here; he'd been required to be here because I'd been seventeen at the time of the incident, but now he's no longer necessary.

He rubs my arm awkwardly.

"See you at home, then," he says, following the rub with a pat.

Abruptly I lean forward and hug him. He's surprised by the unexpected motion, his arms coming up spontaneously to touch me at the waist.

"Thanks, Dad, for being here." I want him to know I appreciate his effort.

He nods, then turns to leave, assuming, I guess, that I'll get a ride home from the Jamison's. Paul, Emma and Rufus follow him, Emma tucking her arm through my father's. I watch him walk out and my eyes land on Jessica, still sitting at the back of the room.

"I'll be right back," I tell Henry.

I make my way to the rear of the room, Jessica standing as I come near.

"I... I hope it's okay that I'm here," she says.

"Why *are* you here?" I ask, genuinely curious.

She looks down, then beyond me, searching for words. Finally her eyes come back to mine.

"A lot of guilt, I guess."

I'm surprised at her honest answer.

"I mean, I can't stop thinking about everything...especially earlier this year, when I...in the bathroom at school..." my mind flashes back to her cornering me and slamming my head against the floor. I could have told her that her beating was amateurish at best compared to what I'd been reared on, but it suddenly seems unimportant.

She shudders at the memory. "I can't help it; all this time you were suffering so much, and I added to it."

"Jessica," I touch her arm, and she wilts miserably under the contact. "It's over now. It can't be undone. I forgive you."

"How can you?" she wails wretchedly. "How can *I*?"

"You can because I can," I tell her. Suddenly I have a thought. "I'll make a deal with you."

She looks at me curiously.

"I might need a favor someday soon, and I will need a...friend...I can ask it of."

"*Anything*," the word is a rush of breath. "I'll do anything so that you can know how sorry I am."

I nod. "Thanks for coming."

She shrugs.

"I wanted to. Besides, everyone at school is waiting to hear. I told them I would be coming so I'm sort of the designated spokesman."

I feel that old rush of sickness flow through me; the wolves again waiting to hear of the lamb's humiliation. My feelings must have shown on my face, because she rushes to correct me.

"Because they *care*. They will be happy for you."

"Happy." The word is bitter on my tongue. *Happy* that I have gotten off for something I *had* done?

Henry comes up behind me then, sliding his arms around my waist from behind.

"Everything okay?" he asks, and I can hear in his tone that he knows at least a little something of Jessica's history concerning me.

"Yes," I say, smiling up at him.

"I guess I should go now," she says. I look back at her, sliding my hands along his arms without conscious thought, but with absolute awareness.

"Thanks, Jessica."

She smiles at me, turning to go. Henry turns me in his arms, and my hands slide up around his neck.

"What was that all about?" he asks.

"It doesn't matter," I say, leaning into him as the day's events catch up to me and I feel the enormity of what has happened wash over me. "I need to get out of here."

We walk out into the hallway where his parents stand talking with Rufus and something about it strikes me as odd, though I can't quite put my finger on just what it is. Henry waves to them, and they come my way, followed by Rufus.

"Thanks," I tell him, "for everything."

"I hope I never have to see you again, at least professionally," he says. "See you later, Paul, Emma."

"Thanks, Rufus," Dr. Jamison says, patting him on the shoulder as one might a friend.

"Why don't you come by the house later for dinner?" Emma asks, turning to me. "Bring your father, too."

"Thanks, Emma. I'll have to check with him, see if he's available," the response is automatic, distracted as I watch my lawyer leave the room, then turn back to the Jamison's.

"Do you know him?" I ask Dr. Jamison.

"Yes, he brings his dogs to me." But even as he says it, he's shifting nervously.

"Coincidence, huh?" I ask suspiciously.

Dr. Jamison shrugs. "He's an old friend. He owed me a favor, Kate. It didn't cost anything."

I look at Emma, her face betraying her knowledge, then at Henry.

"Did you know?"

He nods warily, watching for the explosion he seems to fear will come, then qualifies, holding his hands up towards me. "Not at first. Only after he'd come to your house that day, and I went home to tell my parents about it."

"Why didn't you tell me?"

"Because you have a problem accepting help, and I knew you'd be mad."

I want to argue, but know he's right. So I look at Dr. Jamison instead.

"It really didn't cost anything?"

"No." His look is open and honest. "Lawyers have to do a certain amount of pro bono work each year. So I called him." He looks at Henry. "Henry told me about your first lawyer. Kate, we just wanted to help."

I sigh. I guess I can live with their help, as long as it hadn't cost them anything.

"Okay, thank you then. I really appreciate it." I hug the Jamison's, then wrap my arms around Henry, conveying the message that I'm not angry with him. He hugs me back, tension draining from his body.

"Where do you want to go?" Henry asks me, after he's taken me home to change into jeans and a t-shirt—nice ones that belonged to Claire. It's a beautiful day, sky blue and sun shining.

"Let's swing," I tell him, a fantasy I've been nurturing for some time now.

He follows me out back, and for the first time in my life, I sit on my beloved swing-set—not alone. Henry sits next to me, holding my hand between the chains as we swing softly back and forth.

"Bet I can go higher than you," I challenge teasingly, releasing his hand and pushing back with my feet, laughing as I pump higher and higher, Henry by my side, inexperience slowing him down in spite of his longer legs.

I push myself, watching the familiar pattern of grass, fence, neighbor's backyard, treetops, then finally sky, deep blue and bright white with fluffy round clouds like mounds of whipped cream placed there; then the whole pattern in reverse, and then forward again, Henry passing through my peripheral vision as he swings beside me. I'm laughing, and then suddenly I'm crying, gradually at first with tears running slowly down my cheeks as the laughter tapers off. Memories inundate my mind and soul beginning with the first day I had set eyes on this swing, traveling through the unraveling of my childhood and the loss of a normal life by my parents' hands; through the forced servitude and starvation and torture; through the beatings at the hands of the woman who should have loved me more than anyone else, and whose death was my fault.

My tears have become great gulping sobs and Henry has stopped swinging, calling my name as he tries to slow my swing, to catch me between my flying arcs. He steps behind me, timing it as I swing forward and wraps his arms tightly about my waist, stopping my progress, jerking us both forward with the momentum. He leans backward and I let myself be pulled off the swing.

I drop to the ground in a rounded mass, and he goes with me, curling his body around me from behind, knees against my sides, arms bound tightly about me as he holds my shuddering, heaving form, rocking me as we huddle there together in the dirt and I keen and wail, pouring out my grief in a way I haven't allowed myself since I first woke up in the hospital.

When my cries soften into moans, he turns me sideways and pulls my face against his shoulder. I wrap my arms around his ribs, grateful for the solid strength there. I'm shivering now, a belated reaction, and his heat surrounds me.

"I killed her," I moan.

"Sweetheart, it was an accident," his voice is full of emotion, persuasive.

I shake my head.

"It doesn't matter. It's my *fault*."

"Katy, you were trying to get away. She would have killed—" his voice catches and he stops.

I press tighter against him.

"Maybe," I concede. "But maybe not. I didn't give her the chance to find out." I take a breath, then tell him the one thing I've never told anyone else, ever. "I *wished* for it, Henry. More times than I can count. I even prayed for it. What kind of person prays for her mother's death? What if it wasn't an accident...what if I subconsciously knew what I was doing?"

"Kate, look at me." He turns my face up to his with one hand, his other still clasping me tightly. "Don't do this to yourself. I *saw* you. You almost died! One more swing at you and she would have..." his face is terrible with memory, ravaged with the thought of it. His desolate eyes hold mine, dark with feeling.

"Kate, sweetie, you only pushed her away. It was a freak accident. Do you hear me? An *accident!* She could just as easily have only been knocked out. Or even not been hurt at all, and then come after you again. It wasn't anyone's fault that she hit her head the way she did, especially *not yours*. It was her fault she put you in the position to have to defend yourself in the first place." His tone is urgent, pleading with me to understand.

"I didn't even get to go to her funeral," I whisper.

"She was a monster," he says.

"She was my mother."

He nods, trying to understand, unable to in his own bright world full of love. He hugs me close again.

"I know, Kate." We rock silently for a few minutes, tears still running silently down my face, throat aching with residual strain.

"I loved her," I whisper.

"You have to let it go," he says softly. I know he's right, but I have no idea how I'm ever going to do that.

Twenty-Five

Graduation day comes, and since I have passed all of the tests—and I'm not in jail—I'm being allowed to graduate with everyone else. I'm apprehensive about showing up, as the local newspapers have gotten hold of my story and have run it in not-completely-accurate-but-pretty-close sensationalism. I'm not sure of the reaction to expect of my schoolmates, most of whom I have spent the last twelve years attending school with.

My father actually manages to stay sober once again and we ride to the school together in his car, which I have to admit I'm amazed still runs. I suppose that has much to do with the fact that he has always worked as a mechanic—though for many different companies over the years—and manages to keep it running. The inside of the car is dirty, as if it hasn't been cleaned in years, and littered with empty bottles. I wonder how he has lived all these years without wrapping himself around a tree in a drunken haze, or kept from hurting anyone else.

We meet Henry and his family at the auditorium where the graduation is to be held. My father goes to sit with them, while Henry and I line up in our places. I try to pretend that I don't notice the looks and stares I'm receiving, the whispers behind hands.

Henry's friends come over to say hello to me, as do their girlfriends who look more uncomfortable than usual around me. Then Jessica comes up beside me, placing herself into the line right next to me, with a smile. I have to admit it still makes me nervous to have her so close, but she is still the most welcome presence of all the girls here.

We file out, sitting in the seats and listening to the long, boring speeches that accompany graduation. Then row by row we stand and walk up toward the podium to receive our diplomas. We were instructed beforehand to walk up from opposite sides, take our diploma, shake the administrators hands as we walk to the center of the stage, then exit from the center.

When it comes my turn, and my name is announced, there comes a smattering of applause from behind me. This very quickly rolls into a thunderous applause and I glance around to see what is causing the commotion.

Everyone is looking at me, either grinning or with tears rolling down face, or both. Even the administration and speakers on the stage have stopped and are joining in. They're cheering for me? I look around for Henry, but he's on the opposite side of the floor, too far away for contact. He's touching me anyway, his eyes intently burning into mine, a smile of love and recognition on his face.

Jessica is standing behind me, and I reach out blindly for her—for anything real and solid in this strange world. She sees my need and steps forward to grasp my hand, giving me support in the face of this overwhelming happening. I continue up to the podium, releasing Jessica's hand as I meet the receiving line, getting hugs instead of the traditional handshakes, even from those who aren't supposed to be on this side of the stage coming over. Henry has come up from his side, and met me in the middle, taking my hand and kissing me on the temple, walking me down the middle set of stairs.

It takes some time for the cheers to die down after I have returned to my seat, reluctantly letting Henry go. By this time I'm thoroughly embarrassed. I guess that it's my sudden celebrity that has gotten such a reaction.

Later I'm told it's respect for my courage, and for surviving against such odds. That doesn't sound quite right to me—what choice did I have but to survive? And I don't consider myself courageous at all. Courage seems an honorable word, and killing your own mother is anything but honorable.

We go to dinner with the Jamison's to celebrate the dubious honor of making it through high school. Even my father, who's jittery but trying really hard to be like a dad, comes. It's a night of excitement and laughter for most, but inside I felt a deep dread, because I know that each day brings me closer to the time that I'll have to be without Henry.

"Do you want to come back to my house for a while?"

Henry asks me later as we pull up in front of my house, my father climbing out of the SUV. I watch him go and shake my head.

"I think I need to talk to my father. Things are weird between us, and it's time for us talk about it." *It* being the death of my mother, his wife, because of me. Henry doesn't argue, understanding instinctively what I need most, as he always does.

I follow my father in, watching as he stands nervously near the front window, obviously wanting to escape. I recognize *that* feeling very well, but for once he will have to ignore it for me, his daughter.

"Dad, I need to talk to you."

He glances at me, dread in every line of his face.

"I was gonna go out," he says.

"I know. But I need you now. Just for a little while."

"Okay," he concedes, not happy about it. We walk into the kitchen and he sits at the table. I fill a glass of water for me and pull a soda out for him, bypassing the beer. I need him sober for a little longer.

"Do you blame me?" I ask, as soon as I'm seated.

He's startled. "Blame you for what?" he asks.

"For...mom. For...*killing*...her."

His jaw drops. This obviously isn't what he expected.

"No, Kate, of course not. I know what happened. You didn't *kill* her, not really."

"I did. She's dead because of me. She was your wife and now she's gone because of me."

He reaches across the table and folds his hand over mine, an unexpectedly fatherly gesture.

"Kate, you know how things were. You're a smart girl;

you saw what went on between us. She hasn't really been my...*wife* for a long time now." He glances away guiltily. "Not that I blame that on her, either. There is a lot of fault on my part. I think about it sometimes, wonder how things went so wrong." He looks at me, eyes rife with remorse. "It's mostly my fault, the way things were between her and me. I wasn't there for her when she needed me, and I saw how she became, how important the drugs became. I knew, and I ignored it." He glances at me, "I saw how she was with you."

"*Why*?" I ask, tortured. "Why was she that way with me? Was I so horrible, so unlovable? Why did she hate me?"

He shakes his head, and sighs, a great decisive sigh, as if making a choice.

"There's something you should know, Kate. Something that you probably deserved to know a long time ago." He stands. "Wait here, I have something you should see."

He goes up the stairs with a longing glance toward the front door. I can hear him rummaging around, and finally he returns, carrying a sheet of paper with him. He sits across from me, looking down at the paper as if deciding the virtue in showing me, but then he lays it flat and pushes it across the table to me, not meeting my eyes.

I look down at it. *Certificate of Adoption* is scrawled across the top. My brows furrow in confusion. My mother was adopted? What did that have to do with me? Then I continue reading it, seeing the date of birth of the baby girl, and the names of the adoptive parents and my heart stops. I look up at my father, who's watching me painfully.

"I was adopted?" My voice comes out in a squeak.

"Yes."

"But, I don't understand. She was pregnant, when... I remember her being pregnant when I was young. I have a photo of it."

He nods sadly. "She was. That was an accident. We had tried to avoid pregnancy."

"Why?" I understand even less than before.

"There is quite a history of mental illness on your mother's side, and addiction problems on mine. We decided those weren't genes we wanted to pass on. So we adopted you."

"That's why she hated me? Because I wasn't hers?"

"No, Kate, not at all. She loved you. I know that's hard to believe now, but you had to have seen her when we brought you home. She adored you. She spent all of her time playing with you and taking care of you.

"Even when we first found out she was pregnant, and she talked about abortion—which she couldn't do in the end—she still loved you. As if you were her own flesh and blood. And then she lost the baby." He breaks off, lost in the misery of that memory.

"Neither of us dealt with that well. I suppose we had both been looking forward to that baby more than we knew. Something happened to her then, as if some switch had been flipped. She was on pain pills from the miscarriage, followed by pills for depression when she couldn't shake the grief."

He looks at me. "She had been on pills for her form of psychosis since before we were married, but as she became addicted to the others she quit taking those. I wish I had some excuse for why she did the things she did, but in the end it all came down to that. She had started taking her pills around Thanksgiving again, but then she stopped while you were gone over Christmas.

"I'm ashamed to say that I was so bound up in myself and my own problems that I ignored hers. And yours. I didn't want to deal with any of it. And because of that you spent years being hurt, and we have ended up here, like this."

I can only stare at him, shocked. My whole life has been based on lies and selfishness.

"Around Thanksgiving?" my question is low. I can guess exactly what started her taking them again at that time—she had nearly killed me. I feel a spark of anger ignite. "Do you know why?"

He shakes his head, watching me warily at my tone.

"She hurt me. Badly. I was gone for almost a week while the Jamison's nursed me back to health. Were you even aware of that, *Dad*?" I spit his name out sarcastically.

"Kate—" he begins, but I cut him off.

"You chose to adopt me," I accuse, voice full of venom. "You had a responsibility to me. Both of you did. And your excuse is that you *didn't want to deal with it*?" I stand up angrily, and he looks at the floor, misery in every line of his body. I push away any feelings of compassion in me at the sight of him.

"You're a worthless, self-pitying drunk, and I am not your daughter!" My voice rises in pitch, emotions and thoughts swirling in a muddied chaos in my head. I want to articulate them all, but can't find a place to begin in the raging storm that is my mind. There seems to be only one place to begin.

"I'm leaving!" I exclaim, making a sudden decision, the words finding their way to the surface of their own accord. But as I say them, I feel the rightness of the decision. "I'll be gone within a few days, and you can live out the rest of your miserable, lonely life in any way you choose. I hope you spend it thinking of me, every day, and knowing that *you* did this. *You* had the power to stop it, but you *didn't want to deal*. So now deal with what you have left!"

I grab up the certificate in my fist, taking it with me as I run from the room and up the stairs. I slam the door and stand inside the room that has been both my prison and my sanctuary for so many years. I feel nothing. Nothing except a burning anger at the life that has been dealt me. I jam the chair under the door handle.

A few minutes later I hear the front door close, and the car engine start in the driveway. I open my door, listening to the silence. I'm suddenly seized with an intense desire to be gone from this place. I go back into my room, pulling the old suitcase down from the top of my closet and angrily shoving my few possessions into it, more anger growing at how little I have to show for the years of abuse I have suffered in this house.

I pull out the cell phone I still have from Dr. Jamison, and call information. I dial a new number to call in the favor that I expected to be something completely different when I asked for it. I'm relieved when Jessica answers.

"This is Kate," I tell her. "I need that favor now."

Twenty-Six

I ask Jessica if I can stay with her for a few days, which she and her parents readily agree to. Like me, Jessica is an only child, and she had told her parents about me and her treatment of me over the years in a fit of regret. They were horrified and saddened by her behavior, and were glad she had tried to make it up to me, so they're more than willing to let me come. They have a spare bedroom, which shares a bathroom with Jessica, that they let me use.

It's a little awkward at first, but being in close quarters creates a kind of forced intimacy, and soon Jessica and I become something like friends. Behind the façade she puts up at school is someone who is really a kind person.

"Why?" I ask her one night as we sit on the floor in her room, looking at her old family photos—something I have never had myself, short of my one photo of the day my swing set was delivered. "Why did you hate me so much?"

She chews on the side of her thumb for long seconds, not looking at me. Finally she shrugs.

"It's amazingly stupid when I think about it now." She glances up, and I can see the shame on her face. "Remember we were friends?" I nod. "But you started to get kinda weird." She looks down again.

"I guess now I understand why. But I didn't then." She looks at me again, takes a breath and tells me.

"Even though you got weird, and really quiet, you were so pretty. I was jealous because I wanted to be the prettiest one. I guess that's pretty egotistical, but...." She shrugs again.

"Anyway, I had always thought Henry was the cutest boy in school, and somewhere along the line I decided that if he was the cutest, and I was the prettiest, we should be together. Like a power couple.

"Once I decided that, I started to notice the way he watched you. He always went out of his way to be nice to you. Then I saw the Valentine he gave you."

I remember the day—and the Valentine—clearly, of course. I think I even still have it somewhere.

"You hated me because of a Valentine?" I ask.

"Sort of," she qualifies. "That was only a part of it. After that, you two were always together, holding hands. Because I had decided he should be with me, I turned my anger on you. Like I said, egotistical—and petty."

"But he was gone by the next year."

Jessica cringes at my words, twisting her hands together guiltily.

"By that time, I think hating you was almost a habit. You came to school that year prettier than ever—" I make a choked sound and she stops, looking at me with guilty pain in her eyes. She cocks her head.

"You really don't see yourself clearly." Her eyes fall, and her cheeks darken. "But I guess that's my fault, too, isn't it? I made sure you never saw yourself the way all those boys did on the first day of school."

"Jess, no boys were looking at me. I was skinny and dressed in second hand clothes. They couldn't take their eyes off you."

She smiles at me, grimly. "They noticed you, Kate. So I made sure that the attention you were getting quickly became negative attention.

"You never stood up for yourself, not against me, not against anyone else. It was so easy..." she trails off, hearing her own words. When she looks at me again, she has tears in her eyes.

"I had no idea what you were going through, Kate. That's no excuse, but it makes what I did a hundred-thousand times worse. It's already bad enough, that I'm capable of such cruelty, that I could make someone's life so miserable. Then to know what you were suffering..." Suddenly she reaches out, grabbing both my hands.

"You should despise me, Kate. I'm not worthy of anything from you but your loathing. I'm a horrible person. Even knowing that, I want you to forgive me. Please forgive me, Kate."

I squeeze her hands as her tears slide down her cheeks—those perfect, flawless cheeks that I'd spent so many years jealous of.

"You were pretty horrible," I say, Jessica nodding in agreement. "Why did you come to me, on the night of the prom, and act so nice?"

"I saw you when you came back to school, and I didn't know who'd hurt you so bad, but I suddenly saw what I had been doing to you with a clarity that I hadn't ever had before. I felt bad you'd been hurt, which was pretty foreign to me, feeling bad for you like that.

"So I confessed to my mom—who was horrified that her daughter could be so *mean*. She told me the only way to make it up to you was to be your friend. I just didn't know how to do that." She squeezes my hands. "I know there's no way I can ever possibly make it up to you. I'm so sorry for everything, Kate. For what your mom did to you, for what I did to you, for what others did to you because of me."

"Don't be."

She leans back in surprise at my words.

"I hate pity," I tell her. "I could use a friend, though."

"If you'll let me, Kate, I'll be your friend. I'll spend the rest of my life trying to make it up to you."

I laugh and she finally grins a little.

"Sounds pretty melodramatic, huh?"

"Like a soap opera," I say.

"You have Henry, too."

My smile falters, and I pull my hands from hers.

"I have Henry," I murmur, turning away.

"I'm glad, Kate. I'm so glad you have him; that he could see what all the rest of us were too blind to see."

"Yeah," I agree, "I'm glad I have him, too."

I don't tell her that I won't have him much longer, and

I don't look her way, afraid she'll see the pain and terror the thought of losing him causes me.

It's farther from Jessica's house to Henry's, but with the weather warming up I begin walking the distance, then having Henry drive me back at night. I can tell that he doesn't really understand why I'm so angry with my father, though I think Emma and Dr. Jamison are a little more understanding.

I've been thinking a lot about Henry, trying to find a way we might be able to stay together. I know he will be going away to school, but I have nothing to tether me where I am. I can follow him, maybe, if I work really hard and save some money. Or I can wait for him. I'll wait for him forever if I need to.

The thought of being without him, permanently, petrifies me.

It's because I'm walking to Henry's that I hear the conversation that changes my hopes.

Henry is sitting in his backyard with his father. I don't mean to eavesdrop, but in the end I'm glad I do.

"Henry, don't be foolish," Dr. Jamison says.

"Dad, I know what I'm doing."

"No, I don't think you do. Son, I know you love her, but you'll give up your future for her?"

I freeze, knowing instinctively they're talking about me.

"Yes, I will, I'll give anything up for her."

"And end up angry and bitter because of it. Then you'll hate her, and she doesn't deserve that."

"That's not going to happen," Henry argues, but he doesn't sound so confident now.

"You don't think it will, but I've seen it happen plenty of times. You've had your college career mapped out for as long as I can remember. You can't just give it up."

"I'm not; I'm just...*changing* it."

"Son, you've worked very hard for a very long time to get to this point. How can you even think of it?"

"Because I can't imagine being without Kate. She *needs* me. And I can't hurt her that way, leaving her here alone."

I run away then, not wanting to hear anymore. I had known he would leave, of course I had known that. Even as I think it, I know that I've always thought there would be a way around it, just like all of the times I had managed to get out of my house to be with him when it seemed impossible. Because I can't imagine being without him. Now I can see that he knows how dependant I am on him, that he is willing to change his life, give up his dreams for me—a nobody.

A murderer.

And I know Dr. Jamison is right, that he will hate me for it in the end. I try to imagine Henry looking at me with hate and disgust, and it makes me physically ill picturing it.

I run into the woods, the woods that had once been the site of his prom for me, a stark testament to just how far he'll go to try to please me, just as he had when he had given up his prom to give me my own.

I sit on the ground in the wet leaves. I know what I have to do. I have to destroy myself to save him. I lean over, throwing up on the damp ground at the sickness that grips my stomach at the thought.

I get up and walk back toward his house. I have to do it now, before I lose the courage to.

Henry is now sitting alone in the backyard, hunched over in a lawn chair, deep in thought. I unlatch the gate, and he sits up at the sound.

"Hey," he calls, smiling, happy to see me, which breaks my heart. He gets up and comes over, taking me in his arms and kissing me. I relax into him, savoring the feeling, any excuse to put off what I need to do, wanting one last time to be held by him.

"Your pants are wet," he observes.

"Oh, yeah…I stopped in the trees and sat for a while, thinking."

He cocks his head, giving me an odd look.

"Thinking? About anything important?"

"Actually, yeah. Something I need to talk to you about."

"Okay." He takes my hand and leads me over to the lawn chairs. I sit across from him, not sure where to start, not wanting to do this.

"Is everything okay? Is there a problem at Jessica's? Or with your dad?"

"No, no problems with Jessica or my…dad. Jessica and her parents have been great, really great."

"You can always stay here, you know."

My heart squeezes painfully. With every fiber of my being I want to do that, to give in, move into this warm house, to be surrounded with this family's love. To be with Henry. Above all, to be with Henry.

"Henry, the thing is...I can't see you anymore." I stand up, turning away from him, not wanting him to see what it costs me to say the words, afraid that if I look at him, I'll take them back.

"What?" he's incredulous. "What do you mean?"

"I mean, it's time for us to grow up, to start living for our futures. And I don't see a future with us together."

"What are you talking about?" He's on his feet, and I use all my years of practice at schooling my face into blankness in front of my mother's fury when I face him.

"Henry, we live different lives—in completely different worlds. Our futures will be entirely different. You will be successful in whatever you do, whether you become a doctor or not. You were raised to do that. I was raised to just get by, to wear hand-me-downs, to drive crappy cars and live in run-down houses. That's my future."

"That's not true, not with me. I won't let that be how you have to live."

"But that's the difference between us, Henry. I don't mind that. I don't aspire to be something I'm not. And you—you could never live the way I do."

"You are saying we can't be together because I'm not poor?" He sounds angry now, with pain underneath his words. "I can live that way—as long as it's with you. I *will*, if that's what you want." But his words are untrue—he knows it and I know it.

"You'll be going away to college; I'll be lucky to get a job flipping burgers. You need a wife who can fit into your world, who doesn't have a past like mine, someone with parents who weren't drunks and drug addicts, and crazy to boot. A wife who hasn't been charged with the murder of her mother. Imagine trying to explain that to your other doctor colleagues, or to your patients when you're trying to build a practice."

Henry's eyes are dark with denial, his face devastated. He's shaking his head, and it takes all I have not to put my arms around him and try to ease the pain from his eyes.

"It doesn't matter," he's pleading now. "I don't care what anyone thinks."

"But I do, Henry." That stops him. "Because it would be *me* they would be despising, *me* who would be excluded from their lives, *me* who would be your shame, *me* who would be hurt by it." I turn away from him again because honestly, I don't care one ounce what anyone thinks of me, what anyone might think in the future, but if this is what it takes to get Henry to let me go, then I'll use it.

"Don't do this, Katy. Please."

His voice is broken and I shudder deep within my soul. I don't want to—oh, how I don't want to. But his father's words ring again in my ears. I won't let him ruin his life for me; I'm hardly worth it. If I wasn't worth the love of either my birth or adopted parents, then I'm really not worth the love of someone as pure as Henry.

I pull the cell phone out of my pocket, squeezing it, as if imprinting the feel on my palm will somehow keep him close. I set it on the table.

"Katy, please, *please* don't do this. I want to be with you. I want to *marry* you." He steps forward and turns me back toward him, hands clasped around my upper arms. I close my eyes against the intensity in his eyes, against my own overwhelming desire to give in to him, to be selfish and take what he offers. But behind my closed eyes I see again my imagined picture of him looking at me with hatred and I stiffen my resolve.

"It wouldn't last Henry. You know that."

"Kate, I love you," he says, yearning in his words.

"I love you, too." I struggle to keep my voice light, to suppress the emotion that demands to be released with the words. "I always will. You've been my best friend. I will never forget anything you've done for me. You have no idea how much it means. But now it's time for me to move on."

"No," he moans, pressing his forehead against mine. I reach up, laying my hand against his cheek, allowing myself this one last indulgence.

"Bye, Henry," I say, pulling away, hurrying through the gate, running once I'm beyond the house, running blindly with tears flooding my eyes, not stopping until I can't run anymore.

Twenty-Seven

I end up staying with Jessica throughout the summer. Every time I try to leave, Jessica or her parents talk me into staying just a little longer, until eventually I quit even bringing it up. It just seems easier to stay.

When I came home from breaking up with Henry, and told Jessica about it she sat with me while I cried.

"I can't do this," I tell her.

"Then don't," she says, "Go back to him."

She stays close to me while I work through the depression, dragging me out of bed on the days that I don't want to get up.

"Come on, Kate, let's go get ice cream," she says.

"I don't want to eat ice cream again," I moan.

"Then let's go get a cup of cyanide. I hear they serve the best cyanide west of the Rockies at Joe's."

She also tells me that I'm an idiot, that if she had someone who loved her in the way Henry loves me, she would do anything to keep them, *not* push them away.

She can't see the picture in my head, though, the one where Henry hates me for destroying his dream, the one where being married to a murderer has shattered his perfect life.

I find work at the nursing home, taking care of Alzheimer patients, learning patience and love for people who are suffering so much worse than me, people who don't care about my sudden local celebrity and don't ask me questions about it.

I apply for several scholarships, and receive enough to take a full course of classes at the community college, even enough to cover book costs. Jessica is also going to be attending, though we only have two classes together.

I go to the bank with Grandpa Henry's money and convert it into a money order, which I then mail to him. It comes back a week later. I mail it again to him, with a letter this time, telling him I'm no longer with Henry and no longer need an "emergency fund". It comes back again, this time a new money order for *two*-thousand dollars, with its own letter.

Dear Kate,

I am aware of your misguided break-up with my grandson, but I still hold out hope that you will realize the foolishness of this and will return to him. In the meantime, this money is mine to do with as I please, and it pleases me for you to have it. I am happy you no longer need emergency money, so spend it on yourself. You deserve it. Return it to me and I will again double its value and will continue to do so as long as you keep returning it. Do you want to be responsible for wiping out an old man's life savings?

Love, Grandpa Henry

The letter makes me laugh and cry. I miss Grandpa Henry, more so knowing I'll never see him again. But I know he means what he says, and so I keep the money, this time sending him a letter thanking him for his donation to the Kate Mosley New Life Fund.

"So, I hear you don't drive," Jessica's dad, Tom, tells me over dinner one night.

I glance at Jessica, who pointedly ignores me as she's piling potatoes on her plate. I turn back to Tom.

"That's only kinda true. I have a drivers license; I've just never really had much of an opportunity to actually drive, so I'm not really sure if I still can or not."

"Well, then, let's get going."

He stands up, and I look around, confused. Jessica only shrugs, shoveling a forkful of potatoes into her mouth—to cover a grin, I suspect. Jill, Jessica's mom, only smiles and nods for me to follow her husband.

We head out to the garage, and Tom throws me the keys to the small SUV as he climbs into the passenger seat. I take a breath, climbing into the opposite side.

And just sit.

After long, silent moments, Tom looks over.

"Well?" he prompts.

I turn to him.

"This is really nice, but..."

"But?"

"It seems silly. I don't even own a car."

"No big deal," he says. "You'll be the official family driver from here on out, until you get your own car."

"I'm not going to have money for a ca—" I break off as a thought pops into my head. I look at him with a smile.

"What now?" he grins back.

"Know any good used car dealers?" I ask, sticking the key into the ignition.

Jessica's family is different from the Jamison's, not as loud and exuberant, hugs given sparingly, but they are still so far above what I have ever known. Her parents are quiet and steady, warm and welcoming me into the family from the beginning, as if I already belonged but only just showed up. They clearly love one another; they just aren't as public about it as Emma and Dr. Jamison.

I'm woven into the tapestry of their family so completely that I'm even given some chores to do along with Jessica. When the summer is coming to an end and I begin talking about moving out again, they ignore me, not making a big fuss and I find myself staying—again.

Turns out Tom does have a friend that owns a car dealership and he helps me find a good used car cheap, one that I pay for somewhat guiltily using Grandpa Henry's money.

The pain of losing Henry doesn't ever ease; I just learn to live with it. I avoid places in town that I know he might be. Jessica tries to tell me things she hears about him, but I plug my ears childishly, his name too painful to even hear. I don't want to know what he's doing, even as I yearn for the sight of his face, the touch of his hand, the kiss of his lips so much that I cry myself to sleep every night.

Then it happens, the one thing I had feared.

I'm driving home from work, and as I pull through a stop sign, I see a heartbreakingly familiar car coming the other way. I quickly pull to the side of the road, ducking, peering up over the steering wheel. My heart pounds, my hands sweat. My reaction is completely visceral, and I feel that I'm coming apart at the seams as I sit and watch, hoping and dreading.

It's Emma.

I breathe a sigh of relief, then begin trembling in aftershock. It wasn't who I thought—but was almost as bad. Waves of longing crash over me, and for an insane moment I consider turning my car around and following her. Then I scoff at myself.

"Okay, Kate, get a hold of yourself!" I command.

I try to imagine if it was Henry in the car and the pain that suffuses me is overwhelming. I think that if I were to see Henry somewhere I would probably have a heart attack if my body's current reaction is any indication. At the very least it would undo the progress I've made in learning to try to live without him—no matter how small that progress. I figure getting out of bed, and trying to make a life is better than nothing.

I've met a few new people in my college classes, though I still struggle with trust issues and believing someone would want to know me without malicious intent. I'm seeing a psychiatrist again, at the insistence of Jessica's parents, who are worried about my deep depression after Henry. Having seen and felt the result of untreated depression firsthand in the form of my mother, I agree. I don't need pills—refuse to take them, as a matter of fact—just someone to help me work through everything. She's helping me learn to trust, to believe in myself, and to deal with being without Henry. She keeps encouraging me to date, but I know that isn't going to happen for a very long time, if ever.

Twenty-Eight

My psychiatrist encourages me to make peace with my father. I discovered that my birth parents are unknown, as I had been left on the steps of a hospital—not as romantic in reality as it sounds. So I decide to try to see him.

I pull up in front of the house next door to the house I had grown up in, ironically in the place where I had once made Henry leave me to avoid being seen.

My father is home—odd since it's the middle of the afternoon on a Saturday. He has his head pushed underneath the open hood of his old car. It's a peculiarly normal thing for him to be doing, something I don't remember ever seeing him do before. I watch him for a few minutes, searching for the anger within. There's a little rumble of it deep in my stomach, but mostly it's gone.

I climb out of my car, and he jumps at the sound of my slamming car door, hitting his head against the open hood, cursing as he rubs the spot. His eyes fall on me and his hands still as he watches me come near with disbelief.

"Hi," I say, as I come to the other side of the car from where he stands.

"Hi," he echoes, his voice reflecting his bewilderment. He picks up a rag lying over the fender and wipes his hands.

"Car trouble, huh?" I say.

He looks down at the engine as if there might be something there to explain my presence.

"Yeah, I keep thinking I'm gonna keep this thing going for a few more years, but it has its own ideas." I nod and he looks beyond me to where my car sits. "That yours?" he asks.

"Yeah, I just got it about a month ago."

"Runs okay, huh?"

I shrug. "It seems to."

"You ever need it looked at, I can..." he trails off, looking at me uncertainly.

"Okay, I might take you up on that sometime." My answer surprises him.

He's silent a minute, watching me, shifting nervously. "You wanna come in, have a soda or something?" he asks, sounding as if he expects a no.

"Sure." Again, his eyebrows raise in shock at my reply.

I follow him in, sitting at the table while he washes his hands in the sink. I take the opportunity to look around. I'll be honest, I expected the place to be in complete disarray, dishes piled in the sink, floor splattered. It's clean, and organized. When he opens the fridge to retrieve sodas it's filled with food—and most unusual of all, no beer or other alcohol that I can see. As he sits across from me I really look at him for the first time.

"You look good," I say, and it's true.

His eyes are clear. His face is anxious about me being here but underneath that he is relaxed, no jitters or nervous twitches. His nose is lined with the broken vessels that indicate alcoholism, but it isn't red.

"Thanks. So do you." He takes a sip of his soda, watching me.

"Lot of memories involving this table," I say, running my hands across the clean, worn surface.

"Not all of them good though, huh?"

I look at him, remembering my last time here when I learned I'd been adopted, the time of the failed Thanksgiving dinner, all the meals served but not eaten by me. Then I think of the times I sat here with Henry, or with Emma. And even a few of those times with my father there.

"Not all of them bad, either," I say.

He clears his throat, hands folded around his can of pop.

"Kate, there's something I want to tell you, if it's okay." His eyes are on the table.

"Sure," I wonder what other revelation he might give, if it will explode my world again.

"I'm an alcoholic." He says it so matter-of-factly that my mouth drops open a little. "Not that you didn't already know that. Not that *I* didn't already know that. But I couldn't admit it before. I can now."

He looks up at me.

"I've been going to AA, getting help."

"That's good," I say, meaning it.

"I should have done it years ago, though. Before you were born, before your mom and I were married, I was having drinking problems, and had gotten help then, though it didn't last. I was doing well until I lost my job. That shouldn't have been so bad but I was scared, she was pregnant with the baby we shouldn't have been having, we already had you to be responsible for, this house with its mortgage, other bills. And instead of dealing with it, I turned to alcohol to numb the stress.

"I know it doesn't matter now, with all that has happened, but it's important to me that you understand that most of the past ten years have been a drunken fog for me." He holds up his hands as if I protested. "It's not an excuse for what I have done. Or for what I *haven't* done. Or for anything I allowed to happen to you. I take absolute responsibility for that. I was your father, and I didn't ever act like it. But Kate, I always loved you. I did a really poor job of showing it, but I did."

"Why now?" I ask, curious. "Did something happen to make you decide to get help?"

"You did," he answers, as if it should have been obvious. "The last time you were here. You were so angry. And I realized that that was my doing." He smiles sadly. "When I came home and you weren't here, and then didn't come back, I knew that I had let it destroy my life and take from me the one good thing I had."

"But you didn't come find me."

"No," he shakes his head. "I figured you hated me, and

with good reason. I had no right to ask you to forgive me. But I know about you."

"You do?"

"It took me some time to get sober. When I did I became truly aware of what I'd lost. So I asked around. I found out where you were living and I cornered Tom Bolen at the hardware store. It took some time and several conversations with him to convince him I was genuine in my concern and not trying to harm you before he would tell me anything."

He waves his hand toward the wall next to the opening between the kitchen and living room and I see a white phone hanging on the wall.

"I finally got a phone. I stay sober, so I can keep my job, so I can pay my phone bill, so I can talk to Tom about you." He shakes his head. "Pathetic, huh?"

"No, not pathetic. Responsible. Fatherly."

His eyes flicker with something like hope, and the residual anger that is in my heart melts away. I pull a small notebook and pen out of my purse and scribble a number on it, passing it to him.

"My cell phone number," I tell him. "You can just call me direct now and I'll tell you what's going on."

"I can call you?"

"Sure."

He's staring at the paper, rubbing his thumb lightly over the print.

"Do you think someday you might let me try to be your dad again?" he asks softly.

"I'd like that." I cover his hand with mine. He leans down and kisses my knuckles.

"Can I stay for dinner? I could cook for us," I say.

"You can stay, but I'll cook. I've become pretty handy with my grill out back. I'd like to show off for someone else besides me for once."

I laugh.

"Deal."

Since that day I've talked to him on the phone almost daily. I go to his house a couple of times a week to have dinner with him. This new, sober man is a far cry from the drunken stranger I'd known before. He asked me once about Henry because Jessica's dad had told him I had broken up with him, but I cut him off, refusing to talk about it, and unlike Jessica he let it drop and didn't ask me again. Sometimes, though, I catch him watching me with a sad, puzzled look in his eyes and I know he *wants* to ask, wants to know what could have driven us apart, but he doesn't ask.

The summer fades and rolls into fall, the mountains changing from green to red as the leaves change, and finally to white as winter comes and the snow falls. My life is a half-life, but even at that it's more than it had been before Henry.

I go to school and do well, no longer feeling a need to keep unnoticed with mediocre grades. I go to work and don't have to pretend to be anything because most of the patients have a hard time remembering me anyway from time to time. I go to movies with Jessica, and watch TV with her parents. I spend time with my father, even attending a few of his AA meetings with him. I see my psychiatrist and work through my guilt and lack of self-worth as much as possible. I smile and laugh when I'm supposed to.

I pretend that I'm not keenly aware that he's gone now, wherever his destiny has taken him.

Just before Christmas I move back home with my father. I'm determined to keep a happy face for him, to help him stay sober and not drag him down with my sorrow.

At night I still cry, and dream of Henry, and miss him with an aching loneliness that threatens to overwhelm everything else in my life.

Twenty-Nine

Spring comes early. The snow and ice melt quickly, the spring flowers blooming when they shouldn't be. I still walk as much as possible, so I'm glad about the flowers, especially when I'm on campus, because they are so beautiful. They feel like new life, new beginnings. I like walking from building to building to go to class, the sun warm on my back. I wear Henry's jacket, which I kept, deciding that this little piece of self-torture is worth it to feel closer to him.

When I hear my name being called one spring afternoon by a voice more familiar than my own, I decide that it's the power of wishful thinking, since I'm wearing his jacket. I turn anyway, schooling my smile to not show how much I wish the voice really does belong to him, expecting to see one of my classmates there.

My smile falls, arms going limp as my books scatter across the ground when my eyes light on him. He's here, really here, standing ten feet away. He walks closer, a wry smile crossing his face as he takes in the strewn books. My heart twists painfully at the familiar expression, my hands curling into fists, nails digging in to keep me from crying out in pain.

"Still not big on carrying a back pack, huh?" he asks, gaze coming to my face. I'm nearly knocked over by the pain I see reflected in his eyes. I squat down, scooping my books up to give myself a chance to regroup. Any chance of that is lost as he walks closer, his shoes right next to me now. Slowly I stand up, taking a breath, wanting to run away, but facing him anyway.

"Why are you here?" I intend it to come out sounding careless, remote. Instead the words are nearly breathless, hurt underlying each syllable.

"I don't really know," he says, his words a repeat of his answer the first time I talked to him, when I asked him why he wanted to be my friend.

"You should go." I order my feet to turn and walk away, but they disobey, fixed in place.

"I can't, Kate." The sound of my name on his lips is like a physical blow. I rock back a little from the impact. "Not until I tell you what I came to say."

"Say it then," I mumble, wanting this moment over now because I don't think I can take it for much longer, but also wanting to draw it out so that I can drink in the sight of him, so much better in reality than in my dreams.

"I think it's time for you to stop being such a martyr," his words come out harshly, his jaw clenching. He runs his fingers roughly through his hair, the gesture so endearingly familiar that I ache with it. He takes another step closer. "How much longer do we have to suffer apart until your sense of justice is fulfilled?"

"What?" I gasp. "You think this is some kind of masochism, or self punishment?"

"If not that, then what?" his voice is rising, and a few students nearby look our way.

"It *can't* work, Henry. I told you—"

"You told me a load of crap! I've thought over everything you said, a hundred times a day, every day, and it makes no sense. The only thing that makes sense is that you think you're not good enough for me, you think you don't deserve me. You think you have to self-sacrifice in order to make everyone happy."

This hits so close to home that hurt washes over me. I turn that pain into anger.

"Pretty arrogant, Henry. Sounds like it's *you* that thinks you're too good for me."

"Don't try to turn my words around, Kate."

"You were only with me because you pitied me. I was just some poor creature for you to rescue."

"No!" His denial is vehement. "Not at first. And then, okay, maybe a little." I'm stunned by his admitting it. "But not after that. *You*, Kate, I fell in love with you! With your strength and courage, with your naiveté and innocence, your unschooled sense of humor. With your loyalty and how willingly you gave your love and trust."

"Not exactly flattering, Henry," I flounder around, trying to find a part of his speech that isn't singing through my heart, trying to maintain my anger. I finally find a word. "Loyal! Like a good dog."

"You're turning my words around again," he growls.

His face is only inches from mine as we yell at one another, so close that if I just lean in just a few more inches, our lips will be touching.

I see the moment when Henry realizes the same, when his face changes from anger to intensity, when he starts to make the move forward. I channel every ounce of self-control and will-power I have in me to jerk back and take a step away. His jaw tightens.

"This is stupid, Kate. I *love* you. I want to be with you. Today, tomorrow, *always*. And I *know* you love me. Tell me I'm wrong about you, about why you left me. Tell me you don't love me."

I know I should open my mouth and say the words, say the lie, and then he can move on. I open my mouth. Nothing comes out, so I snap it shut.

"You're wearing my jacket," the accusation is soaked with misery. I pull it tighter around me in response, my throat clogged with tears.

"So here's the deal," he says when I remain silent, clearing his throat and drawing himself up. He reaches out toward me, then stops himself, his hand falling uselessly to his side. "I'm living at home, going to school here, at the university, which I will be doing for the next three years. And after that I don't know where I will be, but wherever it is I want to be there with you. I don't *want* to go without you, but I will. And then I'll come back for you. If I have to wait one day or twenty years, I'll wait for you. So when you decide you're done with *this*..." he trails off searching for the right word. Apparently not finding it, he continues. "When you've punished us enough, you come to me. Because that's what you've reduced me to—a man who will live a pathetically empty life, just waiting for you."

He stares at me a few eternal seconds longer while a thousand thoughts swirl in my head, each fighting to get out, none succeeding. Finally he turns and begins walking away, ignoring the tears running down my cheeks. He pauses, with a murmured, "I'm tortured, Kate," before continuing away from me.

"Henry," his name is out before I can stop it, before I even know I intend to say it. He stops, frozen, and then slowly turns back toward me. His face is creased with misery, hurt shining from his eyes, every line of his body reflecting despair. And I realized that that's because of me.

I love him more than I ever thought it possible to love someone, and here I am, causing him so much pain when all I ever wanted was for him to be happy. With that my decision is made. I wipe my tears away, squaring my shoulders.

"I want to tell you a story," I say. "It's about a girl, who fell in love with a boy. But she didn't think she was worthy of this boys love, or anyone's love. She thought she had to push him away so he could be happy." I watch as slow understanding crosses his features, though still tempered by the idea that I might not be saying what he wants. I begin to walk slowly toward him. "She was a foolish girl, miserable and lonely, crying herself to sleep every night because she missed him so much. But that didn't matter, what mattered was that he was better off without her." He shakes his head, opening his mouth to protest, but I'm in front of him now, and I place my finger lightly on his lips to stop him. Warmth, and a feeling of *rightness,* flows through me at the contact, nearly derailing my train of thought.

"But then one day he came to her, and she could see that he was hurting, that *she* had done that," my hand flattens against his cheek, "that *she* had caused him to ache even though she would rather die a thousand slow, agonizing deaths than cause him one second of pain. And she realized that maybe she'd been wrong." His hand comes up, capturing mine, pressing my palm against his lips. "She decides that maybe she *could* make him happy and she wondered, if she asked *really* nice, if he might forgive her, and give her another chance. That he might let her spend the rest of her life showing him how sorry she is and how much she loves him."

His free hand comes up to my cheek, cupping my jaw.

"I've heard this story," he smiles.

"Oh yeah?" I ask, losing myself in his dark eyes that are now shining with elation. "How does it end?"

"It doesn't end," he says, pulling me close. "It begins, like this."

As his mouth comes down to mine, my heart lifts free of its burden and soars. I'm back where I belong.

Epilogue

Henry

I slide my hand beneath the table, running my fingers lightly, slowly down her arm until our hands meet. She immediately turns her hand over, tangling her fingers with mine. It works out really well, my being left-handed and her being right, so that I can hold her hand whenever I want and not have it interrupt her meticulous note-taking.

She doesn't look my way, keeping her eyes resolutely turned to the front of the room, ostensibly listening to each word the professor spouts. I know her so well, though. The corners of her mouth turn up, and the slightest sigh escapes her lips.

I'll be getting a kiss after class.

I always knew Kate was stubborn; I didn't realize the exact extent until I decided just how our lives should go.

Turns out Kate has her own ideas.

She stayed at the community college for a full additional year, while I attended the university. No matter how much I cajoled, threatened or pleaded, she did what she wanted. It was torture, with both our schedules so full, to see so little of her.

Last year she transferred to the university, and though this is the only class we have together this year, we worked our schedules out so that we are in school as much as possible at the same time—and therefore home at the same time.

Kate lives with her father, whom she has grown very close to. John has turned his life completely around for Kate—a sentiment I completely empathize with. He's finally being the father he denied her of for so many years.

She refuses to marry me.

She says she won't marry me until she finishes her degree and can support me while I go to medical school. She's less than a semester away from her teaching degree.

She wants to teach fourth grade, she says, because for her, that's when she needed someone to recognize how her home life was deteriorating. She wants to be in the position to do that for someone else if needed.

My compassionate, courageous Kate would be just the person to do that.

I stare at Kate, compelling her to look my way. She glances down at her paper where she's taking notes, sliding her eyes sideways to glance up at me from under long, dark lashes.

"I love you," I mouth silently, rubbing my thumb across her palm in her lap. She smiles openly at me.

"Me, too," is her mouthed response.

Absently, I reach up and muss my hair, and her eyes turn liquid. I laugh silently. It never fails to amaze me, the things she loves about me. She's told me repeatedly that she finds the habit "adorable." I'm not sure how I feel about that—it doesn't sound too manly to be "adorable." But then she looks at me like that, when I do it, and suddenly I don't mind being adorable.

I don't know exactly how many times I've proposed to her. A lot. But she's going to have to say yes soon. Not just because I can't wait any longer—though that's certainly true.

This time I have the deal breaker in my pocket. I've been accepted to pre-med in Maine, almost twenty-five hundred miles away—and I'm not going without her. She'll say yes because it's the only way she'll go with me, if we have our union bound legally. She's very firm on that, not living together while unmarried. Part of it is her personal values; part of it, I believe, is that she's afraid I'll leave her still. She doesn't know that I'll never leave, and if *she* goes, I'll follow her to the ends of the earth.

Oh, she'll protest. She'll tell me that she isn't good enough to be a doctor's wife, that others in my profession will shun her. She's wrong.

Kate has never been able to see herself as she truly is. A spurt of anger shoots through me when I think of what was done to her, why she has such a flawed vision of herself. I tamp it down; she's taught me about forgiveness, about letting go, so I'm working on it.

What she doesn't know is what I see. If anyone tries to look down on her, tries to make her think she is less than them, she will raze them with her quiet dignity. She isn't the cowering mouse she used to be.

I look over at her once again, see the curve of her mouth as she bumps her shoulder against mine.

"Quit staring at me," the gesture says. The great thing about gestures is how easy they are to ignore. She glances at me and I see it—that glint of pride and confidence that comes through when she isn't guarding against it.

They won't be thinking she's not good enough for me; they'll be wondering *why* she's with me. I don't really care, as long as she is with me.

"That's it for today," the professor announces, and I quickly shove my books into my backpack, as Kate slowly layers her books by size in her backpack that I bought her. Impatiently, I scoot hers off the edge of the table into the bag, dragging her up with me amidst her protests, hurrying her out of the room.

"Henry, what—"

I cut her words off with my mouth as I push her into a nearby alcove, needing to have her in my arms. She responds immediately, flame meeting flame.

"What was that for?" she asks breathlessly when I let her up for air.

"Does it matter?" I tease.

"Nope," she grins, pulling me back down for another kiss.

Yup, I'm definitely going to have to push for that wedding—and soon. I can't imagine anything better, anything I want more, or anything I will ever want more, than to hold her in my arms.

For always.

About the Author

Cindy C Bennett was born and raised in beautiful Salt Lake City. She lives with her husband, and is the mom of four humans and three dogs. Her two daughters keep her writing with their constant encouragement. Her two sons keep her writing with their willingness to read her books—even if they aren't fantasy, sci-fi, or comics! She volunteers her time working with teen girls between the ages of 12-18, all of whom she finds to be beautiful, fascinating creatures. When she's not writing, reading or answering emails she can often times be found riding her Harley through the beautiful canyons near her home.

Please visit the author's website at
www.cindycbennett.com

and her blog at
http://cindybennett.blogspot.com